Fic ALT

408 food
stairs

Alten, Steve.   COND!

WITHDRAW

Meg : a novel of deep

terror /

6 X 8/02 LT 8/99 7183   SOUTHEAST

10X 7/03 25 1/08

D0978777

MEG

DOUBLEDAY

New York London Toronto Sydney Auckland

Steve Alten

MEG

A NOVEL OF DEEP TERROR

PUBLISHED BY DOUBLEDAY
a division of Bantam Doubleday Dell
Publishing Group, Inc.
1540 Broadway, New York, New York
10036

DOUBLEDAY and the portrayal of an
anchor with a dolphin are trademarks of
Doubleday, a division of Bantam Doubleday
Dell Publishing Group, Inc.

All of the characters in this book are
fictitious, and any resemblance to actual
persons, living or dead, is purely coincidental.

Book design by Jennifer Ann Daddio

Library of Congress
Cataloging-in-Publication Data
Alten, Steve.
Meg : a novel of deep terror / Steve Alten.
— 1st ed.
p.   cm.
I. Title.
PS3551.L764M4   1997
813'.54—dc21   96-40161
CIP

ISBN 0-385-48905-6
Copyright © 1997 by Steve Alten
All Rights Reserved
Printed in the United States of America
July 1997

First Edition

1   3   5   7   9   10   8   6   4   2

FOR DAD . . .

Acknowledgments

Only in America could a guy be flat broke, lose his job, and become wealthy a few days later. The realization of one's goal takes hard work and believing in what you're doing during the tough times, but it also requires the assistance and kindness of others. As a first-time writer, I am extremely grateful to so many wonderful people who have worked very hard on this project.

First and foremost, to my "Dream Team," led by Ken Atchity, literary manager and producer extraordinaire. You took a chance on an unknown and I will forever be in your debt. To his partner Chi-Li Wong and the rest of the people at Atchity Editorial/ Entertainment International for the vision and effort to help make my dreams come true; my gratitude to Ed Stackler and David Angsten for your outstanding editing of the manuscript, and to Warren Zide of Zide Entertainment, your efforts and energy on *Meg* have been boundless, and elevated the project to a whole new level. To Joel McKuin and David Colden of Colden & McKuin, thank you both for your incredible work and kindness; as well as to Jeff Robinov. I cannot imagine a better group, to all of you, this was a TEAM EFFORT. Thank you.

I am grateful to Walt Disney Pictures, its president, David Vogel, and executives Allison Brecker and Jeff Bynum, for taking on *Meg*. To Shawn Coyne, Pat Mulcahy, and the great people at Bantam Doubleday Dell for everything you have done. It has been an honor and a privilege for me to be associated with all of you.

To my parents, for supporting my family through all the tough times, and to my sister Abby, for her encouragement when it was needed the most. Thanks also to Richard and Michelle Przystas for your help as my computer whizzes. Last, to my wife, Kim, for tolerating the long hours, years of struggling, and a husband who may have been a bit grouchy after many sleepless nights of writing.

MEGALODON

Late Cretaceous Period, 70 Million Years Ago
The Coast of the Asiamerica-Northern Landmass (Pacific Ocean)

From the moment the early morning fog had begun to lift, they sensed they were being watched. The herd of *Shantungosaurus* had been grazing along the misty shoreline all morning. Measuring more than forty feet from their duck-billed heads to the end of their tails, these reptiles, the largest of the hadrosaurs, gorged themselves on the abundant supply of kelp and seaweed that continued to wash up along the shoreline with the incoming tide. Every few moments, the hadrosaurs raised their heads nervously like a herd of deer, listening to the noises of the nearby forest. They watched the dark trees and thick vegetation for movement, ready to run at the first sign of approach.

Across the beach, hidden among the tall trees and thick undergrowth, a pair of red reptilian eyes followed the herd. The *Tyrannosaurus rex*, largest and most lethal of all terrestrial carnivores, stood twenty-two feet above the forest floor. Saliva oozed from its mouth as *T. rex* watched, quivering with adrenaline. The two largest duckbills had just ventured out into shallow water, lowering their heads to forage among the thick strains of kelp.

The killer crashed from the trees, his eight tons pounding the sand and shaking the earth with every step. The duckbills rose on their hind legs and scattered in both directions along the beach. The two reptiles in the surf turned to see the carnivore closing on them, jaws wide, fangs bared, its bone-chilling roar drowning the crash of the surf. The pair of hadrosaurs turned instinctively, plunging into deeper waters to escape. They strained their long necks forward and began to swim, their legs churning to keep their heads above water.

T. rex plunged in behind them, crashing through the surf and into deeper waters. But as it neared its prey, the *T. rex*'s feet sank into the muddy sea floor. Unlike the buoyant hadrosaurs, the thickly muscled *T. rex* could not swim and became hopelessly bogged in the mire.

The hadrosaurs now swam in thirty feet of water. But having escaped one predator, they now faced another.

The six-foot gray dorsal fin rose slowly from the sea, gliding silently across their path. The current created by the creature's sheer mass began pulling the hadrosaurs into deeper waters. The duckbills panicked at the sudden change. They would take their chances with the *Tyrannosaurus*. Within the deep waters lurked certain death. They turned, thrashing and paddling frantically until they once again felt the familiar mud beneath their feet.

T. rex let out a thundering growl. In water to its chest, the predator struggled to keep from sinking farther into the soft sea floor. The duckbills broke in either direction, passing within fifteen yards of the frustrated hunter. The *T. rex* lunged at them, snapping its terrible jaws, howling in rage at its fleeing prey. The duckbills bounded through the smaller waves and staggered onto the beach. Collapsing on the warm sand, too exhausted to move, the two hadrosaurs looked back once more to face their would-be killer.

The *Tyrannosaurus* could now hold his huge head only a few feet above water. Insane with rage, it slashed its tail wildly in an attempt to free one of its hind legs. Then, all at once, it stopped struggling and stared out to sea. From the dark waters, slicing through the gray fog, the great dorsal fin was approaching.

The *T. rex* cocked its head and stood perfectly still, realizing too late that it had wandered into the domain of a superior hunter. For the first and last time in its life, the *Tyrannosaurus* felt the icy grip of fear.

If the *T. rex* was the most terrifying creature ever to walk the earth, then *Carcharodon megalodon* was easily lord and master of the sea. The red eyes of the *Tyrannosaurus* followed the gray dorsal fin, feeling the tug of current caused by the unseen mass circling below. The fin disappeared beneath the muddy waters. *T. rex* growled quietly, searching through the haze. The towering dorsal fin rose again from the mist, now racing directly for him. The *T. rex* roared and struggled, vainly snapping its jaws in futile protest.

From the beach, the two exhausted hadrosaurs watched as *T. rex* was slammed backward through the ocean with a great *whoosh,* its huge head disappearing beneath the waves. In a moment the dinosaur surfaced again, wailing in agony as its rib cage was crushed within the jaws of its hunter, a fountain of blood spouting from its mouth.

The mighty *Tyrannosaurus rex* vanished beneath the swirling scarlet water. A long moment passed, and the sea remained silent. The hadrosaurs turned and lumbered toward the trees. Suddenly they turned, cowering at an explosion in the water. Clutching *T. rex* in its gargantuan mouth, the sixty-foot shark, nearly three times the size of its prey, burst from the water, its enormous head and muscular upper torso quivering as it fought to remain suspended above the waves. Then, in an incredible display of raw power, the Meg shook the reptile from side to side between nine-inch serrated teeth, spraying pink froths and gouts of gore in every direction. The twenty-ton Megalodon and its mutilated prey crashed back into the sea, sending a great swell of water high into the air around them.

No other scavengers approached the Megalodon as it fed in the tropical waters. It had no mate to share its kill with, no young to feed. The Meg was a companionless creature, territorial by nature. It mated when it must and killed its young when it could, for the only challenge to its reign came from its own kind. It could adapt and survive the natural catastrophes and climatic changes that caused the mass extinctions of the giant reptiles and countless prehistoric mammals. And while its numbers would eventually dwindle, some members of its species might survive, isolated from the world of man, hunting in the isolated darkness of the ocean depths.

THE PROFESSOR

November 8, 1997   7:42 P.M.
The Scripps Institute, Anderson Auditorium
La Jolla, California

"Imagine a great white shark, fifty to sixty feet in length, weighing close to forty thousand pounds. Can you visualize that?" Professor Jonas Taylor looked at his audience of just over six hundred and paused for effect. "I find it hard to imagine myself sometimes, but this monster did exist. Its head alone was probably as large as a Dodge Ram pickup. Its jaws could have engulfed and swallowed four grown men whole. And I haven't even mentioned the teeth: razor-sharp, seven to nine inches long, with the serrated edges of a stainless-steel steak knife."

The forty-two-year-old paleontologist knew he had his audience's attention. It had been several years since he had returned to the Institute. Lecturing in front of a nearly sold-out crowd was not something he had anticipated. Jonas knew his theories were controversial, that there were as many critics in the audience as there were supporters. He loosened his collar a little, tried to relax.

"Next slide, please? Ah, here we have an artist's rendition of a six-foot diver as compared with a sixteen-foot great white and our sixty-foot *Carcharodon megalodon*. I think this gives you a fairly good idea why scientists refer to the species as the king of all predators."

Jonas reached for the glass of water, took a sip. "Fossilized Megalodon teeth from around the world prove that the species dominated the oceans as long as seventy million years. What's really interesting is that we know that the Megalodon survived the cataclysmic events that occurred about sixty-five and forty-five million years ago, respectively, when the dinosaurs and most prehistoric species of fish perished. In fact, we have Megalodon teeth that indicate these predators disappeared only a hundred thousand years ago. From a geological standpoint, that's a tick of the clock."

A twenty-six-year-old male grad student raised his hand. "Professor Taylor, if these Megalodons were alive a hundred thousand years ago, why did they become extinct at all?"

Jonas smiled. "That, my friend, is one of the great mysteries in the paleo-world. Some scientists believe that the staple of the Megalodon's diet had once been large, slow-moving fish and that they could not adapt to the smaller, swifter species that exist today. Another theory is that falling ocean temperatures contributed to the species' demise."

An elderly man raised his hand from his seat in the first row. Jonas recognized him, a former colleague at Scripps. A former critic.

"Professor Taylor, I think we'd like to hear *your* theory of the disappearance of *Carcharodon megalodon*."

Murmurs of approval followed. Jonas loosened his collar a little more. He rarely wore suits, and this eighteen-year-old wool one had seen better days. "Those of you who know me or follow my work are aware of how my opinions often differ from those of most paleontologists. Many in my field spend a great deal of time theorizing why a particular species doesn't exist. I prefer to theorize why a seemingly extinct species *might* exist."

The elderly professor stood. "Sir, are you saying you think *Carcharodon megalodon* may still be roaming the oceans?"

Jonas waited for quiet. "No, Professor, I'm simply pointing out that, as scientists, we tend to take a rather negative approach when investigating certain extinct species. For instance, it wasn't long ago that scientists unanimously believed that the coelacanth, a species of lobe-finned fish that thrived three hundred million years ago, had been extinct for the last seventy million years. And then, in 1938, a fisherman hauled a living coelacanth out of the deep ocean waters off South Africa. Now scientists routinely observe these 'living fossils' in their natural habitat."

The elderly professor stood up again amid murmurs from the crowd. "Professor Taylor, we're all familiar with the discovery of the coelacanth, but there's a big difference between a five-foot bottom feeder and a sixty-foot predator!"

Jonas checked his watch, realizing he was running behind schedule. "Yes, Professor, I agree, but my point was simply that I prefer to investigate the possibilities of a species' survival rather than justify reasons as to how it became extinct."

"And again, sir, I ask for your opinion regarding Megalodon." More murmurs.

Jonas wiped his brow; Maggie was going to kill him. "Very well. First, I disagree entirely with the theory regarding Megalodon being unable to catch quicker prey. We have learned that the conical tail fin of the great white, the modern-day cousin of the Megalodon, is the most efficient design for propelling a body through water. We also know the Megs existed as recently as a hundred thousand years ago. Then, as now, the predator would have had an abundant supply of slower-moving whales to feed upon.

"I do, however, agree that the diminishing ocean temperatures affected these creatures. May I have the next slide, please? I'm sorry, one more."

A slide showing several different maps of the planet over a three-hundred-million-year period appeared above. "As we see from these maps, our planet's continental masses are constantly moving as a result of seven major tectonic plates. This map"—Jonas pointed to the center diagram—"is how the earth looked about forty million years ago, during the Eocene. As we can see, the landmass that would become Antarctica separated from South America at about this time and drifted over the South Pole. When the continents drifted toward the poles, they disrupted the transport of poleward oceanic heat, essentially replacing the heat-retaining water with heat-losing land. As the cooling progressed, the land accumulated snow and ice, which further lowered global temperatures and sea levels. As most of you know, the most important factor controlling the geographical distribution of a marine species is ocean temperature.

"Now, as the water temperatures dropped, the warmer tropical currents became top-heavy with salt and began running much deeper. So, in essence, the ocean temperatures were cooler along the shallower surface waters, with a tropical current, heavy with salt, running much deeper.

"Based on the locations of fossilized Meg teeth, we know that these creatures inhabited warmer tropical seas, perhaps due to the fact that their food sources would have also adapted to the drop in ocean temperatures by moving into the deeper tropical ocean currents. We also know that *Carcharodon megalodon* survived beyond the climatic changes that killed off the dinosaurs around sixty-five million years ago, as well as the mass extinctions among marine species that occurred forty million years ago.

"Now, about two million years ago, our planet experienced its last ice age. As you can see from this diagram, the deeper tropical currents that had provided a refuge for many marine species were suddenly cut off. As a result, many species of prehistoric fish, including *Carcharodon megalodon,* perished, unable to adapt to the extreme drops in oceanic temperatures."

The elderly professor called out from his seat. "So then, Professor Taylor, you *do* believe that the Megalodon became extinct as a result of climatic changes." The older man smiled, satisfied with himself.

"Not exactly. Remember, I said I prefer to theorize on how a species might still exist. About fifteen years ago, I was part of a scientific team that first studied deep-sea trenches. Deep-sea trenches form the 'hadal' zone, an area of the Pacific Ocean about which scientists know virtually nothing. We discovered that these deep-sea trenches occur along the edges of two oceanic plates, where one plate melts back into the earth by a process called subduction. Inside these trenches, countless hydrothermal vents spew mineral-rich waters at temperatures that sometimes exceed seven hundred degrees Fahrenheit. So, in some of the deepest, most unexplored locations of the Pacific Ocean, a tropical current of water can run along the very bottom. To our surprise, we discovered that these hydrothermal vents supported new life forms never before imagined."

A middle-aged woman stood and asked excitedly, "Did you discover a Megalodon?"

Jonas smiled and waited for the crowd's laughter to subside. "No, ma'am. But let me show you something that was discovered back over one hundred years ago which might be of interest." Jonas pulled out a glass case, roughly twice the size of a shoe box, from behind the podium. "This is a fossilized tooth of *Carcharodon megalodon*. Scuba divers and beachcombers have turned up fossilized teeth like this by the thousands. Some are nearly fifty million years old. This particular specimen is actually special because it's not very old. It was recovered in 1873 by the world's first true oceanic exploration vessel, the British HMS *Challenger*. Can you see these manganese nodules?" Jonas pointed to the black encrustations on the tooth. "Recent analysis of these manganese layers indicated the tooth's owner had been alive during the late Pleistocene or early Holocene period. In other words, this tooth is a mere ten thousand years old, and it was dredged from the deepest point on our planet, the Mariana Trench's Challenger Deep."

The crowd erupted.

"Professor! Professor Taylor!" All eyes turned to an Asian-American woman standing in the back of the auditorium. Jonas looked at her, caught off guard by her beauty. Somehow she seemed familiar.

"Yes, go ahead, please," said Jonas, motioning for the audience to be quiet.

"Professor, are you saying that the Megalodon may still exist?" Silence. It was the question the audience wanted answered.

"Theoretically, if members of the Megalodon species inhabited the waters of the Mariana Trench two million years ago, waters that maintain a deep tropical layer as a result of hydrothermal vents, then one could logically say that a branch of the species might have survived. The existence of this ten-thousand-year-old fossil certainly justifies the possibilities."

"Professor!" A middle-aged man with a young son sitting next to him raised his hand. "If these monsters still exist today, why haven't we seen them?"

"A good question." Jonas paused. A beautiful blond woman, tan, thirty years old, her figure flawless, was walking down the center aisle. Her classic topaz evening gown managed to expose her long legs. Her escort trailed behind, thirtyish, wearing a ponytail and tuxedo. The pair took the two empty seats reserved in the front row.

Jonas composed himself, waiting for his wife and best friend to be seated. "Sorry. Your question was why we haven't actually seen a Megalodon, assuming members of the species still exist. First, if a Megalodon did inhabit the deepest waters in the Mariana Trench, it couldn't leave that tropical bottom layer. The Challenger Deep is seven miles down. The water temperature above the warm layer is near freezing. The Meg could never survive the transition through six miles of icy waters in order to surface.

"It's also unusual for Megalodon, or any shark for that matter, to leave behind evidence as to their existence, especially in the abyss. Unlike mammals, sharks do not float to the surface when they die, as their bodies are inherently heavier than seawater. Their skeletons are composed entirely of cartilage. So unlike dinosaurs and many species of bony fishes, there are no Megalodon bones to leave behind, only their gruesome, fossilized teeth."

Jonas caught Maggie's eye. It seemed to burn into his skull. "One other thing about the Mariana Trench. Man has only ventured down to the bottom twice, both expeditions occurring in 1960 and both times in bathyscaphes. That means we simply went straight down and back up again. The reality is, we've never come close to exploring the trench. In fact, we know more about many distant galaxies than we do about a 1,550-mile isolated section of the Pacific Ocean, seven miles down."

Jonas looked at Maggie and shrugged. She stood, pointing to her watch.

"You'll have to excuse me, ladies and gentlemen. This lecture has lasted a bit longer than expected—"

"Excuse me Dr. Taylor, one important question." It was the Asian woman again. She seemed perturbed. "Before you began studying these Megalodons, your career was focused entirely on piloting deep-sea submersibles. I'd like to know why, at the peak of your career, you suddenly quit."

Jonas was taken back by the directness of the question. "I have my reasons." He searched the audience for another raised hand.

"Wait a minute, I need to know." She was standing now, walking into the center aisle. "Did you lose your nerve, Professor? There had to be a reason. You haven't been in a submersible for what? Seven years?"

"What's your name, miss?"

"Tanaka. Terry Tanaka. I believe you know my father, Masao Tanaka of the Tanaka Oceanographic Institute."

"Yes, of course. In fact, you and I met several years ago on a lecture circuit."

"That's right."

"Well, Terry Tanaka, I can't get into details right now. Let's just say I felt I was ready to retire from piloting deep-sea submersibles so I could spend more time researching prehistoric species like the Megalodon." Jonas collected his notes. "Now, if there are no other questions . . ."

"Dr. Taylor!" A balding man with tiny wire-rim glasses stood in the third row. He had bushy, elfin eyebrows and a tight grin on his face. "Please, sir, one last question if I may. As you mentioned, the two manned expeditions into the Mariana Trench occurred in 1960. But, Professor, isn't it true that there have been more recent descents into the Challenger Deep?"

Jonas stared at the man. "I'm sorry?"

"Come now, Professor, you made several dives there yourself."

Jonas was silent. The audience began to murmur.

The man raised his bushy eyebrows, moving his glasses. "Back in 1989, Professor. While you were doing work for the Navy?"

"I'm . . . not sure I understand." Jonas glanced at his wife.

"You *are* Professor Jonas Taylor, aren't you?" The man smiled smugly as the audience broke into light laughter.

"Look, I'm sorry, I really must be leaving now. I have another engagement. Thank you all for attending."

A smattering of applause trickled out amid murmurs from the crowd as Jonas Taylor stepped down from the podium. He was quickly approached by students with questions, scientists with theories of their own, and old colleagues desperate to say hello before he left. Jonas shook as many hands as he could, apologizing for having to run.

The ponytailed man in the tuxedo squeezed his head through the swarming crowd. "Hey, Jonas, the car's parked outside. Maggie says we need to leave now."

Jonas nodded, finished signing a book for an admiring student, then hurried to the exit at the back of the auditorium, where his wife, Maggie, was waiting impatiently.

As he reached the door, he caught a glimpse of Terry Tanaka, looking at him from behind the moving crowd. Her eyes seemed to burn into his as she mouthed the words "We need to talk." Jonas held up his watch and shrugged. He had enough of the verbal assaults for one night.

As if in response, his wife yelled through the exit door, "Jonas, let's go!"

GOLDEN EAGLE

They drove along the Coronado peninsula in Bud Harris's limousine, Jonas facing them in the backseat. Bud was mumbling into the car phone and fingering his ponytail like a schoolgirl. Maggie looked very much at home on the wide leather seat, her slender legs crossed, a glass of champagne balanced in her fingertips. She's grown used to his money, Jonas thought. He imagined her in a bikini, tanning herself on Bud's yacht.

"You used to be afraid of the sun."

"What are you talking about?"

"Your tan."

She stared at him. "It looks good on-camera."

"Melanoma doesn't look so good."

"Don't start with me, Jonas. I'm not in the mood. This is the biggest night of my career, and I had to practically drag you out of that lecture hall. You knew about this dinner for a month, and you're wearing that twenty-year-old wool suit."

"Maggie, this was my first time back on the lecture circuit in over two years, and you come prancing down the aisle—"

"Hey, whoa, guys." Bud hung up the car phone and held his hands up. "Let's all just calm down a second. Maggie, this was a big night for Jonas too, maybe we should have just waited in the limo."

Jonas remained silent.

Maggie wasn't through. "I've waited years for this opportunity, worked my ass off while I watched you flush your career down the toilet. Now it's my turn, and if you don't want to be here, that's fine by me. You can wait in the fucking limo. Bud will escort me tonight, won't you?"

"Keep me out of this," said Bud.

Maggie frowned and looked out the window. Tension hung in the air. After a few long minutes, Bud broke the silence. "Henderson thinks you're a shoo-in. This really could be the turning point in your career Maggie, assuming you'll win."

Maggie turned to face him, managing to avoid looking at her husband. "I'll win," she said defiantly. "I know I'll win. Pour me another drink."

Bud grinned, filled Maggie's glass, then offered the bottle to Jonas. Jonas shook his head and sat back in his seat, staring absently at his wife.

Jonas Taylor had met Maggie almost nine years earlier in Massachusetts while he trained as a deep-sea pilot at the Woods Hole Oceanographic Institute. Maggie had been in her senior year at Boston University, majoring in journalism. The petite blonde had at one time vigorously pursued a modeling career, but lacked the required height. She had reset her sights on making it as a broadcast journalist.

Maggie had read about Jonas Taylor and his adventures in the Alvin submersible and thought he would be a good subject for the university paper. She knew he was a bit of a celebrity in his own right and thought him handsome, with an athletic body.

Jonas Taylor was amazed that anyone like Maggie would be interested in deep-sea diving, or himself for that matter. His career had left him little time for a social life, and when the beautiful blonde seemed interested, Jonas jumped at the opportunity. They'd begun dating almost immediately, with Jonas inviting Maggie to the Galápagos Islands as part of an *Alvin* exploration team during spring break of her senior year. He even allowed her to accompany him on one dive into the Galápagos Trench.

Maggie was impressed by the influence Jonas had among his colleagues in the field, and loved the excitement and adventure associated with ocean exploration. Ten months later they married and moved to California, where Jonas was contracted to work in conjunction with the U.S. Navy. Maggie loved California. In no time she became addicted to the celebrity life and longed for her own career in the media. With her husband's help, she knew she could break into the business.

And then, disaster. Jonas had been piloting a new deep-sea submersible on a top-secret Navy expedition into the Mariana Trench. On his third dive into the abyss he had panicked, surfacing the sub too quickly to decompress properly. Two crewmen had died, and Jonas had been blamed for the accident. The official report had called it "aberrations of the deep," and the accident destroyed Jonas's reputation as a reliable argonaut. It would be his last expedition in a submersible.

Maggie quickly realized that her ticket to stardom was in serious jeopardy. No longer able to cope with the stresses of deep-sea diving, Jonas became consumed with paleontology, writing books, studying prehistoric marine creatures. His income dwindled quickly, changing the lifestyle Maggie had grown accustomed to. She found herself part-time work as a freelance writer for a few local magazines, but it was all dead-end work. Her dreams of becoming a celebrity seemed over, her life suddenly unbearably boring.

Then Jonas introduced her to his former college roommate, Bud Harris. Harris, thirty-five at the time, had recently inherited his father's shipping business in San Diego. He and Jonas had spent three years living together in an off-campus apartment at Penn State University and had kept in touch after graduation.

Maggie was working as a part-time writer for the *San Diego Register*. She was always looking for stories, and she and Jonas both thought Bud's shipping business would make an interesting article for the Sunday magazine. Maggie spent a month trailing Bud around the harbor, with trips to his dock facilities in Long Beach, San Francisco, and Honolulu. She interviewed him on his yacht, sat in on board meetings, took a ride on his hovercraft, even spent an afternoon learning how to sail.

The article she wrote became the *Register*'s cover story and made a local celebrity of the wild and woolly millionaire. His San Diego charter business boomed. Not one to forget a favor, Bud helped Maggie get a television reporting job with a local station. Fred Henderson, the station manager, was a yachting partner of Bud's. Maggie started by doing two-minute fillers for the ten o'clock news, but it wasn't long before she maneuvered herself into a staff position, producing weekly features on California and the West. Now *she* was becoming a local celebrity.

Bud climbed out of the limo, held a hand out for Maggie. "Maybe *I* ought to get an award. Whaddya think, Maggie? Executive producer?"

"Not on your life," Maggie replied, handing her glass to the chauffeur. The alcohol had settled her down a bit. She smiled at Bud as the three ascended the stairs. "If they start giving you awards there won't be any left for me." They passed through the main entrance to the famous Hotel del Coronado, beneath a gold banner welcoming "The 15th Annual San Diego MEDIA Awards."

Three enormous crystal chandeliers hung from the vaulted wooden ceiling of the Silver Strand Ballroom. A band played softly in the corner as well-heeled guests picked at hors d'oeuvres and sipped drinks, wandering among tables draped with white-and-gold tablecloths. Dinner would soon be served.

Jonas never thought he'd feel underdressed in a suit. Maggie had told him of the affair a month ago but had never mentioned it was black tie.

He recognized a few television people in the crowd, provincial stars from the local news. Harold Ray, the fifty-four-year-old co-anchor of Channel 9 Action News at Ten, smiled broadly as he said hello to Maggie. He'd helped secure network funding for Maggie's special about the effects of offshore oil drilling on whale migrations along the California coast. This piece was one of the three competing for top honors in the "Environmental Issues" documentary category. Maggie was the favorite to win.

"You just may take home the Eagle tonight, Maggie."

"What makes you think so?"

"I'm married to one of the judges!" Harold said, laughing. Eyeing Bud's ponytail, he asked, "Is this young man your husband?"

"I'm afraid not," Bud replied, shaking his hand.

"Not what? Not young or not her husband?" He laughed again.

"He's my . . . executive producer," Maggie said, smiling. She glanced at Jonas. "This is my husband."

"Jonas Taylor. Glad to meet you, Mr. Ray."

"*Professor* Jonas Taylor?"

"Yes."

"Didn't we do a piece on you a couple years ago? Something about dinosaur bones in the Salton Sea?"

"You may have. There were a lot of newspeople out there. It was an unusual find—"

"Excuse me, Jonas," Maggie interrupted, "I'm just dying for a drink. Would you mind?"

Bud pointed a finger in the air. "A gin and tonic for me, pal."

Jonas looked at Harold Ray.

"Nothing for me, Professor. I'm a presenter tonight. One more drink and I'll start reporting the news up there."

Jonas made his way to the bar. The air was humid in the windowless ballroom, and Jonas's wool jacket felt prickly and hot. He asked for a beer, a glass of champagne and a gin and tonic. The bartender pulled a bottle of Carta Blanca out of the ice. Jonas cooled his forehead with it and took a long draft. He looked back at Maggie, who was still laughing with Bud and Harold.

"Would you like another beer, sir?" The drinks were ready. Jonas looked at his bottle and realized that he had emptied it. "I'll have one of those," he said, pointing at the gin.

"Me too," a voice said behind him. "With a lime."

Jonas turned. It was the balding man with the bushy eyebrows. He peered over his wire-rimmed bifocals with the same tight grin on his face. "Fancy meeting you here, Doctor."

Jonas regarded him suspiciously. "Did you follow me here?"

"Heavens no," the man replied, scooping up a handful of almonds from the bar. He gestured vaguely at the room. "I'm in the media."

The bartender handed Jonas his drink. "You here for an award?" Jonas asked skeptically.

"No, no. Simply an observer." He put out his hand. "David Adashek. With *Science Journal*."

Jonas shook his hand warily.

"I enjoyed your lecture tremendously. Fascinating, about the Mega . . . What did you call it?"

Jonas sipped his drink, eyeing the reporter. "What is it you want, mister?"

The man finished a mouthful of almonds and took a swig of his drink. "I was given to understand that seven years ago you made some dives for the Navy in the Mariana Trench. Is that true?"

"Maybe it is, maybe it isn't. Why do you want to know?"

"Rumor has it the Navy was looking for a site to bury radioactive waste from an aging nuclear weapons program. That's a story I think my editors would have a great deal of interest in."

Jonas was stunned. "Who told you this?"

"Well, no one told me exactly—"

"Who was it?!"

"I'm sorry, Professor. I don't reveal my sources. Given the clandestine nature of the operation, I'm sure you can understand." Adashek slipped an almond into his mouth, chewing it noisily like a stick of gum. "Funny thing, though. I interviewed the fellow about it four years ago. Couldn't get a word out of him. Then last week he calls out of the blue, says if I want to know what happened I ought to talk to you. . . . Did I say something wrong, Doc?"

Jonas slowly shook his head, looked at the man. "I've got nothing to tell you. Now, you'll have to excuse me, it looks like they've begun serving dinner." He turned, walking back toward his table.

Adashek bit his lip, eyeing Jonas narrowly.

"Another drink, sir?" the bartender asked.

"Yeah," Adashek said sharply, scooping up a handful of nuts.

From the other side of the room, a pair of dark Asian eyes followed Jonas Taylor as he made his way across the ballroom, watching as he took a seat next to the blonde.

．　．　．

Four hours and six drinks later, Jonas stared at the Golden Eagle now perched on the white tablecloth, a TV camera clutched in its claws. Maggie's whale film had beat out a Discovery Channel project on the Farallon Islands and a Greenpeace documentary on the Japanese whaling industry. Maggie's acceptance speech had been largely a passionate "save the whales" plea. Her concern for the cetaceans' fate had inspired her to make the film, she had said. Jonas had wondered if he was the only one in the room who didn't believe a word she was saying.

Bud had passed out cigars. Harold Ray made a toast. Fred Henderson stopped by to offer his congratulations and say if he wasn't careful Maggie would get snapped up by a major station in Los Angeles. Maggie feigned disinterest. Jonas knew she'd heard the rumors—she had started them herself.

They were all dancing now. Maggie had taken Bud's hand and led him onto the floor, knowing Jonas wouldn't object. How could he? He didn't like to dance.

Jonas sat alone at the table, chewing the ice from his glass and trying to remember how many gins he'd downed in the last three hours. He felt tired, had a slight headache, and all signs pointed to a long evening still ahead. He got up and walked to the bar.

Harold Ray was there, picking up a bottle of wine and a pair of glasses. "So how was Baja, Professor?"

Jonas momentarily wondered if Ray was drunk. "Excuse me?"

"The cruise."

"What cruise?" He handed his glass to the bartender, nodded for a refill.

Ray laughed. "I told her three days was no vacation. Look at you, you've already forgotten."

"Oh, you mean . . . last week." Then it hit him. The trip to

San Francisco. The tan. "I'm afraid I didn't enjoy it as much as Maggie did."

"Too many margaritas?"

Jonas shook his head. "I don't drink." The bartender handed him his gin and tonic.

"Neither do I!" said Ray, laughing as he returned to his table.

Jonas stared for a long moment at the glass in his hand, then scanned the dance floor for Maggie. The band was playing "Crazy." The lights were low and couples were dancing close. He located Maggie and Bud, clinging together like a pair of drunks. Bud's hands were caressing her back, working their way down. Jonas watched as Maggie absentmindedly repositioned his hands to her buttocks.

Jonas slammed his drink down, then made his way awkwardly across the dance floor. They were still holding each other, lost to the world, their eyes dreamily closed.

Jonas tapped Bud on the shoulder. They stopped dancing, turned to him. Bud stared at his friend, a look of apprehension coming over him. "Jonas?"

Jonas let loose with a hard right to Bud's jaw. Several women screamed as Bud crashed into another couple and went sprawling to the floor. The band stopped playing.

"Keep your hands off my wife's ass."

Maggie looked aghast at Jonas. "Are you crazy?!"

Jonas rubbed his knuckles. "Do me a favor, Maggie. Next time you take a cruise to Baja, don't come back." He turned and left the dance floor, the alcohol spinning the room as he strode toward the exit.

Jonas stepped out the front entrance and ripped off his tie. A uniformed bellboy asked him for his parking stub.

"I don't have a car."

"Would you like a taxi, then?"

"He doesn't need one. I'm his ride." Terry Tanaka stepped out the door behind him.

"*You?* Jesus, when it rains it pours. What is it, Terry, you want to harass me some more?"

She smiled. "Okay, I deserved that. Just don't take a swing at me or you'll find yourself on your back."

Jonas sat down on the curb, combing his fingers through his hair. His head was throbbing. "What is it you want?"

"I followed you here. I'm sorry, believe me, it wasn't my idea. My father insisted."

Jonas glanced back at the door. "This isn't exactly a good time . . ."

She handed him a photograph. "It's about this."

His eyes took in the image. He looked back at the woman. "What the hell *did* this?"

UNIS

Jonas let her take him home, cooling his knuckles in the wind as they drove. His eyes remained on the road, but he kept studying the photograph in his mind.

Taken 38,000 feet beneath the surface of the western Pacific in the deep canyon waters of the Mariana Trench, the black-and-white photograph showed a spherical UNIS (Unmanned Nautical Informational Submersible), a remote-sensing device used to monitor conditions at the ocean floor. Jonas was quite familiar with the most recent research on these remarkable robots. In a joint Japanese-American earthquake detection project, twenty-five titanium UNIS submersibles had been deployed by the Tanaka Institute along a 125-mile stretch of the Mariana Trench to monitor tremors at the bottom of the world's deepest underwater canyon.

"The deployment was a success," Terry told him as they reached the freeway. "Even my father was happy." Masao Tanaka and the Tanaka Oceanographic Institute in Monterey had designed the UNIS systems for the joint project. Within two weeks of deployment the Institute's surface ship, the *Kiku,* was receiving a steady stream of data, and scientists on both sides of the Pacific were studying the information eagerly.

Then something went wrong. "Three weeks after the launch," Terry explained, "the Japanese called to say that one of the UNIS robots had stopped transmitting data. A week later, two more units shut down. When another one stopped a few days after that, my father decided we had to do something."

Terry looked at Jonas. "He sent my brother down in the Abyss Glider."

"D.J.?"

"He's the most experienced pilot we have."

"No one should descend that far alone."

"I agree. I told Dad that I should have gone with him in the other Glider."

"You?"

Terry glared at him. "You have a problem with that? For your information, I happen to be a damn good pilot."

"I'm sure you are, but at thirty-five thousand feet? What's the deepest you've ever soloed?"

"I've hit sixteen thousand twice, no problem."

"Not bad," admitted Jonas.

"Not bad for a woman, you mean."

"Hey, hey, I meant not bad for anyone. Very few humans have been down that deep. Damn, Terry, take it easy."

She smiled. "Sorry. It gets frustrating, you know. Dad's strictly old-fashioned Japanese. Woman are to be seen and not heard, that kind of attitude."

"So go on," said Jonas. "How did D.J. do in the Marianas?"

"He did well. He found the UNIS, filmed everything. The photo came from his video."

Jonas took another look at the photograph. It showed a UNIS submersible lying on its side at the bottom of the deep-water

25

canyon. *The sphere had been cracked open.* Its tripod legs were mangled, a bolted bracket torn off, and the titanium skin of the sphere itself severely battered and scarred.

Jonas studied the image. "Where's the sonar plate?"

"D.J. found it forty yards down-current. He hauled it up—it's at the Institute in Monterey. That's why I'm here. My father would like you to take a look at it."

Jonas stared at her skeptically.

"You can fly up with me in the morning," she said. "I'm taking the Institute's plane back at eight."

Lost in thought, Jonas almost missed his driveway. "There—on the left."

She turned down the long, leaf-littered driveway, then parked in front of a handsome Spanish colonial buried in foliage.

As Terry switched off the engine, Jonas turned to her and narrowed his eyes. "Is that *all* your father wants?"

Terry paused a moment. "As far as I know. We don't know what happened down there. Dad thinks maybe you could help provide some answers, give us your professional opinion—"

"My professional opinion is that you should stay the hell out of the Mariana Trench. It's far too dangerous to be exploring, especially in a one-man submersible."

"Hey, listen, *Doctor* Taylor. Maybe you lost your nerve after so many years in retirement, but D.J. and I haven't. What the hell happened to you anyway? I was only seventeen when we first met, but I remember you being full of piss and vinegar."

"Terry, the Mariana Trench is too deep, just too dangerous."

"Too dangerous? What is it you're so afraid of, a sixty-foot great white shark?" She smirked. "Let me tell you something, Jonas, the data we collected in the first two weeks was invaluable. If the earthquake detection system works, it will save thousands of lives. Is your schedule so damn busy that you can't take a day to fly up to the Institute? My father's asking for your help. Just examine

26

the sonar plate and review the video that my brother took and you'll be home to your darling wife by tomorrow night. I'm sure my father will even give you a personal tour of his new whale lagoon."

Jonas took a breath. He considered Masao Tanaka a friend, a commodity he seemed to be running short of lately. "When would we leave?" he asked.

"Meet me tomorrow morning at the commuter airport at seven-thirty sharp."

"The commuter . . . we're taking one of those puddle jumpers?" Jonas swallowed hard.

"Relax. I know the pilot. See you in the morning." She looked at him another moment, then walked back to her car. Jonas stood there, watching her drive away.

Jonas shut the door behind him and switched on the light, feeling for a moment like a stranger in his own home. The house was dead quiet. A trace of Maggie's perfume lingered in the air. She won't be home until late, he thought.

He went into the kitchen, pulled a bottle of vodka from the cabinet, then changed his mind. He turned on the coffeemaker, replaced the filter and added some coffee, then filled the slot with water. He ran the faucet, sucked cold water from the spigot and rinsed out his mouth. He shut off the water and for a long moment stood at the sink, staring out the back window into the darkness while the coffee brewed. It was black out there. All he could see was his reflection in the glass.

When the coffee was done, he grabbed a mug and the entire pot and went into his study.

Sanctuary. The one room in the house that was truly his own. The walls were covered with contour maps of the ocean's continental margins, mountain ranges, abyssal plains, and deep-sea trenches. Several fossilized Megalodon teeth littered the tables. Some stood upright in glass cases, others lay on stacks of notes like paperweights. A framed painting of a great white shark hung above his desk, and next to it an anatomical diagram of the creature's internal organs.

Jonas set the coffee mug down beside the computer, then positioned himself at the keyboard. A set of jaws from a twelve-foot great white gaped at him from high above his monitor. He punched a few keys to access the Internet, then typed out the web address of the Tanaka Oceanographic Institute.

Titanium. Even Jonas found it hard to believe.

NIGHT OWLS

Jonas gulped the hot liquid and waited for the menu to appear before him. He typed in the word: UNIS.

UNIS

Unmanned Nautical Informational Submersible

Originally designed and developed in 1979 by Masao Tanaka, CEO of the Tanaka Oceanographic Institute, to study whale populations in the wild. Reconfigured in 1997 in conjunction with the Japan Marine Science Technology Center (JAMSTEC) to record and track seismic disturbances along the deep-sea trenches. Each UNIS system is composed of a three-inch-thick titanium outer shell. The unit is supported by three retractable legs and weighs 2,600 pounds. Each UNIS system is designed to withstand pressures of 35,000 pounds per square inch. UNIS communicates information back to a surface ship by way of fiber-optic cable.

UNIS INSTRUMENTATION:

Electrical Fields	Mineral Deposits	Salinity
Seismic Equipment	Topography	Water Temperature

Jonas reviewed the engineering reports of the UNIS systems, impressed by the simplicity of the design. Positioned along a seismic fault line, the UNIS remotes could detect the telltale signs of an impending earthquake.

Southern Japan had the misfortune of being geographically located on the convergence of three tectonic plates. Periodically, these plates grind against each other, generating about one-tenth of the world's annual earthquakes. One devastating quake in 1923 had killed over 140,000 people.

In 1994, Masao Tanaka had been desperately seeking funds to complete his dream project, a monstrous cetacean lagoon, or whale sanctuary. JAMSTEC had agreed to fund the entire project if the Tanaka Institute would provide twenty-five UNIS remotes to monitor seismic activity within the Challenger Deep. Three years later, the systems had been successfully deployed. But after a few weeks of transmitting critical data to the surface ship seven miles above, something had gone wrong. Now Masao Tanaka needed Jonas's help to discover the cause of the breakdowns.

Jonas took a long swig of coffee. The Challenger Deep, he thought to himself. Submarine experts referred to it as "hell's antechamber."

Jonas just called it "hell."

Twenty miles away, Terry Tanaka, freshly showered, wrapped in the hotel towel, sat on the edge of her queen-sized bed at the Holiday Inn. Taylor had really irked her. The man was obstinate, with strong chauvinistic ideas. Why her father had insisted that their team required his input was beyond her. Pulling out her briefcase, Terry decided that she needed to review the personnel file on Professor Jonas Taylor.

She knew the basics by heart. Educated at Penn State; advanced degrees from the University of California–San Diego and Woods Hole Oceanographic Institute. Previously a full professor at the Scripps Institute and author of three books on paleobiology. At one time, Jonas Taylor had been considered one of the most experienced submersible pilots in the world. He had piloted the *Alvin* submersible seventeen times, leading multiple explorations to four different deep-sea trenches in the 1980s. And then, seven years ago, for some unknown reason, he had simply given it all up.

"It doesn't make sense," Terry said aloud. Thinking back to the lecture earlier in the evening, she remembered the bushy-eyebrowed man who had practically accused Jonas of piloting an expedition into the Mariana Trench. Yet nothing in his personnel file indicated any trip into the Challenger Deep.

Terry put the file aside and powered up her laptop computer. She entered her personal code, then accessed the Institute's computers.

She punched up: Mariana Trench.

FILE NAME: MARIANA TRENCH

LOCATION:
Western Pacific Ocean, east of Philippines, close to island of Guam.

FACTS:
Deepest known depression on earth. Measures 35,827 feet deep (10,920 m), over 1,550 miles long (2,500 km), making the trench the deepest abyss on the planet and the second

longest. The deepest area of the Mariana Trench is called the Challenger Deep, named after the *Challenger II* expedition that discovered it in 1951. Note: A 1 kg weight dropped into the sea above the trench would require more than an hour to reach bottom.

EXPLORATION (MANNED):
On January 23, 1960, the U.S. Navy bathyscaphe *Trieste* descended 35,800 feet (10,911 m), nearly touching bottom of the Challenger Deep. On board were U.S. Navy Lt. Donald Walsh and Swiss oceanographer Jacques Piccard. In the same year, the French bathyscaphe *Archimède* completed a similar dive. In each case, the bathyscaphes simply descended and returned to the surface ship.

EXPLORATION (UNMANNED):
In 1993, the Japanese launched *Kaiko,* an unmanned robotic craft, which descended to 35,798 feet before breaking down. In 1997, 25 UNIS robotic submersibles were successfully deployed by the Tanaka Oceanographic Institute along the Challenger Deep's seafloor.

Terry skimmed through the file. Nothing about Jonas Taylor here. She keyed in: Naval Exploration.

NAVAL EXPLORATION: (see) TRIESTE, 1960.
SEACLIFF, 1990.

Seacliff? Why hadn't the name appeared in the data above? She probed further.

SEACLIFF: ACCESS DENIED.
AUTHORIZED U.S. NAVAL PERSONNEL ONLY.

For several minutes, Terry attempted to gain access to the file, but it was hopeless. She felt a knot in her stomach.

She put the laptop away, thinking of tonight's lecture. Her first meeting with Jonas Taylor had been ten years ago at a symposium held at her father's institute. Jonas had been invited to speak about his deep-sea dives aboard the *Alvin* submersible. At the time, Terry was seventeen and had worked closely with her father, organizing the symposium, coordinating travel and hotel arrangements for more than seventy scientists from around the world. She had booked Jonas's ticket and met him at the airport herself. She recalled developing a schoolgirl crush on the deep-sea pilot with the athletic build. Terry looked at his picture again in her file. Tonight, Professor Taylor had appeared confident, yet, in a way, a little helpless. A handsome face, tan, with a few more stress lines around the eyes. Dark brown hair turning gray near the temples. Six foot one, she guessed, about 195. Still had the athletic build.

What had happened to the man? And why had her father insisted on locating him? As far as Terry was concerned, Jonas Taylor's involvement was the last thing the UNIS project needed.

Jonas woke up in his clothes. A dog was barking somewhere in the neighborhood. He squinted at the clock. Six A.M. He was lying on the couch in his den, a ream of computer printouts scattered all around him. He sat up, his head pounding, his foot knocking over the half-empty coffeepot, staining the beige carpet brown. He rubbed his bloodshot eyes, looked up at the computer. His screen saver was on. He tapped the mouse, revealing a diagram of the

UNIS remote, glowing on the screen. His memory came flooding back.

The dog stopped barking. The house seemed unusually quiet. Jonas got up, went into the hallway, walked down to the master bedroom.

Maggie wasn't there. Their bed hadn't been touched.

MONTEREY

Terry spotted him crossing the tarmac from the parking lot.

"Good morning, Professor," she said, just a little bit too loud. She smiled. "How's your head?"

Jonas shifted his duffel bag to his other shoulder. "Talk softer." He eyed the plane warily. "You didn't tell me it was . . . so small."

"It's not. For a Beechcraft." She was finishing her preflight checklist. The plane was a twin-turbo, with a whale logo and "TOI" painted on the fuselage.

Jonas set down his bag, looked around. "Where's the pilot?"

She put her hands on her hips and smiled.

"*You?*" he said.

"Hey, let's not start that shit again. Are you going to have a problem with this?"

"No, I just . . ."

Terry went back to her inspection. "If it makes you feel any better, I've been flying for six years."

Jonas nodded uneasily. It didn't make him feel better. It just made him feel old.

"Are you all right?" she asked as he fumbled with his seat belt. Jonas looked a little pale. He hadn't said a word since he'd boarded the plane. "If you'd rather sit in back there's plenty of room to stretch out. Barf bags are in the side pocket." She smiled.

"You're enjoying this."

"I didn't think that an experienced deep-sea pilot like you would be so squirmish."

"Guess I'm used to being in control. Just fly the damn plane. Up front will be fine," he said, his eyes impulsively scanning the dials and meters on the control panel. The cockpit was a little tight, the copilot seat felt jammed up against the windshield.

"That's as far back as it goes," Terry told him as he searched for a lever to adjust the seat.

He swallowed dryly. "I need a glass of water."

She noticed his trembling hands. "The green cabinet, in back."

Jonas got up and struggled back into the cabin.

"There's beer in the fridge," she called out.

Jonas unzipped his duffel bag, found his dop kit, and took out an amber medicine bottle filled with small yellow pills. Claustrophobia. His doctor had diagnosed the problem after the accident, a psychosomatic reaction to the stress he had endured. A deep-sea pilot with claustrophobia was as useless as a high diver with vertigo. The two just didn't mix.

Jonas chased down two of the pills with water from a paper cup. He stared at his trembling hand, crumpling the cup into his fist. He closed his eyes a moment, then took a long, deep breath. When he slowly opened them and looked at the crinkled cup in the palm of his hand he was no longer shaking.

"You okay?" Terry asked through the door of the cockpit.

Jonas looked up at her. "I told you, I'm fine."

．　．　．

The flight to Monterey lasted two and a half hours. Jonas settled in and began to enjoy it. Above the coast of Big Sur, Terry spotted a pair of whales migrating south along the shore. "Blues," she said.

"Cruising to Baja," he added, staring down at the endangered species.

"Jonas, listen. About the lecture. I didn't mean to come off so harshly. It's just that Dad insisted that I find you, and frankly, I didn't see the purpose of wasting your time. I mean, it's not like we need another submersible pilot."

"Good, because I wouldn't be interested if you did."

"Well, we don't." She felt her blood beginning to boil again. "Maybe you could convince my father to allow me to follow D.J. down in the second Abyss Glider?"

"Pass." He gazed out his window.

"Why not?"

Jonas looked at the girl. "First, I've never seen you pilot a sub, which is a hell of a lot different than flying a plane. There's a lot of pressure down there—"

That did it. "Pressure? You want pressure? Terry pulled back on the wheel and rolled the Beechcraft into a series of tight 360s, then sent the small plane into a nauseating nosedive.

The plane righted itself at 1,500 feet as Jonas puked across the dashboard.

THE REPORTER

David Adashek adjusted his wire-rimmed bifocals, then knocked on the double doors of Suite 810. No reply. He knocked again, this time louder.

The door opened, revealing a groggy Maggie Taylor standing behind it, wearing nothing but a white robe. It was untied, exposing her tan breasts.

"David, Christ, what time is it?"

"Almost noon. Rough night?"

She smiled, still half asleep. "Not as rough as my husband's, I'm sure. Sit." She pointed to a pair of white sofas that faced a big-screen TV in the living area.

"Nice suite. Where's Bud?"

Maggie curled up on the far sofa opposite Adashek. "He left about two hours ago. You did a nice job of harassing Jonas at the lecture."

"Is all this necessary, Maggie? He seems like a decent enough guy—"

"So *you* marry him. After almost ten years, I've had enough."

"Why not just divorce him and get it over with?"

"It's not that simple. Now that I'm in the media's eye, my agent says we have to be very careful about what the public's perception will be. Jonas still has a lot of friends in this town. He has to come off as a lunatic. People have to believe that his actions brought this divorce on. Last night was a good start."

"So what's next?"

"Where's Jonas now?"

Adashek pulled out his notes. "He went home with the Tanaka woman—"

"Jonas? With another woman?" Maggie laughed hysterically.

"It was innocent. Just a ride home from the awards. I followed him to the commuter airport earlier this morning. They're headed to Monterey. My guess is to that new whale lagoon the Tanaka Oceanographic Institute is constructing."

"Okay, stay with him, and keep me informed. By the end of next week, I want you to go public with the Navy story, emphasizing the fact that two of the crew were killed. Once the story hits, you'll do a follow-up interview with me, then I'll push for the divorce, public humiliation and all."

"You're the boss. Listen, if I'm going to be following Jonas, I'll need some more cash."

Terry pulled a thick envelope out of her robe pocket. "Bud says to save the receipts."

Yeah, thought Adashek, I'm sure he needs the write-off.

LAGOON

"There it is." Terry pointed to the shoreline as they descended toward the sparkling Monterey Bay.

Jonas sipped the warm soda, his stomach still jumpy from Terry's little air show. His head pounded, and he had already made up his mind to leave immediately after meeting with Masao. As far as he was concerned, Terry Tanaka was the last person Jonas would ever recommend to Masao to descend to the bottom of the Challenger Deep.

Jonas looked down and to his right at the empty man-made lagoon situated on a ten-mile-square parcel of beachfront real estate just south of Moss Landing. From the air it looked like a giant oval-shaped swimming pool. Lying parallel to the ocean, the structure was just over three-quarters of a mile in length and a quarter mile wide. It was eighty feet deep at its center, with walls two stories high and enormous acrylic windows at each end. A concrete canal at the midpoint of the lagoon's oceanside wall connected it with the deep waters of the Pacific.

The lagoon held no water yet. Construction workers crawled

like ants over the walls and scaffolding. If the schedule held, in less than a month the massive doors of the canal entrance would be opened and the lagoon would fill with seawater. It would be the largest man-made aquarium in the world.

"If I hadn't seen it with my own eyes, I wouldn't have believed it," Jonas said as they prepared to land.

Terry smiled proudly. Masao Tanaka had made the building of the aquarium his life's work. Designed as a living laboratory, the lagoon would serve as a natural yet protective environment for its future inhabitants, the largest creatures ever known to exist on earth. Each winter tens of thousands of the mammals migrated through California's coastal waters to breed. When the aquarium was complete, its doors would open to welcome them, the giant cetaceans—the grays, the humpbacks, and perhaps even the endangered blues.

Masao's dream was becoming a reality.

Forty-five minutes later, Jonas found himself smiling into the eyes of the lagoon's founder.

"Jonas! My God, it's so good to see you." Masao Tanaka, a good foot shorter than Taylor, was positively beaming at the man. "Let me look at you. Ah, you look like shit. Smell like it too! Hah. What's the matter? You don't like flying with my daughter?"

"No, as a matter of fact, I don't." Jonas gave the girl a look to kill.

Masao looked at his daughter. "Terry?"

"His fault, Dad. It's not my problem if he can't handle the pressure. I'll see you in the projection room." She walked off the tarmac, heading toward the three-story building at the end of the lagoon.

"My apologies, Taylor-san. Terry is very headstrong, she is

41

somewhat of a free spirit. Is that the term? It is difficult raising a daughter without a female role model."

"Forget it, I really came up to see you and your whale lagoon. Amazing."

"I'll give you a tour later. Come, we'll get you a fresh shirt. Then I want you to meet my chief engineer, Alphonse DeMarco. He is reviewing the video D.J. took in the trench. Jonas, I really need your input."

Jonas followed Masao to the projection room. They entered the dark room where the video was already being viewed. Jonas took a seat next to Terry as DeMarco greeted Masao.

The video showed a spotlight cutting a beam through the clear, dark water. The wreckage of the UNIS loomed into view. It was lying on its side at the bottom of a canyon wall, wedged in between boulders and mud.

Alphonse DeMarco stared at the monitor in the video-editing suite. "D.J. found it a hundred yards down from its initial position."

Jonas rose from his seat and approached the monitor. "What do *you* think happened?"

DeMarco stared at the screen as the spotlight roamed over the scarred metal surface of the broken submersible. "The simplest explanation is it got caught in a landslide."

"A landslide?"

"I'm sure you know they're a frequent occurrence down there. Just look at all of those rocks."

Jonas walked to the table behind them. The retrieved half-shell of the sonar plate lay there like a severed piece of abstract sculpture. Jonas touched the torn edge of the metal dish. "It's titanium casing over four-inch steel supports. I've seen the stress-test data—"

"The shell may have developed a crack on impact. The currents are incredibly strong."

"Is there any evidence—?"

"The UNIS recorded an increase in turbulence almost two minutes before we lost contact."

Jonas paused, then looked back at DeMarco. "What about the others?"

"Two of the other missing UNIS systems recorded similar changes in turbulence. If a landslide got this one, we can probably assume the same thing happened to the others."

Jonas turned toward the monitor. "You've lost four units," he said. "Isn't it pushing the limits of probability to say they've all been destroyed in landslides?"

DeMarco removed his glasses and rubbed his eyes. He'd had this argument with Masao more than once. "We knew the trenches were seismically active. Cables that cross other canyons are broken by landslides all the time. All this means is the Mariana Trench is even more unstable than we'd expected."

"Changes in deep-sea currents often precede landslide activity," chimed in Terry.

"Jonas," said Masao, "this entire project depends on our ability to determine what happened to these robots and correct the situation immediately. I have decided that we must retrieve this UNIS. My son cannot do the job alone. The job requires two subs working together; one to clear the debris and steady the UNIS while the second sub attaches the cable—"

"Dad!" Terry suddenly realized why her father had insisted on locating Jonas.

"Stop the tape." Jonas had seen something on the monitor. "Go back a little," he said to the editor.

"That's good. Let it play."

They stared at the shifting image on the screen. The spotlight circled to the opposite side of the UNIS sphere, partially submerged in boulders and mud. The light shone into the debris near its base.

"There!" Jonas said. The editor froze the frame. Jonas pointed to a tiny white fragment wedged under the submersible. "Can you blow that up?"

The man punched some buttons and a square outline appeared on the monitor. Moving a joystick, he positioned the square around the object, then pulled it out to fill the screen.

The triangular object was larger, but fuzzy and unclear. Jonas stared at the screen. "It's a tooth," he stated.

DeMarco moved closer, scrutinizing the image. "You're nuts, Taylor."

"DeMarco," commanded Masao in an authoritative voice. "Show the proper respect to our guest."

"I'm sorry, Masao, but what our professor here is saying is impossible. You see that?" He pointed to a bolt dangling from a steel strut. "That's a bolt for a girder beam," he said. "It's three inches long." He pointed to the fuzzy white object below it. "That would mean that . . . thing—whatever it is—is at least seven, eight inches long."

He looked at Masao. "There's no creature on earth with teeth *that* big."

Jonas held a photograph of the blown-up video frame in his hand as he and Terry followed Masao down the corridor which led to the giant aquarium lagoon. Terry had located a staff T-shirt for the professor.

"If it *is* a tooth, how do we know it wasn't just uncovered in the landslide?" Terry asked.

"We don't. But it looks white, Terry. Every fossilized Megalodon tooth we've found has been gray or black, denoting its age. A white tooth would indicate that its owner had only recently perished, or perhaps could still be alive."

"You certainly seem excited about this," said Terry, trying to keep up with her father.

Jonas stopped. "Terry, I need to recover that tooth; it's very important to me."

She looked up at him, almond eyes blazing. "No way. If anyone accompanies my brother into the trench, it will be me! Why is this so important to you anyway, Jonas?" Before he could answer, Masao called out.

"Hey, I'm not babysitting here. You wanna see my lagoon, you keep up!"

Terry glared at him. "This discussion isn't over, Jonas."

They reached a doorway through the towering wall of the aquarium and entered the giant lagoon. Jonas stopped, awestruck by its enormity.

Masao Tanaka stood in front of them proudly, a tight smile etched across his face. "We do nice work, eh, my friend?"

Jonas could only nod in agreement.

Masao turned his back to Jonas and Terry. "This lagoon has been my dream since I was six years old. Forty million dollars, almost seven years of planning, four years of construction, Jonas. I did all I could, gave it everything I had."

He turned and faced them again, tears in his eyes. "It's too bad she is never gonna open."

MASAO

Jonas sat in the bamboo chair and gazed upon the setting sun as it kissed the Pacific horizon. Masao Tanaka's home had been built into the Santa Lucia Mountains in California's Big Sur Valley. The cool ocean breeze and magnificent view were intoxicating, relaxing Jonas for the first time in as long as he could remember.

The Tanakas had invited Jonas to spend the night. Terry was in the kitchen at her father's request, preparing a plate of jumbo shrimp for the barbecue. Masao emerged from the house, checked on the gas grill, then walked around the pool and took a seat next to Jonas.

"Terry says dinner will be ready soon. I hope you're hungry, Jonas. My daughter is a very good cook." He smiled.

Jonas looked at his friend. "I'm sure she is. Now, tell me about the lagoon, Masao. What made you build it in the first place? And why did you say it may never be completed?"

Masao shut his eyes and breathed deeply. "Jonas, you smell that sweet ocean air? It makes you appreciate nature, eh?"

"Yes."

"You know, my father was a fisherman. Back in Japan, he would take me out almost every morning. I guess he had to. My mother died when I was only four, so there was no one else to take care of me but my father.

"When I was six, we moved to America to live with relatives in San Francisco. Four months later, the Japanese attack Pearl Harbor. All Orientals are locked in detention camps. Jonas, my father was a very proud man. He could never accept the fact that he was in a prison, unable to fish, unable to live his life. One morning, my father just decided to die. Left me all alone, locked up in a foreign land, unable to speak or understand a word of English."

"You were all alone?"

Masao smiled. "Yes, Jonas, until I saw my first whale. From the prison gates, I could see them leap. The humpbacks, they sang to me, kept me company, occupied my mind. My only friends." He closed his eyes for a moment, in deep thought.

"You know, Jonas, Americans are funny people. One minute, you can feel hated by them, the next loved. After eighteen months, I was released and adopted by my American family, David and Kiku Gordon. I was very lucky. They loved me, supported me, put me through school. But when I felt depressed, it was my whales that kept me going."

"Now I understand why this project means so much to you," said Jonas.

"Learning about whales is very important. In many ways they are superior to man. But capturing and imprisoning them in small tanks, forcing them to perform stupid human tricks so they can receive their rations of food, is very cruel. This lagoon, it will allow me to study the whales in a natural environment. The lagoon will remain open so the whales can enter and exit of their own free will. No more small tanks. Having been locked up myself, I could never do that. Never." Masao closed his eyes again. "You know, Jonas, humans could learn a lot from whales."

"So why won't your lagoon ever open?"

Masao shook his head. "For three years I searched for financing for the project. No bank in the United States would support my dreams. Finally, I met with JAMSTEC. They don't care about building lagoons, they just want to buy my UNIS systems to monitor earthquakes. It seemed like a good deal. They agreed to underwrite my lagoon and the Tanaka Institute agreed to work on the Mariana Trench/UNIS project. But when the UNIS systems began breaking down, JAMSTEC froze all our funding."

"You'll finish the lagoon, Masao. We'll figure out what happened."

"What do you think happened?" Masao's eyes blazed into Taylor's, searching for answers.

"Honestly, Masao, I don't know. DeMarco may be right. The UNIS robots could have anchored themselves too close to the canyon wall. But I can't imagine a boulder being able to crush titanium like that."

"Jonas, you and I are friends."

Jonas looked at the older man. "Of course—"

"Good. I tell you my story, now you tell your old friend Tanaka the truth. What happened to you in the Mariana Trench?"

"What makes you think I was in the Mariana?"

Masao smiled knowingly. "We've known each other . . . what? Ten years? You lectured at my Institute at least a half dozen times. Now you underestimate me? I have contacts in the Navy too, you know. I know what the Navy says happened. Now I want to hear your side."

Jonas rubbed his eyes. "Okay, Masao, for some reason it seems that the story is being leaked anyway. There were three of us on board a new Navy deep-sea submersible, the *Seacliff*. I was the pilot, the other two crewmen were scientists with the Navy. We were measuring deep-sea currents in the trench to determine if plutonium rods from nuclear power plants could be safely buried within the Challenger Deep."

Jonas closed his eyes. "I guess we were hovering about four thousand feet from the bottom. It was my third descent in eight days, too much really, but I was the only qualified pilot. The scientists were busy conducting tests. I was just looking out the porthole, staring down into the black abyss, when I thought I saw something circling below."

"What can you see in darkness, Jonas?"

"I'm not sure, but it appeared to be glowing, totally white, and very big. At first I thought it could be a whale, but I knew that was impossible. Then it just disappeared. I figured I had to be hallucinating."

"So what happened next?"

"I . . . to tell you the truth, Masao, I'm not sure. I remember seeing this huge head, or at least I thought I did."

"A head?"

"Triangular, Masao. Monstrous, as big as a truck, all white with huge teeth. They say I panicked, dropped every weight plate the sub had and rocketed toward the surface. Never decompressed . . . just panicked."

"Jonas, this head, it was this Megalodon you lecture about?"

"I guess that's been my theory all of these years."

"Did the creature pursue you?"

"No, apparently not. I blacked out with the others . . ."

"Two men died."

"Yes."

"What happened to you?"

Jonas rubbed his eyes again. "I spent three weeks in a hospital, then went through months of psychoanalysis. Not a fun time."

"You think this creature crushed our UNIS robot?"

Jonas looked to the horizon. "I don't know. The truth is, I've begun to doubt my own memories of the event. If it was a Megalodon I saw, how did it simply disappear? I was looking straight down at it, then *poof,* gone."

Masao sat back in his chair. "Jonas, I believe you saw something, but I don't think it was a monster. You know, D.J. tells me there are giant patches of tubeworms all along the bottom. Thousands in a single growth. D.J. says these worms glow in the dark, all white. You never did make it to the very bottom of the trench, did you, Jonas?"

"No, Masao."

"D.J. made it. That boy loves deep-sea diving, says it's like being in outer space. Jonas, I think what you saw was a patch of tubeworms. I think the currents pushed them out of your sight line. That's why they seemed to disappear. You were exhausted, staring into the darkness. The Navy worked you too hard, three dives in eight days is not safe. And now you've spent seven years of your life hypothesizing how these monsters may still be alive."

Jonas sat in silence.

Masao placed his hand on Jonas's shoulder. "My friend, I need your help. And I think maybe it's time to face your fears. I want you to return to the Mariana Trench with D.J., but this time you'll make it all the way to the bottom. You'll see these patches of giant tubeworms for yourself. You were once a great pilot, and I know in my heart you still are. You can't live in fear your whole life."

Tears began forming in Jonas's eyes. "Okay . . . okay, Masao, I'll go back." He choked back a laugh. "Boy, your daughter is going to be very pissed off. She wants to be the second pilot, you know."

Masao smiled grimly. "I know. D.J. says she's good too, but she's very emotional. One must be extra cautious seven miles below the surface, eh? My daughter will get her opportunities on other dives, but not in this hellhole."

"I agree."

"Good. And when all of this is over, my friend, you will come work with me at the lagoon, okay?"

Jonas laughed. "We'll see."

Masao waited until after dinner to tell his daughter of his plans. Jonas excused himself, exiting the kitchen for the living room as the conversation in Japanese heated up. He had no idea what was being said, but it was obvious that Terry Tanaka was livid.

THE *KIKU*

Terry rose from her seat on the aisle and headed back toward the plane's rest room. Jonas pushed aside the laptop computer and laid his head back against the seat.

They were on an American Airlines flight five hours out of San Francisco. DeMarco and Terry had been talking Jonas through the computerized "flight" simulator, a laptop program for instructing pilots in the operation of the Abyss Glider II. The AG II was the one-man, deep-sea submersible that had carried D. J. to the bottom of the Mariana Trench. Jonas would accompany him in a second AG on the trip to retrieve the UNIS. He was already familiar with the basic operations of the submersible, having piloted the AG I, the sub's shallow-water predecessor, several years earlier. Now all he needed was to familiarize himself with the new deep-sea design. There'd be plenty of time for that. It was a twelve-hour flight across the Pacific to Guam, plus a stop in Honolulu for refueling.

Terry's attitude toward Jonas had turned cold. She was visibly hurt that her father had ignored her qualifications to back up D.J., and felt Jonas had lied to her about not being interested in piloting the sub in the Mariana Trench. She would help train Jonas on the simulator, but nothing more.

The Abyss Glider simulator used two computer joysticks to "steer" the submersible by simulating adjustment of its midwing and tail fins. Because most of the trip to the bottom was in complete darkness, the pilot had to learn to "fly blind," navigating the craft to the bottom using readouts alone. For this reason, piloting with the simulator was very much like piloting the real thing. So similar, in fact, that Jonas had to stop working, close his eyes, and try to relax.

Jonas thought about his conversation with Masao Tanaka. It had never occurred to him that he could have been focused on tubeworms. *Riftia.* Jonas had seen smaller varieties of the species growing in clusters around every hydrothermal vent he had ever explored. The tubeworms were a luminescent white, possessing neither mouths nor digestive organs. They relied on thick colonies of bacteria living inside their bodies. The worms supplied hydrogen sulfide, which they extracted from the sulfur-rich waters of the trench. The bacteria inside the worms used the hydrogen sulfide to make food for themselves and their host.

Until man began exploring the deep-sea trenches, no life was thought to exist at the very bottom of the ocean. Man's knowledge of existence was limited to what he understood: Where there is light, there is food. If there is no light, then no food. Since no light could penetrate the deepest trenches of the sea, then photosynthesis could not exist to allow life to take a foothold.

But Jonas had seen it for himself. The hydrothermal vents supported a unique food chain by spewing searing-hot water and vast amounts of chemicals and mineral deposits out of cracks in the seabed. The high sulfur content, poisonous to most species, became food for a variety of deep-sea bacteria. The bacteria, in turn, were living inside worms and mollusks, breaking down other chemicals into usable food. The massive clumps of tubeworms also consumed the bacteria, and a variety of newly discovered species of fish ate the tubeworms. The process was called chemosynthesis: bacteria receiving energy from chemicals rather than energy from the sun. Despite man's common beliefs, life flourished in the darkest, seemingly most uninhabitable location on the planet.

D.J. had told Masao that the tubeworm clusters sometimes covered a fifty-foot expanse along the bottom. It was possible, thought Jonas, that he has been staring at a worm cluster, fallen asleep, and imagined the triangular head. Jonas felt ill. Two men had died for his mistake. The Megalodon defense he had convinced himself of for all of these years somehow had lessened his guilt. Coming to grips with the fact that he might have imagined the whole event made him feel sick.

One way or another, Jonas knew Masao was right; he had to face his fears and return to the trench. If a white Megalodon tooth could be found, it would justify seven years of research. If not, so be it. One way or the other, it was time to get on with his life.

Fifteen rows behind Jonas and DeMarco, David Adashek closed the hardback, *Extinct Species of the Abyss* by Dr. Jonas Taylor. He removed his bifocals, positioned his pillow against the window, and fell asleep.

The Navy helicopter flew low above the waves. The pilot glanced over his shoulder at Jonas and DeMarco. "There she is, people."

"It's about time," DeMarco said, and turned to wake Terry. She'd been sleeping since they'd left the naval station in Guam.

Jonas trained his eyes on the horizon, a faint line separating the gray ocean from the gray sky. He couldn't see anything. Maybe *I* should have slept, he thought, rubbing his eyes. He was certainly tired enough. They'd been traveling for over fifteen hours.

He looked once more and now could see the ship, a flat speck quickly growing larger. In less than a minute they were close enough to read the name on the hull: *Kiku.*

The *Kiku* was a decommissioned Oliver Hazard Perry class Guided Missile Frigate, disarmed and reconfigured for ocean research. The Tanaka Institute had purchased the 445-foot-long steel ship from the Navy three years ago, rechristening it the *Kiku,* after Masao's mother.

The frigate was perfect for deep-sea research. Removing the SAM missile launcher from her bow gave the crew plenty of deck space on which to work. Situated in the stern, along the transom, was a reinforced-steel winch, designed to lift even the heaviest submersible into and out of the sea. Behind the winch was a massive spool containing over seven miles of steel cable.

Forty feet of deck separated the winch from two hangars located in the stern. One held the twin pair of Abyss Gliders, the one-man submersibles that D.J. and Jonas would descend in; the other stored the ship's helicopter. Steel tracks embedded within the deck allowed the crafts to be rolled in and out of their respective hangars.

The small pilothouse overlooked the bow from the second deck and contained the navigator's console board, which drove the two GE LM 2500 gas-turbine engines. A short corridor connected the pilothouse to the Command Information Center (CIC). This once-secured room was always cool, always kept dark, illuminated only by the soft blue overhead lights and the colorful computer console screens situated along the interior walls. The weapons stations which had controlled the frigate's SAM and Harpoon missiles, the antisub torpedoes, and a variety of other guns and countermeasures had been replaced with computers that now monitored the deployed UNIS systems, retrieving data from the robots implanted along the Challenger Deep seven miles below the ship.

The *Kiku*'s CIC also contained the hull-mounted Raytheon SQS-56 sonar and Raytheon SPS-49 radar systems, the exterior dishes of which could be seen rotating on two towers rising twenty-five feet above the upper deck. All of these systems were linked to a computer integration program that displayed the information across a dozen computer consoles.

Below the control deck were the galley and the crew quarters. The triple-stacked coffinlike bunks of the Navy had been torn out, the interior reconfigured to accommodate more private quarters for the crew of thirty-two. Below this deck were the engine room and the main machinery that drove the twin-shaft propellers. The *Kiku* was a fast ship, capable of speeds up to twenty-nine knots.

As the helicopter approached the aft deck, Jonas immediately recognized the large reinforced-steel winch attached to the ship's transom which had been used to lower the twenty-five UNIS submersibles to the bottom of the Mariana Trench. Terry peered out the window, pressing close to Jonas. A young man in his early twenties stood face into the wind, waving at the airship's passengers. His body was lean and taut with muscles, his skin a deep tan. Terry waved back excitedly. "D.J.," she said with a grin.

Terry's brother grabbed her bags the moment she stepped off the chopper. Terry hugged him, then turned to Jonas. With their black hair, dark eyes, and bright smiles they almost looked like twins.

"D.J., this is Professor Taylor," she said. D.J. dropped the bags and shook Jonas's hand. "So, you're going to be descending with me into the Challenger Deep. Sure you're up to it?"

"I'll be fine," said Jonas, feeling D.J.'s competitive nature.

D.J. turned to Terry. "Does the professor know Dr. Heller's on board?"

"I don't know. Jonas, did Dad happen to mention that to you yesterday?"

Jonas felt the breath squeeze out of his chest. "Frank Heller's part of this crew? No, your father definitely did not mention that to me."

"Is that going to be a problem, Dr. Taylor?" asked D.J.

Jonas regained his composure. "Frank Heller was the physician in charge of a series of dives I piloted for the Navy seven years ago."

"I take it you haven't kept in touch," said DeMarco.

"To put it lightly, there's not a whole lot of love lost between the two of us. If Masao had told me Heller was part of this mission, I doubt I would have come."

"Guess that's why Dad didn't tell you," chuckled D.J.

"If I had known, I would have told you myself," said Terry. "It's not too late to recall the chopper."

Jonas stared at Terry, his patience wearing thin. "I'm here. If Frank has a problem with that, I guess he'll have to deal with it."

D.J. looked at his sister. "How did he do on the program simulator?"

"Not bad. Of course, the program lacks controls for the mechanical arm or escape pod."

"Plan on at least one practice run before we descend then, Doc," said D.J. "We'll wait till you get your sea legs."

Jonas ignored him. "Whenever you're ready. Can you show me the Gliders?"

As they approached the hangars, a large dark-skinned man in a red knit cap walked on deck with two Filipino crew members.

"Professor Taylor," D.J. said, "this is Captain Barre." Leon Barre was French-Polynesian, strong as an ox with a baritone voice. A tiny silver cross dangled from his neck. He gripped Jonas's hand, shook it once. "Welcome aboard the *Kiku*."

"Glad to be here, Captain."

Barre tipped his hat to Terry. "Madam," he said reverently.

DeMarco slapped the big man's shoulder. "You putting on a little weight, Leon?"

Leon's face darkened. "The Thai woman, she fattens me like a porker."

DeMarco laughed, turned to Jonas. "The captain's wife is a hell of a cook. We could use a little of that, Leon. We're starving."

The captain grunted an order to the Filipino sailor at his side. The sailor rushed off toward the main cabin. "We eat in an hour," the captain said, then turned and followed his men inside.

Jonas, D.J., DeMarco, and Terry walked across the wide deck to where the two Abyss Glider submersibles were perched on dry mounts.

D.J. turned around to face Jonas. "What do you think?"

"They're beautiful," Jonas said.

"A few modifications since you last took a ride," remarked D.J.

"I piloted the AG I in shallow waters. The AG II was still on the drawing board back then."

"Come on, Taylor," said DeMarco. "I'll give the nickel tour."

The subs were ten feet long by four feet wide and resembled nothing more than fat torpedoes with wings. They were one-man vessels, the pilot entering through the tail section, then using a joystick to "fly" the vessel, lying prone within the sub. The clear nose cone of the Abyss Glider allowed the pilot to see nearly 360 degrees of his deep-water surroundings.

"Lexan," said DeMarco, pointing at one of the nose cones. "This plastic's so strong, it's used as bulletproof glass in presidential limousines. The entire escape pod's made of the stuff. The AG I's were refitted with it several years ago."

Jonas inspected the plastic cone. "I didn't realize these subs contained escape pods. It wasn't in the original model."

"You have a good memory," said D.J. "The AG II's were specifically designed for the Mariana Trench. Since there's always the risk that a wing or tail fin will catch on to objects at the bottom, as you enter the tail section you're actually entering the Lexan escape pod. If the Glider gets into trouble, pull the escape lever located in a metal box along your right and the interior chamber will slide right out from the heavier tail and wing sections. It's like being in a bubble. You'll rise right to the top."

DeMarco frowned. "I'll give the tour, if you don't mind, D.J. After all, I did design the damn things."

D.J. smiled at the engineer. "Sorry."

DeMarco took center stage once more, obviously in his element. "As you're aware, Taylor, the challenge in deep-water exploration is to design and build a hull that is both buoyant and strong enough to withstand tremendous pressures. The other problem is the length of time it can take for a submersible to travel to the bottom. The *Alvin,* the French *Nautile,* and the Russian *Mir I* and *II* are all bulky vessels that can descend at a rate of only fifty to one hundred feet per minute. At those speeds, it would take us well over five hours just to enter the Challenger Deep."

"And," added D.J., "those subs can't even descend beyond twenty thousand feet."

"What about JAMSTEC's *Shinkai 6500?*" asked Jonas. "I thought she was designed to reach bottom."

"No, the *Shinkai* was designed for a maximum depth of twenty-one thousand feet," corrected DeMarco. "You're thinking of JAMSTEC's latest unmanned sub, the *Kaiko.* Until D.J. piloted the AG II last week, the *Kaiko* was the only vessel, manned or unmanned, to reenter the Challenger Deep since the *Trieste* in '60. She spent just over a half hour at a depth of 35,798 feet, two feet shy of the record, before suffering mechanical problems."

"Now the record's mine," said D.J. "Guess I'll be sharing it with you soon, Doc."

"Should've been me," mumbled Terry.

"Anyway," continued DeMarco, ignoring the siblings' exchange, "those other subs have hulls made of a titanium alloy, similar to our UNIS systems. Half your power source is exhausted in just piloting the heavily weighted sub along the bottom, just so you can drop the weighted plates later to surface. These Abyss Gliders, however, are made from a reinforced, positively buoyant ceramic capable of withstanding forces over sixteen thousand pounds per square inch. With her maneuverable wings, she'll fly to the bottom at a rate of six hundred feet per minute and float back to the surface without the use of weights. Saves a ton of battery power."

"D.J., how will we bring the damaged UNIS to the surface?" asked Jonas.

"Look beneath the belly of the sub," instructed D.J. "There's a retractable mechanical arm with a claw. The arm has a limited extension of about six feet directly in front of the nose cone. The claw was designed to gather specimens. When we make our descent, you'll take the lead. I'll follow you in my sub, which will have a steel cable attached to my mechanical claw. The damaged UNIS has several eye bolts along its outer casing. Once you clear the debris away from the UNIS, I'll attach the cable and the *Kiku*'s winch will haul the unit back on board."

"Doesn't sound too bad."

"It's really a two-man job," said D.J. "I tried to attach the cable on my first descent, but there was too much debris covering the UNIS. I couldn't maintain the claw's grip on the steel cable and clear the rocks away. The currents are real strong too."

"Maybe you were nervous," added Terry.

"Bullshit," responded her brother.

"Come on, D.J.," teased Terry. "You told me it's kind of scary down there. It's not what you're looking at or even the constant darkness. It's the claustrophobia, knowing that you're seven miles down, surrounded by thousands of pounds of pressure. One mistake, one crack in the hull, and your brains implode from the change in pressure." Terry glanced at Jonas, looking for a reaction.

"Terry, you're just jealous." He looked at Jonas, his face full of animation. "I loved it! What a rush, man, I can't wait to go back. I thought bungee jumping and parachuting were cool, but this beats the shit out of them!"

Jonas looked at DeMarco with concern. "You consider yourself an adrenaline junkie?"

D.J. calmed himself. "No, no . . . I mean, yeah, I'm an adrenaline junkie, sure, but this is different, Doc. The Challenger Deep . . . it's like being the first person to explore another planet. These huge black smokers everywhere, and the weirdest fish you ever saw. But what am I telling you? You've been on dozens of trench dives before."

Jonas tugged on one of the red vinyl flags with the Tanaka logo that was attached to the back of each sub. He looked up at the younger pilot. "I've piloted more than my share of dives into deep-sea trenches, but the Mariana Trench is a whole different ball game. My suggestion is to leave the cowboy attitude behind." Jonas looked back toward the *Kiku*'s interior chambers. "Where can I find Dr. Heller?"

D.J. threw a glance at his sister. "He's in the CIC, I think."

Jonas turned and walked away.

HELLER

"End of the hall on your right," D.J. said, pointing down the narrow corridor. He heaved Jonas's duffel bag onto his shoulder. "I'll leave this in your cabin. Number ten. Right below." Jonas nodded. D.J. headed down the narrow stairwell.

Jonas walked down the corridor to a doorway labeled "Operations." He stepped into the dark cabin humming with computers, video monitors, radar and sonar equipment. A gaunt man with short-clipped gray hair and heavy, black-framed glasses was bent over a control panel, pecking at computer keys with his long fingers. He turned and looked at Jonas without speaking, his moist gray eyes swollen behind the thick lenses. He turned back to his computer, studied the monitor. "Another fishing expedition, Taylor?"

Jonas paused a moment before he answered. "That's not why I'm here, Frank."

"Why *the hell* are you here?"

"I'm here because Masao asked for my help."

"The Japanese have no sense of irony."

62

"We're going to have to work together, Frank. The only way to find out what's going on down there is to haul up the damaged UNIS. D.J. can't do it alone—"

"I know that." Heller rose quickly and crossed the room to refill his coffee. "What I don't understand is why *you* should be the one to go with him."

"Because nobody else has been down there in the last thirty years."

"Oh yes they have," Heller said bitterly. "Only they died making the trip."

Jonas broke eye contact. "Frank, I want to talk to you about that. I . . ." Jonas searched for the right words. "Look, there hasn't been a day that's gone by in the last seven years that I haven't thought about the *Seacliff* incident. To be honest with you, I'm still not sure what happened. All I know is that I *believed* I saw something rise up from the bottom to attack our sub, and I reacted."

Heller moved to Jonas, stood face to face, inches away. His eyes burned with hatred. "Guess that little confession makes everything all right in your book, but it changes nothing with me. You were daydreaming, Taylor. You hallucinated, thought you saw an extinct monster, of all things, and killed two of your team, tossing aside years of training. You panicked. And you know what really ticks me off? You've spent the last seven years making a career of justifying the possible existence of this Megalodon, substantiating your fabricated excuse so you wouldn't look so bad." Heller was shaking with emotion. He took a step back and leaned against his desk. "You make me ill, Taylor. Those men didn't deserve to die. Now here we are, seven years later, and you still can't face up to the truth."

"I don't know what the truth is, Frank. If it makes a difference, maybe I was looking at a cluster of tubeworms and then hallucinated. I don't know. I know I screwed up. I almost died down there myself. Now I've got to deal with this thing for the rest of my life."

"I'm not your priest, Taylor. I'm not here to take your confession or to hear about your guilty feelings."

"And what about your contribution to the accident?" Jonas yelled. "You were the physician of record. You told Danielson that I was medically fit to make a third descent into the trench. Three dives within eight days! Do you think that may have had anything to do with my ability to function?"

"Bullshit!"

"Why is it bullshit, *Doctor* Heller?" Jonas paced across the room, his blood boiling. "You said it yourself, wrote it on the official report: 'psychosis of the deep.' You and Danielson forced me to pilot those dives without sufficient rest, and the two of you railroaded me, set me up to be the Navy's fall guy."

"It was your fault!"

"Yes," whispered Jonas, "it was my piloting error, but I never would have been placed in that position without your involvement or Danielson's. So, after seven years, I've decided to go back down to finally face my fears, to figure out for myself what happened. Maybe it's time you faced up to your own responsibilities." Jonas headed toward the door.

"Hold it, Taylor. Look, maybe you shouldn't have been in the trench on that third dive. As for me, Danielson was my commanding officer, but I still believed you were mentally fit. You were a damn good pilot. But let's just make sure that the reason you're making this dive with D.J. is to assist him and not to go off looking for some tooth."

Jonas opened the door, then turned to face Heller. "I know my responsibilities, Frank. I hope you remember yours."

NIGHTFALL

Twenty minutes later, having showered and changed, Jonas entered the galley, where a dozen crewmen were noisily feasting on fried chicken and potatoes. He saw Terry, seated next to D.J., a vacant chair to her left.

"Is this seat taken?"

"Sit," she ordered.

He sat down, listening to D.J., who was involved in a heated debate with DeMarco and Captain Barre. Heller's absence was conspicuous.

"Doc!" D.J. sprayed half his mouthful of chicken out with the word. "You're just in time. You know that practice dive we had scheduled for tomorrow? Well, forget about it."

Jonas felt butterflies in his stomach. "What are you saying, D.J.?"

Captain Barre turned to Jonas, swallowed a mouthful of food, and said, "Storm front moving in from the east. No time for practice dives. If you're gonna descend this week, it's gonna be tomorrow, first light."

"Jonas, if you're not ready yet, I think you should be man enough to admit it and let me step in," interjected Terry.

"Nah, he'll be fine, right, Doc?" said D.J., winking. "After all, you've been down to the Mariana Trench before."

"Who said that?" Jonas felt the room go quiet, all eyes on him.

"Come on, Doc. It's all over the ship. Some reporter in Guam interviewed half the crew by radio an hour after you boarded."

"What? What reporter? How the hell—?" Jonas no longer felt hungry.

"It's true, Jonas," said Terry. "Same guy who was questioning you at the lecture. He claims two people died on the sub you were piloting. Told us you panicked because you hallucinated, claiming to have seen one of those Megalodons."

D.J. looked him squarely in the eye. "So, Doc, any of this true?"

The room was dead silent. Jonas pushed his tray away from him. "It's true. What this reporter, or whoever your source is, left out is that I was exhausted at the time, having already completed two deep trench dives during the same week. I was pushed into service, okayed by the medical officer. To this day I'm not sure if what I saw was real or I imagined it. But as far as tomorrow is concerned, I made a commitment to your father to complete the mission and I intend to keep that commitment. I've piloted subs on more deep-sea missions than you've had birthdays, D.J., so if you have a problem with me escorting you down, then let's get it out on the table right now!"

D.J. smiled nervously. "Hey, I've got no problem with you. Take it easy. Actually, Al DeMarco and I were just talking about this creature, this giant prehistoric shark of yours. Al says that it would be impossible for a creature of that size to exist in water pressures as great as those in the trench. Now, me, I'm on your side. I say it's possible. Not that I believe your theory, 'cause I don't. But I've seen dozens of different species of fish down there.

Now, if those little fish can withstand the water pressures, why couldn't this mega-shark, or whatever the hell you call it." D.J. was grinning from ear to ear. Several crew members began snickering.

Jonas stood up to leave. "You'll excuse me. I think I've lost my appetite."

D.J. grabbed his arm. "No, wait, Doc, come on now. Tell me about this shark. I really want to know. After all, how will I recognize it if I see it tomorrow?"

"It'll be the big shark with the missing tooth!" blurted out Terry. Laughter cascaded around them.

Jonas sat back down. "Okay, D.J., if you really want to know about these monsters, I'll tell you. The first thing you have to realize about the shark family is that they've been around for about four hundred million years. Compare that with humans, whose ancestors fell from the trees only about two million years ago. And of all the species of sharks ever to have inhabited the ocean, the Megalodon was undisputed king. What little we know about these monsters is that nature endowed the creatures not just to survive but to dominate every ocean and marine species. So we're not just talking about a shark here, we're talking about a formidable war machine. Forget for a moment that this species was a sixty-foot version of a great white shark. The Meg was the supreme hunter of the planet, during the reign of the dinosaurs, endowed with over seventy million years of killer instincts. Besides its massive size and murderous seven-inch serrated teeth, the creature also possessed eight highly efficient sensory organs."

Leon Barre began chuckling. "Hey, Doc. How you know all this shit about some dead fish nobody's ever seen?" Snickers could be heard from some of the men. The room quieted once more, awaiting Jonas's response.

"For one thing, we have their fossilized teeth, which not only tells us about their enormous size but reveals their predatory tendencies. We also have fossilized evidence from the species they fed on."

"Go on about their senses," said D.J., now truly curious.

"Okay." Jonas gathered his thoughts. He noticed that the other members of the crew had grown silent, now listening as well. "The Megalodon, just like its modern-day cousin the great white, possessed eight sensory organs that allowed it to search, detect, identify, and stalk its prey. Let's start with its most amazing sensory organ, called the ampullae of Lorenzini. Along the top and underside of the Meg's snout were tiny, jelly-filled capsules beneath the skin which could detect electrical discharges in the water. Let me put that in layman's terms. The Megalodon could detect the faint electrical field of its prey's beating heart or moving muscles hundreds of miles away. That means if the Megalodon was circling our ship, it could still detect a person enjoying a leisurely swim off the beaches of Guam."

The room was silent now, all eyes focused on Jonas.

"Almost as amazing as the ampullae of Lorenzini was the Megalodon's sense of smell. Unlike man, the creature possessed directional nostrils that not only could detect one part of blood or sweat or urine in a billion parts of water but could determine the exact location of the scent. That's why you see great whites swimming with a side-to-side motion of their heads. They're actually smelling the water in different directions. A full-grown adult Megalodon's nostrils were probably the size of a grapefruit.

"Now we come to the monster's skin, a sensory organ and weapon combined in one. Running along either side of the Meg's flank was an organ referred to as the lateral line. Actually, the line is more of a canal that contains sensory cells called neuromasts. These neuromasts were able to detect the slightest vibrations in water, even the flutter of another fish's heartbeat."

Al DeMarco stood up. "You'll have to excuse me. I've got work to do."

"Ah, come on, Al," said D.J. lightheartedly. "There's no school tomorrow. We'll let you stay up late."

DeMarco gave D.J. a stern look. "Tomorrow happens to be a big day for all of us. I suggest we all get some rest."

"Al's right, D.J." agreed Jonas. "I've already mentioned the best parts anyway. But to quickly answer your first question, the Megalodon possessed an enormous liver that probably constituted one-fourth of its entire weight. Besides serving the creature's normal hepatic functions and storing fatty energy reserves, the liver would have allowed the Megalodon to adjust to changes in water pressure, even at depths as great as those in the Challenger Deep."

"All right, Professor," said DeMarco. "Let's assume, just for argument's sake, that a Megalodon shark did exist in the trench. Why hasn't it surfaced? After all, there's a helluva lot more food topside than along the bottom."

"That's easy," said Terry. "If it rose from seven miles down, it would burst."

"No, I don't agree," said Jonas. "Changes in water pressure, even drastic changes, affect sharks differently than humans. The Megalodon would already have adapted to the crushing pressures seven miles down. A full-grown adult Megalodon would weigh upward of forty-five thousand pounds, and about seventy-five percent of that is water, contained primarily in the muscles and cartilage. The creature's liver would be enormous, enabling the Meg to reduce its specific gravity, in a sense decompressing as it rose. The journey would be strenuous but the Meg would survive."

"So what would be the problem then?" said Terry.

"Obviously, you weren't paying much attention during my lecture, were you?" Jonas responded. "Remember, I said that my theory for the existence of Megalodons in the Mariana Trench was based on the presence of a warm layer of water prevailing along the bottom of the gorge, a result of the hydrothermal vents.

Above that warm layer is six miles of freezing-cold water. The rest of the Megalodon species perished a hundred thousand years ago because of the drop in water temperatures resulting from the last ice age. Any Meg surviving in the trench did so because they were able to escape the colder waters above. The creatures would be trapped below. Even if they did attempt to surface, they'd never survive the cold."

"Conveniently, Taylor, it appears you have all the answers," said DeMarco, the cynicism rising in his voice. "But your creative solutions still haven't told us what food source would be available in the Mariana Trench to sustain a predator the size of a sixty-foot great white?"

"Maybe they've run out of food," said Terry, sarcastically. "That's why they're eating our UNIS robots."

D.J. laughed, then abruptly grew serious. "Would a Meg eat a UNIS, Doc?" Terry and DeMarco burst out laughing.

"No, D.J.," said Jonas, "these creatures have a sense of taste. They can tell by rubbing their snouts against a foreign object if something is edible or not. But the UNIS systems do emit electrical impulses which can easily be detected by a Meg. These signals may have irritated the shark, its instincts forcing it to attack."

"So if they don't eat titanium robots, what do they eat?" said D.J. with a smile.

Jonas hesitated. "To be honest, I just don't know. My assumption has always been that the Megalodon's food source would also have migrated to the deeper waters of the trench to inhabit the warmer currents. Nature has a tendency to allow a species to adapt to certain limitations over thousands, even millions of years. I think the trench waters, which maintain a much lower oxygen content than our surface waters, would effectively slow the creatures' metabolism down, greatly decreasing their appetites. Megalodons, being territorial predators, would probably thin out their numbers by devouring any weaker members of their own species.

And those huge growths of tubeworms are a readily available source of protein—"

"Do you really believe a sixty-foot predator could exist on nothing but tubeworms?" scoffed DeMarco. "What nonsense. We both know there's nothing inhabiting the Mariana Trench large enough to sustain even one Megalodon."

"How do you know, DeMarco?" Jonas retorted. "Unfortunately, your close-minded attitude is typical among those who arrogantly consider themselves 'men of science.' The notion of a species existing in an unexplored environment like the Challenger Deep is impossible for you to comprehend simply because you haven't seen the species with your own eyes. It's far easier to criticize my theories than to consider the possibilities of existence. If you remember, it was only a short time ago that Man refused to accept the notion that life could exist without photosynthesis, but it does. Who really knows what life forms inhabit the unexplored Challenger Deep? For your information, the unmanned submersible, Kaiko, recently recorded schools of unidentified fish inhabiting the deep waters of the Mariana Trench. We also know giant squids, over sixty feet long, weighing close to two tons, inhabit the abyss. Surely these creatures would be adequate dining for a limited number of Megs. And what if other prehistoric species also managed to survive without our knowledge or blessings?"

DeMarco shook his head in disbelief. "Your theories are based totally on conjecture, Taylor, fueled by your own vivid imagination, motivated by your guilt. I've had enough of this nonsense for one night." DeMarco headed out the door.

D.J. whistled. "Well Doc, personally I'm glad you just hallucinated these things," he said, winking at his sister. "Now all of us can sleep real good. Good night, Terry." D.J. kissed his sister and followed DeMarco out of the galley. Seconds later, their laughter could be heard down the corridor.

Jonas felt humiliated. "Good night, Terry." He stood up, leaving his dinner on the table, and headed out on deck.

It was a calm sea, but clouds could be seen moving in from the east. Jonas watched the half-moon dance along the black surface of the Pacific. He thought about Maggie. Did he still love her? Did it really matter anymore? He gazed at the black water and felt the butterflies return, unaware that, one deck up, Frank Heller was watching.

Jonas awoke sometime before dawn. His cabin was pitch black, and for a moment he didn't know where he was. When he remembered, a shiver of fear flared in his gut. In a few hours he'd be in similar darkness with seven miles of frigid water over his head. He closed his eyes and tried to go back to sleep. He couldn't. An hour later D.J. knocked on his door to wake him.

It was time.

DESCENT

D.J. was in the water, his Abyss Glider already twenty feet beneath the surface by the time Jonas walked on deck in his wet suit. He had eaten a light breakfast and popped two of his yellow pills for the descent, keeping another two in his shoulder pocket. Despite the pills, he still felt anxious. Carefully, he crawled into his sub through the tail section.

A steel cable from the giant winch at the stern of the *Kiku* had been lowered and attached to the claw of D.J.'s submersible's mechanical arm. Capturing the latched hook at the end of the cable had proved more difficult than expected. D.J. had struggled with it for nearly half an hour before a frogman was forced to enter the water and secure it firmly to the claw.

There were two smaller winches on either side of the *Kiku*, designed only for lowering the Abyss Gliders into and out of the water. One of them held Jonas's sub, which was slowly being lowered into the choppy surf. Two frogmen on either side of the harness escorted him down. The big winch in the stern would be used strictly to feed the steel cable from D.J.'s sub, eventually hauling the damaged UNIS to the surface.

Lying on his stomach within the capsule, Jonas watched as the two frogmen detached the harness from around his sub. He saw Terry looking down at him from the rail of the *Kiku,* her image dissolving as the water closed around him. One of the frogmen knocked on the Lexan nose cone, giving the all-clear sign. The AG II was free. Jonas started the twin engines, pressed forward on the throttle, and adjusted the midwings, aiming his vessel down.

The vessel responded at once. Jonas noticed the sub felt much heavier, perhaps even sluggish compared with the light-weight AG I he had test-flown years before. Still, no other sub-mersible Jonas had ever piloted could compare with the Abyss Glider's design. Jonas found D.J. at thirty feet, the UNIS recovery cable now firmly hooked in his sub's mechanical claw.

They made visual contact and D.J. smiled, giving Jonas the pilot's thumbs-up. "Age before beauty, Professor," his voice came over the radio.

Jonas moved the joystick forward, and his fourteen-foot Glider began its descent. D.J. followed him with the steel cable in tow. They were cruising at a thirty-degree angle, looping downward in a slow spiral.

Within minutes the sunlight faded to a deep shade of gray, and then . . . total blackness. Jonas checked his depth gauge: a mere 1,250 feet. Descending in the required prone position of the Abyss Glider felt strange to Jonas. If not for the harness, his body would have slid forward until his head collided with the interior tip of the nose cone. "Relax and breathe," he whispered to himself. "You've got a long way to go."

"Everything all right, Taylor?" Dr. Heller's voice over the radio had an air of insinuation. Jonas realized Frank was assigned to monitor the two pilots' vital signs. He must have noticed Jonas's heart rate increase on the console's cardiac monitor.

"Yeah . . . I'm fine," he said. He took a deep breath, tried to focus on the nothingness before him, fighting the urge to turn on the spotlight. Using the spotlight now would only waste the sub's batteries.

Strange sea creatures began to appear before his eyes, glowing softly as they swam through the dark. "Abyssopelagic animals," Jonas whispered to himself, saying the technical name for these unique groups of fish, squid, and prawns. Jonas watched as a four-foot culper eel hovered in front of him. Deciding to attack the larger sub, the eel opened its mouth as if to swallow the nose cone, hyperextending and unhinging its jaws, revealing vicious rows of needle-sharp teeth. Jonas tapped the glass. The eel darted away in silence. He looked to his left. A deep-sea anglerfish circled nearby, an eerie light appearing over its mouth. Jonas knew the species possessed a rod fin that actually lit up like a lightning bug's tail. Small fish would mistake the light for food and swim straight toward it, right into the angler's wide-open mouth.

Jonas hadn't noticed the cold creeping up on him. He glanced at his temperature gauge. Forty-two degrees outside. He adjusted the thermostat to heat the pilot's capsule.

And then it happened, a wave of panic that jerked Jonas right off his stomach, slamming his head against the inside of the pod. It was a feeling comparable only to being buried alive in a coffin, unable to see, unable to escape. Sweat poured from his body, his breathing became erratic, and he found himself hyperventilating. He reached for the two pills, then, afraid of an overdose, flicked on the exterior lights of the sub.

The beam revealed nothing but more blackness, but it served its purpose, to reorientate its pilot. Jonas took a breath, then wiped the sweat from his eyes. He turned down the heat, the cooler air helping.

D.J. was calling him over the radio. "What's with the light, Doc? We have strict orders."

"Just testing to make sure they work. How're you doing back there?"

"Okay, I guess. This damn cable's all tangled around the mechanical arm. Kind of like my telephone cord gets."

"D.J., if it's a problem, we should head back—"

"No way, Doc. I've got it under control. When we get to the bottom, I'll flip around a few dozen times and unwind." D.J. laughed at his own joke, but Jonas could hear the tension in the younger pilot's voice.

Jonas called up to DeMarco. "Al, D.J. says his cable's twisting around the mechanical arm. Can you do anything topside to relieve some of the pressure?"

"Negative. D.J.'s got the problem under control. We'll monitor him. You concentrate on what you're doing. DeMarco out."

Jonas looked at his watch. They had been descending now for forty-five minutes. He rubbed his eyes, then attempted to stretch his lower back within the tight leather harness.

The capsule was cramped, it reminded Jonas of the time he had to submit to ninety minutes' worth of MRIs. The massive machine had been situated only inches above his head, the sword of Damocles waiting to crush his skull. Only the red glow from the Abyss Glider's control panel gave him a sense of direction, keeping him from insanity. Jonas felt the telltale signs of claustrophobia creeping up again, but this time he fought the urge to flick on the 7,500-watt searchlight. His eyes moved over the damp Lexan interior of the pilot capsule. The water pressure surrounding him was over 16,000 pounds per square inch. He stared out into the blackness, felt a shiver of fear come over him. He was dropping below 34,000 feet—deeper than he'd ever gone before.

Jonas felt a slight trace of vertigo, which he hoped had more to do with the rich oxygen mixture in the submersible than with his medicine. His eyes moved from the inky water to the control panel readouts. The outside ocean temperature was thirty-six degrees . . . and rising! Thirty-eight, forty-two.

He spoke into the mike on his headset. "Here we are, D.J."

"You're about to enter the tropical currents, Doc. It's gonna get very hot as we pass above the black smokers. Hey, can you see that cluster of tubeworms down there?"

"Where?" Jonas focused hard but could see nothing.

"Two o'clock," said D.J. "Wait, the haze from the black smokers must be blocking our view."

Jonas felt his heart pounding through his ears. The layer of haze from the black smokers! It resembled a thick cloud of air pollution hanging above a steel plant, except that in the trench the heavy mineral deposits formed a ceiling above the sea floor. That's why the white image had disappeared before his eyes seven years ago. Camouflaged by the darkness, the mineral deposits and black smoke had obscured his view!

"Taylor!" Heller's voice shattered his thoughts. "What's going on? Your cardiac monitor just jumped off the scale."

"I'm okay . . . just excited." Jonas looked at his digital temperature readout as it continued climbing. Fifty degrees, sixty . . . and still rising. Eighty-five. They had fully entered the warm layer of the canyon, heated by the hydrothermal vents.

"Doc, switch on your searchlight. You need to avoid direct contact with the water spewing out of those big chimney stacks. It's so hot it could melt your sub's ceramic seals."

"Thanks for the warning, D.J." Jonas flipped the switch, revealing the tops of dozens of chimneys, some thirty feet high. Black smokers. Jonas knew the strange geological formations well. As the superheated water from the hydrothermal vents shot upward from the earth's mantle, they deposited sulfur, copper, iron, and other minerals along the sides of the seabed cracks. Over time, the cooling deposits left chimneys that resembled skinny volcanoes, rising high above the ocean floor. The water billowing out of these towering stacks was black from its high sulfur content, earning the name black smoker.

Jonas maneuvered his sub between two of the smoking towers, his visibility virtually eliminated as he passed through the murky layer. His temperature gauge rocketed past 230 degrees, and then he was through, the 7,500-watt searchlight cutting a path through the now-clear black water.

Jonas Taylor opened his eyes wide, awestruck by the view. D.J. was right. He had entered a different world.

THE BOTTOM

Jonas adjusted his midwing, decreasing his angle of descent. He hovered twenty feet above the seabed and slowed, waiting for D.J.

Spread out before him were row upon row of giant clams, pure white and glowing, each over a foot in diameter. There were thousands of them, lying in formation around the vents as if worshipping their god. The searchlight picked up movement along the bottom, vent crustaceans, hundreds of albino lobsters and crabs, glowing in the darkness of the abyss, all completely blind.

Jonas knew that many species of fish living in the dark sea depths made their own light by means of chemicals called luciferins or through the luminous bacteria that lived in their bodies. Nature had endowed the species with white skin and a luminescent glow to attract prey and locate each other.

Life. The amount and variety within the trenches had shocked scientists, who had incorrectly theorized that no life form could exist on the planet without sunlight. Jonas felt awed at being in the Challenger Deep. In the most desolate location on the planet, nature had found a way to allow life to exist.

Next to a patch of giant clams and mussels, Jonas could see a magnificent cluster of massive tubeworms, flowing like clumps of spaghetti in the warm currents. Pure white and fluorescent, except for the tips, which were blood red. Twelve feet long, five inches thick, in groups too numerous to begin to approximate. The tubeworms fed on the bacteria in the water. In turn, eelpouts and other small fish fed off the tubeworms.

A bizarre food chain, located at the bottom of the world, a world existing in total darkness. What species is at the top of this food chain? wondered Jonas. Giant squids? Undiscovered genera? Seven miles down, separated from 16,000 pounds per square inch of water pressure by a few inches of alloy, Jonas now felt thankful that he had been wrong about the Meg's existence.

Jonas slowed the AG II. He could see the bright glare of the second sub's searchlight approaching from behind. He picked up the radio. "You can take over from here, D.J."

D.J.'s sub slowly "flew" around and ahead of Jonas, careful to maintain sufficient distance. The two aquanauts wanted to remain within sight of one another, but didn't want Jonas to get caught in D.J.'s trailing cable.

DeMarco's voice came over the radio. "The canyon wall should be to port, approximately one-five-zero feet."

Jonas followed D.J. along the ocean floor until he could see the vertical wall of the submerged mountain range, known as seamounts. The subs entered a valley surrounded by high walls. It was as if God had lifted the Grand Canyon and submerged it under seven miles of ocean. Jonas was traveling back in time, knowing the seamounts were at least 200 million years old. He maneuvered within the gulley, keeping D.J.'s sub within sight.

"Doc, it's a bit rough ahead, so hold on," warned D.J. As if on cue, Jonas felt his tail section begin wagging like a dog's tail. "We may have had another landslide down here."

"I hope you're wrong about that," Jonas said. "Can you see anything up there?"

"Not yet, but I've picked up the damaged unit's homing signal on my radar. North along this gulley. You'll see," said D.J., "the valley will open up again. The UNIS had positioned itself about sixty feet from the canyon wall on our left before it broke down."

Jonas looked to his right. Sure enough, the seamounts disappeared, revealing more black ocean. On his left, the canyon wall still loomed tall, disappearing upward, well beyond his view.

Jonas saw the red blip appear on his console screen.

"There it is!" D.J. said after a long silence.

The shell of the destroyed UNIS looked like a piece of scrap metal buried beneath several rocks. D.J. positioned his sub well above the remains, shining his spotlight over it like a streetlamp. "It's all yours, Doc. Go ahead and take a look."

Jonas moved closer to the UNIS, floating into the light of D.J.'s sub. He aimed his own spotlight at the shattered hull and drifted past it to the other side. Something's different, he thought, looking at the debris around the base. It's *moved*.

"You see anything?" D.J. asked over the radio.

"Not yet," Jonas said, straining his eyes for a glimpse of something white. He moved closer, peering into the rocks. *And there it was!*

"D.J., I can't believe it! I think I've located that tooth!" Jonas could barely maintain his excitement. He extended his sub's mechanical arm, aiming the claw above the eight-inch white triangular object, then lifting it carefully out of the mound of sulfur and iron.

"Hey, Doc." D.J. was laughing hysterically.

Jonas looked at the object he had traveled seven miles down to obtain.

It was the remains of a dead albino starfish.

THE MALE

Terry Tanaka, Frank Heller, and Alphonse DeMarco nearly fell out of their chairs in uncontrollable fits of laughter. Jonas could hear them over the radio. For a moment, he seriously considered ramming his submersible into the canyon wall.

"I'm sorry for laughing, man," said D.J. "Hey, wanna laugh at my stupidity? Take a look at my sub's mechanical arm."

Jonas looked up. The steel cable had wound in a dozen chaotic loops around the six-foot mechanical limb, so much so that the arm was barely visible beneath the cable. "D.J., that's not funny. You've got a lot of untangling to do before you can free yourself up."

"Don't worry. I can handle it. You work on clearing those rocks."

"Taylor!" DeMarco's voice burst from the radio. "Maybe you thought you saw a sixty-foot starfish . . ." Jonas could hear Terry's high-pitched laugh.

Jonas lowered the mechanical arm, trying to focus on the task at hand. He felt his blood boiling, beads of sweat dripping down his sides. Within minutes, he had managed to clear the debris from the UNIS.

"Nice job, Doc." D.J. was slowly revolving the mechanical arm in tight counterclockwise circles. Gradually, the steel cable began freeing itself from around the extended appendage.

"You need some help?" asked Jonas.

"No, I'm fine. Stand by."

Jonas hovered the Abyss Glider twenty feet off the bottom. Masao had been right, all of them had. He had hallucinated, allowed his imagination to wander in the abyss, violating a major rule of deep-sea exploration. One mistake, one simple loss of focus, had cost the lives of his crew and his reputation as an aquanaut.

What was left for him now? Jonas thought about Maggie. She'll want a divorce, no doubt. Jonas was an embarrassment. She had turned to Bud Harris, his own friend, for love and support while Jonas had built his new career on a hallucination. Today's return dive into the Challenger Deep in search of evidence of the Megalodon's existence would make him the laughingstock of the paleontologist community. A starfish, for Christ's sake . . .

Blip.

The sound caught him off-guard. Jonas located his radar. A red dot had appeared on the abyssal terrain, the map indicating the source of the disturbance was approaching fast.

Blip. Blip, blip, blip . . .

Jonas felt his heart racing. Whatever it was, it was big!

"D.J., check your radar," commanded Jonas.

"My radar . . . whoa, what the fuck is that?"

"DeMarco!"

Alphonse DeMarco had stopped laughing. "We see it too, Jonas. Has D.J. attached the cable yet?"

Jonas looked up, the sub's mechanical arm was twisting wildly, attempting to free the last loops. "No, not yet. How big would you estimate this object to be?"

"Jonas, relax. I know what you're thinking. But DeMarco says you're probably looking at a school of fish."

Jonas watched the radar, unconvinced. The object appeared to be heading straight for them, as though the subs were a homing beacon . . .

"D.J., stop twisting!" commanded Jonas.

"Huh? I'm nearly—"

"Shut down everything, all systems. Do it now!" Jonas shut off his sub's power, the 7,500-watt searchlight going dark. "D.J., if this object is a Meg it's homing in on the vibrations and electrical impulses from our subs. Kill your power!"

D.J.'s heart raced. He stopped twisting the mechanical arm. "Al, what should I do?"

"Taylor's crazy. Attach the cable and get the hell out of there."

"D.J. . . ." Jonas stopped speaking, his eye catching a massive object circling less than five hundred yards away.

It was glowing.

THE GLOW

D.J.'s searchlight flickered off, dropping a cloak of darkness around the two submersibles. Jonas couldn't see his own hand now, but he could feel it shaking. He kept it close to the power switch for his own light.

The object came into view, a vague, pale glow circling back and forth within the overwhelming blackness. It was sizing up its prey, gliding silently five hundred yards from the subs, gradually closing.

Jonas felt his throat tightening.

There was no doubt. Jonas could see the conical snout, the thick triangular head, the crescent-moon tail. He estimated the Megalodon to be a good forty-five feet long, 30,000 pounds. Pure white. Fluorescent, just like the giant clams, just like the tubeworms. The beast turned again, remaining parallel to the canyon wall. Jonas saw the claspers: a male.

D.J.'s voice whispered across the radio. "Okay, Professor Taylor. I swear to you, I'm a believer. So what's your plan?"

"Stay calm, D.J. It's sizing us up. It's not sure if we're edible. No movements, we have to be careful not to trigger a response."

"Taylor, report!" Heller's voice ripped through the capsule.

"Frank, shut up," whispered Jonas. "We're being watched."

"D.J.," Terry's voice whispered over the radio.

D.J. didn't respond. He was mesmerized by the creature before him, paralyzed with fear.

Jonas knew they had only one chance; somehow they had to make it past the tropical layer into the frigid open waters above. The Meg couldn't follow. Jonas noticed the sub had begun to heat up on the hot silt floor of the canyon. Dripping with sweat, he watched as the glow of the male's hide grew larger, brighter. Jonas caught a glimpse of a bluish-gray eye.

The monster turned. It was coming straight for them.

The massive creature bloomed ghostlike in the pitch black. Mouth agape, rows of jagged teeth.

Jonas ignited the searchlight, blasting 7,500 watts into the nocturnal eyes of the Megalodon. The male whipped its head sideways to the right, a bolt of lightning disappearing with a flicker of its tail into the darkness.

D.J. screamed over the radio. "Holy shit, Doc—"

The concussion wave created by the fifteen-ton creature plowed into the two submersibles. D.J.'s Glider twisted and spun, tugging on the steel cable. Jonas's ship was swept against the canyon wall, striking tail-first, crushing the sub's twin propellers.

The Megalodon circled from above, diving down toward the crippled AG II, now lying upside down against the base of the seamount. Jonas opened his eyes as the approaching glow filled the capsule. The monster's thick white snout lifted, the upper jaw pushed forward, exposing multiple rows of razor-sharp seven-inch teeth. Jonas closed his eyes, actually registering a millisecond of gratitude that his death would be delivered by the pressure change and not by the hideous teeth of the creature.

At the last moment, the Megalodon broke from its attack, whipping its body around in a tight circle, away from the sea floor. The wall of water created by the movement of its massive tail tossed the powerless submersible over and over again, until it finally settled itself right-side up against the canyon wall.

Jonas felt the warm liquid oozing down his forehead as he melted into unconsciousness.

THE KILL

D. J. Tanaka accelerated his AG II in a ninety-degree climb. He ignored the constant barrage begging him to respond, choosing instead to focus on the race at hand. Blood pounded in his ears, but his hands were steady. He knew the stakes were high, life and death. The adrenaline junkie grinned.

He glanced quickly over his left shoulder. The albino monster banked sharply away from the canyon wall, rocketing away from the seabed like a guided missile homing in on its escaping prey. D.J. estimated he had a twelve-hundred-foot lead, the frigid waters a good two to three thousand feet away. It was going to be close.

The Glider burst through the thick haze created by the black smokers. D.J. looked back. The Meg was nowhere in sight. He checked his exterior temperature gauge. Fifty-two degrees and falling. I'm going to make it, he told himself.

The glow on the right side of the capsule registered in D.J.'s vision a split second before the gargantuan mouth exploded sideways into the submersible, the impact that of a locomotive collid-

ing with an automobile. Spinning upside down in complete darkness, D.J. tried to scream, the sickening crunch of ceramic and
Lexan glass deafening his ears as his skull imploded and crushed his
brain.

The Megalodon snorted the warm blood into its nostrils, its entire
sensory system quivering in delight. It rammed its snout farther
into the tight chamber, unable to reach the remains of D. J. Tanaka's upper torso.

Clutching the crippled sub in its jaws, the male descended
toward the tropical currents below with its kill.

Jonas came to in complete darkness and an all-consuming silence.
A sharp pain shot up his leg. His foot was caught on something.
He worked it loose and turned his body. A warm liquid had
drained into his eye. He wiped it away. Blood, he realized, though
he could not see his hand in front of his face.

How long had he been out?

The power had shut down, but the compartment was steaming
hot. I must be lying on the bottom, Jonas thought. He reached
out blindly, feeling for the controls, only to find he had slipped
out of the pilot's harness and fallen to the other end of the capsule.
He felt his way back into the cockpit and groped for the controls
on the panel. He flipped the power switch, but nothing happened.
The AG II was dead in the water.

From above and outside the sub he saw something. A flare of
light refracted in the Plexiglas. Jonas pushed forward into the
Lexan bubble, craning his neck upward.

He caught sight of the male, swimming slowly toward the sea
floor, a strange object dangling between its upper jaw and snout.

"Oh God . . . ," Jonas cried out, recognizing the remains of the Glider. D.J.'s submersible dangled from the predator's jaws, the steel cable still attached, the slack now looping and winding itself around the Megalodon's torso.

Frank Heller sat frozen in his chair. "We need to know what's going on down there," he said, pointing at the blank monitors.

Terry continued in vain to make radio contact. "D.J., can you hear me? D.J.?"

DeMarco was speaking rapidly with Captain Barre over an internal phone line. He and his crew were stationed in the stern, manning the giant winch.

"Frank, Leon says there's movement registering on the steel cable. D.J.'s sub is still attached."

Heller jumped to his feet, moving to the TV monitor showing the winch on the rear deck. "We've got to haul him up before he dies down there. If he's lost power, we're his only chance."

"What about Jonas?" Terry asked.

"We have no way of reaching him," DeMarco answered, "but we might be able to save your brother."

Heller leaned forward in his console and spoke into the mike. "Leon, are you there?"

Leon Barre's voice boomed over the speaker. "You ready to haul him up?"

"Do it."

Jonas froze, watched as the male passed directly overhead, its belly quivering as its jaws opened and closed. The ravenous predator continued to torque its snout into the remains of the submersible, unconcerned about the steel cable that now encircled it.

Jonas focused beyond the creature, catching a shadow of movement. The slack was being taken in from above. Seconds later, the steel cable pulled taut against the monster's white hide, tearing into the shark's tender pectoral fins.

The crushing embrace of the cable sent the male Megalodon into spasms. It spun its torso in a fit of rage, whipping its caudal fin to and fro in a futile attempt to struggle free. The more it fought, the more entangled it became.

Jonas stared in helpless fascination as the Megalodon fought in vain, unable to release itself from the steel bonds. With its pectoral fins pinned to its side, it couldn't stabilize itself. It shook its monstrous head from side to side, causing powerful concussion waves which pummeled the canyon wall. The creature's efforts served only to exhaust it.

After several minutes, the predator stopped thrashing, ceasing all movement. Within the tangled steel, the only sign of life came from the occasional flutter of its gills. Slowly, the *Kiku*'s winch began pulling the entrapped Megalodon up toward the frigid waters above.

The thrashing movements of the dying male sent vibrations cascading throughout the Challenger Deep.

THE FEMALE

It appeared out of nowhere, sweeping directly over Jonas, its deathly glow illuminating the black landscape like an enormous moon. Its sheer mass took several seconds to pass overhead. Until he caught sight of its towering tail fin, Jonas thought it might be some kind of submarine.

The female Megalodon was at least fifteen feet longer than the male, weighing well over twenty tons. A casual slap of her caudal fin sent a concussion wave exploding against the damaged sub, lifting and pushing it down the gully. Jonas braced himself as the AG II skidded across the canyon floor, flipping twice before settling in another cloud of silt. He pressed his face to the window and, as the muck settled, saw the female rise toward the male, still struggling in the cable.

Closing to within two body lengths, the female charged upward in a burst of acceleration and drove her hyperextended jaws around the soft underbelly of her mate. The colossal impact drove the smaller Megalodon fifty feet upward while the attacker's nine-inch serrated teeth tore open its white hide, exposing its heart and stomach.

The *Kiku*'s winch bit into the slack, gaining momentum, pulling the cable upward even as the female swallowed a massive hunk of her mate's digestive tract. Jonas could just make out the diminishing glow of the female as she continued rising with the carcass, her snout buried deep within the male's bleeding body, her swollen white belly quivering in spasms as she engulfed huge chunks of flesh and entrails. The female was pregnant, almost to term, her unborn pups' hunger insatiable. She refused to abandon her meal, even though she was now feeding in icy waters never before ventured. But the tropical-temperatured blood of her mate was bathing her in a thick river of warmth, escorting her upward as she rose out of the depths, making the journey tolerable. And so she continued feeding, her murderous jaws entrenched deep within the wound, shredding the spleen and duodenum as hundreds of gallons of warm blood gushed over her torso, protecting her from the cold.

She's moving through the cold, Jonas realized. Trapped in his sub, Jonas watched the thrashing white glow disappear overhead, leaving the blackness of the canyon to close back around him.

Terry, DeMarco, and Heller had come out on deck, where the ship's medical team and at least a dozen other crew members peered over the railing, waiting for their missing comrade to surface.

Captain Barre stared at the iron O-ring that suspended the pulley from the steel frame of the winch. It was straining under the weight of its load, threatening to snap apart at any moment.

"I don't know what's on the other end of this," he said gravely, "but it sure as hell is more than D.J.'s sub."

ESCAPE

Jonas knew he'd suffocate if he didn't act quickly. The wings of his sub had been mangled in the crash, and the engine was out of commission. It would be impossible to ascend with the dead weight of the mechanical end of the craft. He had to find the emergency lever and jettison the Lexan escape pod.

Jonas was drenched in sweat, beginning to feel dizzy again. He couldn't be sure if it was from loss of blood or the steadily diminishing oxygen. Waves of panic accelerated by the claustrophobia rattled his nerves. His fingers groped along the floor beneath his stomach, locating the small storage compartment. Jonas leaned backward, pulling open the hatch, straining to reach the spare tank of oxygen. He unscrewed a valve and released a steady stream of air into the pod.

Now he rolled back into the cockpit's harness, strapping himself into position. Feeling along his right, he found the metal latch box, opened it, then gripped the emergency lever, readying himself.

Jonas yanked back hard on the handle, and a bright flash

seared the darkness behind him, jolting him against the pilot's harness as the capsule exploded into the water and over the canyon floor. The pod had two short stabilizing wings, but still it twisted under the impact from the explosion, spiraling through the water.

Gradually the Lexan pod lost its forward momentum and began a gentle ascent. The clear capsule was positively buoyant, and it rose quickly. Still, it would be several hours before it reached the surface, and Jonas knew he had to concentrate on keeping warm. His clothes were soaked with perspiration and the temperature was plummeting.

The green surface waters began to bubble with a bright pink froth. Then the enormous white head of the male Megalodon broke the surface. Below, the steel cable held together the few hunks of flesh and connective tissue still attached to the long spinal column and caudal fin, which dangled in the water beneath it.

The crew of the *Kiku* stared in amazement as the remains of the devoured monster were hauled out of the water and across the broad deck of the ship. Twisted into the cable, dangling from the monstrous head of the giant shark, were the mangled remains of D. J. Tanaka's sub.

Terry collapsed to her knees, staring blankly at the incomprehensible disaster before her.

Jonas had been rising steadily in the darkness for two hours. Loss of blood and the bitter cold of the deep sea had rendered him barely conscious. He had lost all feeling in his toes and hands. He still could see nothing in the pitch-black water, but knew he'd eventually see light if he could only hang on.

. . .

Frank Heller lowered his binoculars and scanned the seascape with his naked eye. From the bridge he could see all three Zodiac search boats, scattered within a quarter-mile periphery of the *Kiku*.

DeMarco stood beside him at the rail. "The Navy choppers better get here soon," he said.

"It's too late. If he doesn't surface in the next ten minutes . . ." Heller didn't finish the sentence. They both knew that if Jonas hadn't been killed by the Megalodon, he'd certainly die from exposure to the cold.

Heller turned to look for the hundredth time at the giant white head and the spinal column of the monster on the deck below. The science team was examining the carcass. One member was taking photographs.

"If that . . . *thing* killed D.J. . . . what on God's earth killed it?" he said.

DeMarco stared down at the bloody head. "I don't know. But it sure as shit wasn't a landslide."

Terry stood at the bow of the yellow Zodiac as it bounced through the choppy water. She searched the waves ahead of her for a glimpse of the other AG II pod. Until they found it, she had no time for grieving, no time for the pain in her heart. She had to locate Jonas while any chance remained.

Leon Barre steered from the rear of the boat. "I'm going to circle back," he shouted.

"Wait!" Terry saw something in the swells. She pointed off the starboard bow. "Over there."

The red vinyl flag was just visible over the crest of the waves.

Leon guided them to the capsule, which bobbed gently in the water. They could see Jonas's body through the Lexan escape pod.

"Is he alive?" Leon asked, peering over the bow.

Terry leaned over the water as they drew close.

"Yes," she said gratefully. "He's alive."

HARBOR

Frank Heller couldn't figure out how the news had spread so quickly. It had taken less than twelve hours for the *Kiku* to reach the Aura Harbor naval base in Guam. Two Japanese television crews and one from the local station were waiting for them on the dock, along with press reporters and photographers for the Navy, the *Manila Times,* and the local Guam *Sentinel.* They surrounded Heller the moment he disembarked, bombarding him with questions about the giant shark, the dead pilot, and the surviving scientist who'd been airlifted ahead for medical treatment.

"Professor Taylor suffered a concussion and is being treated for hypothermia and blood loss, but I understand he is recovering well," Heller told them.

The cameramen trained their lenses on Heller, but when the carcass of the Megalodon was hoisted up on the crane, they scrambled for a shot.

An insistent young Japanese woman pressed her microphone at Heller. "Where will you take the shark?"

"We'll be flying the remains back to the Tanaka Oceano-graphic Institute as soon as possible."

"What happened to the rest of it?"

"We're not certain at this point. The shark might have been ripped apart by the cable that entangled it."

"It looks like it's been eaten," said the balding American with bushy eyebrows. "Is it possible another shark attacked this one?"

"It's possible, but—"

"Are you saying there are more out there?"

"Did anyone see—?"

"Do you think—?"

Heller raised his hands. "Please, please—one at a time." He nodded to a heavyset man from the Guam paper with his pen raised in the air.

"I guess what we want to know, Doc, is whether it's safe to go in the water?"

Heller spoke confidently. "Let me put your fears to rest. If there *are* any more of these sharks in the Mariana Trench, six *miles* of near-freezing water stands between them and us. Apparently, it's kept them trapped down there for at least two million years. It'll probably keep 'em down there a few million more."

"Dr. Heller?"

Heller turned. David Adashek stood before him. "Isn't Profes-sor Taylor a marine paleontologist?" Adashek asked innocently.

Heller glanced furtively at the crowd. "Yes. He has done some work—"

"More than some work. I understand he has a theory about these . . . dinosaur sharks. I believe they're called Megalodons?"

"Yes, well, I think I'll leave it to Dr. Taylor to explain his *theories* to you. Now if—"

"Is this a—?"

"If you don't mind, we've all got a lot of work to do." Heller pushed off through the crowd, ignoring the flurry of questions that followed him.

"Gangway!" came a thundering voice from behind. Leon Barre was supervising the transferal of the Megalodon carcass onto the dock.

A photographer pushed to the front and shouted, "Captain, could we get your picture with the monster?"

Barre waved his arm at the crane operator. The Megalodon head came to a stop in midair, its spine and caudal fin dragging on the dock and its jaws open to the sky. The cameramen scrambled for an angle, but the carcass was so long it would not fit into the frame. Barre walked up beside the giant head, turned to face them. The monstrous predator made the burly man look like a small child.

"Smile, Captain," someone shouted.

Barre continued staring grimly. "I am," he grunted.

THE *MAGNATE*

Maggie was lying topless on the teakwood deck of the yacht. The sun beat down upon the oil glistening on her body.

"You always said a tan looks good on-camera." Bud stood over her in his swim trunks, his face lost in the glare.

Maggie shielded her eyes, squinted up at him. "This is for you, baby," she said with a smile. "But not now." She turned over on her stomach and watched a tiny television. "Now you can fetch me another drink."

"Sure, Maggie," he said, his eyes drifting down her back. "Anything you say." He shuffled off to the cabin of the *Magnate* to mix a vodka and tonic.

A minute later she screamed his name. Bud ran out on deck. Maggie was sitting up, clutching the towel to her breasts, staring openmouthed at the TV. "I don't believe it!"

"What?!" Bud hurried over, looked at the TV. The Megalodon's head and fang-filled jaws filled the monitor, dangling from the crane of the *Kiku*.

". . . could be the giant prehistoric shark known as the Megalodon, ancestor of the great white. No one seems to know how the shark could have survived, but Dr. Jonas Taylor, who was injured in the capture, may be able to provide some answers. The professor is currently recovering at the naval hospital in Guam.

"In China today, negotiations for a trade . . ."

Maggie rushed for the cabin, Bud shouting after her, "Where're you going?"

"I need to call my office." She ran into the pilothouse, wrapping herself in a towel. "Phone!" she screamed at the captain. He pointed behind her, staring an extra few seconds as she exposed her back to him.

Maggie frantically dialed the office. Her secretary told her a Mr. David Adashek had been trying to contact her all morning. She took down the number, then dialed the overseas operator to connect her to Guam. Several minutes later, the line was ringing.

"Adashek."

"David, what the fuck is happening?"

"Maggie? I've been trying to call you all morning. Where the hell have—?"

"Never mind that. What's going on? Where did that shark come from? Where's Jonas? Has anyone spoken with him yet?"

"Hey, slow down. Jonas is recovering in the Guam naval hospital, with a guard posted at his door so no one can speak with him. The shark's for real. Looks like you were wrong about your husband."

Maggie felt ill.

"Maggie, you still there?"

"Shit, this could be the story of the decade. Jonas is a major player, and I missed the whole thing."

"True, but you are Jonas's wife, right? Maybe he can tell you about the *other* shark."

Maggie's heart skipped a beat. "What other shark?"

"The one that devoured the monster that killed the Tanaka kid. Everybody's talking about it, but the Tanaka Institute's people are in denial. Maybe Jonas would talk to you."

Maggie's mind raced. "Okay, okay, I'm coming to Guam, but I want you to stay on the story. Try to find out what the authorities are going to do to locate this other shark."

"Maggie, they don't even know if it surfaced. The crew of the *Kiku* are swearing that it never left the trench, claiming the thing's still trapped down there."

"Just do as I say. There's an extra thousand in it for you if you can get me some inside information from any reliable source about this second shark. I'll call you as soon as I land in Guam."

"You're the boss."

Maggie hung up. Bud was standing next to her. "What's going on, Maggs?"

"Bud, I need your help. Who do you know in Guam?"

RECOVERY

The Navy MP on duty outside Jonas's room at the Aura naval hospital rose to attention as Terry approached the door.

"Sorry, ma'am. No press allowed."

"I'm not with the press."

The MP eyed her suspiciously. "You sure don't look like family."

"My name is Terry Tanaka. I was with—"

"Oh . . . excuse me." The MP stepped aside. "My apologies, ma'am. And . . . my condolences." He averted his eyes.

"Thank you," she said softly, and entered Jonas's room.

Jonas lay near the window, a gauze bandage wrapped around his forehead. His face looked exhausted, pale and scarred.

"I'm sorry . . . ," he said, his voice still weak.

Terry nodded silently. "I'm glad you're all right."

"Have you talked to your father?"

"Yes. . . . He'll be here in the morning."

Jonas turned toward the white light of the window, unsure of what to say. "Terry, this is my fault—"

"No, you tried to warn all of us. We just ridiculed you."

"I shouldn't have let D.J. go. I should have—"

"Just stop it, Jonas," Terry snapped. "I can't deal with my own guilt, let alone yours. D.J. was an adult, and he certainly wasn't about to listen to you. Let's face facts. He wanted to go, despite your warnings. We're all devastated . . . in shock. I don't know what's going to happen next. I can't think that far ahead—" Tears flowed from her almond eyes.

"Take it easy, Terry. Come here." She sat down on his bed, hugging him while she cried on his chest. Jonas smoothed her hair, trying to comfort her.

After a few minutes, she sat up, turned away from Jonas to wipe her eyes. "You're seeing me in rare form. I never cry."

"You don't always have to be so tough."

She smiled. "Yeah, I do. Mom died when I was very young. I've had to take care of Dad and D.J. all these years by myself."

"How's your dad doing?"

"He's a wreck. I need to get him through this. I don't even know what to do. . . . Do you have a funeral? There's no body . . ." The tears clouded in her eyes.

"Speak to DeMarco. Have him arrange a service."

"Okay. I just want this to be over. I want to get back to California."

Jonas looked at her a moment. "Terry, this shark business isn't over yet either. You need to know something. There were two Megs in the trench. The one that the *Kiku* hauled up, it was attacked by a larger female. She was rising with the carcass . . ."

"Jonas, it's okay. Everyone on board was watching. Nothing else surfaced. Heller says the other creature, this female, couldn't survive the journey through the icy waters. You told us that yourself—"

"Terry, listen to me." He tried to sit up. The pain forced him down again. "The male's carcass, there was a lot of blood. Megalodons are like great whites. They're not warm-blooded like mammals, but they are warm-bodied. Some scientists call it gigantothermy, the ability of large creatures to maintain high body temperatures by means of large body size, low metabolic rates, and peripheral tissues as insulation—"

"Jonas, stop lecturing. You're losing me."

"The Megalodon is able to maintain high internal temperatures. Its blood is warmed internally as a result of the movement of its muscles. We're talking seven to twelve degrees warmer than its external environment, and the tropical currents in the trench were quite warm."

"What's your point?"

"When the *Kiku* began hauling up the remains of D.J.'s sub, the male Megalodon became caught in the steel cable. I saw the larger Meg, the female rising with the carcass, rising within the warm-blood stream. I watched her disappear above the warm layer into colder waters."

"How hot would a Megalodon's blood be?"

Jonas closed his eyes, calculating. "Living in the trench, blood temperature could be well above ninety degrees. If the female remained within her dead mate's blood stream, she could have made it to the thermocline. She's very big, maybe sixty feet or more. A shark that size could probably cover the distance from the trench to the warmer surface waters in twenty minutes."

Terry looked at him a long moment. "I have to go. I want you to get some rest."

She squeezed his hand, then left the room.

SHARKS

Jonas awoke and stared at his hand. It was covered with dried blood. He was in the Abyss Glider capsule, bobbing on the surface of the ocean. Sunlight glared through the Plexiglas sphere, half in water, half in air.

I've been dreaming, he thought. I've been dreaming . . .

He crawled to the window, peered out at the sky. The horizon was empty.

How long have I been out? Hours? Days?

The water beneath him rippled with sunlight. He stared down into it, waiting for the shark. He knew she was down there.

Out of the gray depths, the Megalodon appeared, rising up toward him like a rocket, jaws wide, teeth bared, her mouth a black abyss—

Jonas woke in a sweat, gasping for breath. He was alone in his hospital room. The digital clock read 12:06 A.M.

He fell back on the damp sheets and stared at the moonlit ceiling. He took a deep breath and exhaled slowly.

The fear was gone. Suddenly he realized he felt better. The fever, the drugs—something had worn off. I'm hungry, he thought.

He got out of bed, put on a robe, and walked into the hall. It was empty. He heard the sound of a TV down the corridor.

At the nursing station he found the MP sitting alone with his feet on a desk, his shirt open, downing a submarine sandwich while he watched the late news. The boy jumped when he sensed Jonas standing behind him.

"Mr. Taylor . . . you're up."

Jonas looked around. "Where's the nurse?"

"She's stepped out a minute, sir. I told her I'd . . . I'd cover for her." He stared at the bandage on Jonas's head. "You sure you ought to be out of bed, sir?"

"Where can I find something to eat?"

"Cafeteria's closed till six."

Jonas looked desperate.

"Y'all can have some of this." He picked up another half of the bulging sandwich, held it out for Jonas.

Jonas stared at it. "No, that's all right—"

"Please. Go ahead and have as much as you'd like."

"All right, sure, thanks." Jonas took the sandwich and began to eat. He felt like he hadn't tasted food in days. "This is great," he said between bites.

"Salami and cheese sub is hard to come by out here," the young man said. "Only place I know is halfway around the island. Me and my buddies, we make the trip once a week, just to kind of remind us of being back home. I don't know why they don't open something closer to the base. Seems to me . . . ."

The kid continued talking, but Jonas wasn't listening. Something had caught his eye on the television. Fishermen at a dock were unloading a great quantity of sharks from their boats.

"Excuse me," Jonas said. "Can you turn that up?"

The MP stopped talking. "Sure." He raised the volume.

". . . over one hundred sharks were caught off Zamora Bay. Local fishermen apparently have found an expanse of ocean off Saipan that has yielded the largest catches this century. They're hoping their luck will hold out through tomorrow. In a related story, twelve pilot whales and two dozen dolphins beached themselves along Saipan's northern shore. Unfortunately, most of the mammals died before rescuers could push them back out to sea.

"In other news . . ."

Jonas turned off the volume on the TV. "Saipan. That's in the middle of the northern Marianas, isn't it?"

"That's right, sir. Third island up the chain."

Jonas looked away, thinking.

"What is it, sir?" the MP asked.

Jonas looked at him. "Nothing," he said. He turned and headed back down the hall. Then he stopped, came back, handed the boy the rest of his sandwich. "Thanks."

The MP watched Jonas hurry back to his room. "Sir," he called after him, "you sure you're all right?"

SAIPAN

The two-passenger helicopter bounced twice upon the dirt runway before its weight settled down onto its supports. Retired Navy captain James "Mac" Mackreides glanced over at his passenger, who looked a bit shaken after the forty-five-minute flight.

"You okay, Jonas?"

"Fine." Jonas took a deep breath as the chopper's rotary blades gradually slowed to a stop. They had landed on the perimeter of a makeshift airfield. A faded wooden sign read: WELCOME TO SAIPAN.

"Yeah, well, you look like hell."

"Your flying hasn't improved any since you were discharged."

"Hey, pal, I'm the only game in town, especially at three A.M. in the fucking morning. What's so damn important anyway that you needed to fly out to this godforsaken island now?"

"You mentioned that your fisherman friend knows the location of a recent whale kill. I need to examine that carcass."

"At this time of night? We need to get you laid, pal."

"Seriously, Mac, this is important. Where's your friend? I thought he was supposed to meet us here."

"See that path to the left? Follow that down to the beach and you'll see a half dozen fishing boats tied up. Philippe's will be the last boat down the beach. He said he'd wait for you there. I'll be at the tavern getting shit-faced. Find me when you're done playing. If I'm with a woman, wait ten minutes. If she's ugly, wait five."

"If you're shit-faced, what difference does it make?"

"This is true. As for my friend Philippe, just remember, you pay half now, half when you get back, or he might just leave you to swim back to shore."

"Thanks for the advice," said Jonas. He watched his friend limp toward the rusty green building that Mac had referred to as a tavern. Jonas hefted his knapsack and headed in the other direction, to the beach. The stars were covered by the incoming clouds, but the Pacific Ocean was as smooth as glass.

Jonas Taylor had met James Mackreides seven years ago in what both men referred to as the Navy's "loony bin." Following the incident on board the *Seacliff,* Jonas had spent several weeks in a naval hospital, then had been ordered to spend ninety days in a psychiatric ward for evaluation. It was there that the Navy's team of psychiatrists attempted to convince the aquanaut that he had hallucinated the events in the Mariana Trench. After two months of "help," Jonas found himself in a state of deep depression, separated from Maggie, his career in ruins. Unable to leave the mental ward, he felt alone and betrayed.

Until he met Mac.

James Mackreides lived to buck authority. Drafted and sent to fight in Vietnam when he was twenty-three, Mac had been made a captain in the 155th Assault Helicopter Corps, stationed in Cambodia, long before any U.S. armed forces were supposed to be in there. Trained by the Navy to fly Cobras, Mac survived the insanity of Vietnam by deciding himself when, where, and if it was time to wage war. If an assignment seemed ridiculous, he never questioned his orders, he just did something else. When ordered to bomb the Ho Chi Minh Trail, Mac would organize his troops for battle, then lead his squadron of choppers to a U.S. hospital, pick up a group of nurses, and spend the day on the beaches of Con Son Island. Later that night, he'd submit his report on the outstanding job his men did in "banging" the enemy. The Navy never knew any better. On one such adventure, Mac's team landed one of their two-million-dollar helicopters in a delta, shot it to pieces, then blew it up with a claymore mine. Mac reported to his superiors that his squadron had been under heavy fire, but his men had heroically managed to hold their own against superior forces. For their bravery, Mac and his men received Bronze Stars.

This was not to say that Mac and his men did not see their fair share of combat. Mac simply refused to risk the lives of his men if he determined certain actions to be senseless. Of course, in the end, the whole Vietnam War became senseless.

After the war, Mackreides continued flying for the Navy. An advocate of the free-enterprise system, he supplied small-time operators from Guam to Hawaii with everything under the sun, using Navy choppers to expedite deliveries. Another commanding officer finally got wise when he caught his enlisted men lining up for helicopter tours of the Hawaiian Islands. Mac was charging fifty dollars apiece, his package featuring a six-pack of beer and twenty minutes with a local whore.

The "flying bordello" incident earned Mackreides his discharge, a mandatory psychiatric evaluation, and an extended stay at the Navy's mental institution. It was either that or a military prison. Confined against his will, Mac found himself suffocating, with no outlet to express his disdain for authority. Then he met Jonas Taylor.

In Mac's professional opinion, Jonas was yet another victim of the Navy's blame game, the refusal of higher-ups to take responsibility for their actions. This made Taylor a kindred spirit of sorts. Mackreides felt a moral obligation to help Jonas recover.

Mac decided the best remedy for his newfound buddy's depression was a road trip. Stealing the Coast Guard's helicopter had been easy, landing in the parking lot of Candlestick Park a breeze. Getting into the 49ers-Cowboys game proved to be the tough part. After partying all night, they returned to the hospital the next morning by cab, drunk, stupid, and happy. The Coast Guard located the chopper two days later, parked at a body shop, a naked woman painted on either side of the cabin.

The two had remained close friends ever since.

The last boat anchored in the shallow water along the beach hardly looked seaworthy. A mere eighteen-footer, the wooden vessel lay low in the water, its gray planks showing specks of red paint that had worn away over the years. On board, a large black man in a sweaty T-shirt and jeans was busy hauling in a crab trap.

"Excuse me?" Jonas said as he approached. The man continued working. "Hey, excuse me . . . you Philippe?"

"Who wants to know?"

"My name's Dr. Jonas Taylor. I'm a friend of Mac's."

"Mac owes me money. You got me money?"

"No. I mean, I've got enough for you to take me out to the site of the whale kill, but I don't know anything about . . ."

"Dead humpback floating about two miles out. Cost you fifty American."

"Fine, half now, half when we get back." Jonas held up the bills for Philippe's approval.

"Okay, le's go."

Jonas held out twenty-five dollars, then pulled back. "Just one thing. No motor on the way out."

"Whatchu speaking 'bout dere, Dr. Jonas? You want me to row us out two mile? Nah, you keep you money . . .''

"Okay, double. Half now, half when we get back." The islander looked Jonas up and down for the first time.

"Okay, Doc, one hundred. Now you tell me why you no want no motor?"

"Let's just say I don't want to disturb the fish."

Jonas knew he needed some kind of evidence to prove his theory that the female had surfaced. The large fishing hauls off the Saipan coast were a possible indicator that something was disturbing the local shark population. The whale and dolphin beachings could also indicate the massive predator's presence. But neither events were the proof Jonas required. If the humpback that Philippe had located had been killed by the female, the oversized bite radius would be all the evidence Jonas needed. Paddling out to the site was simply a necessary precaution.

Even with Jonas manning an oar, it took nearly an hour to reach the spot. Shirtless and sweaty, the two men let the boat drift against the black oozing carcass.

"There she is, Doc. Looks like de sharks been eatin' at her all day. Not much left."

The dorsal surface of the dead whale floated along the calm sea, its stench overpowering. Jonas used his paddle to manipulate the bloated carcass, bobbing it up and down along the surface. It was much too heavy to flip over.

"Whatchu tryin' to do?" asked Philippe.

"I need to see what killed this whale. Can we flip it over?"

"Twenty-five dollar."

"Twenty-five? You planning on getting in the water for that much?"

"Nah. Too many sharks. Look dere."

Jonas spotted the fin. "Is that a tiger shark?"

"Yeah, dat's a tiger. Don't worry, Doc, it get too frisky and I kill 'em wit' me six-shooter!" Philippe pulled the pistol from his waistband.

"Philippe, please . . . no noise!" Jonas shone his flashlight over the clear surface of the black water. Waves lapped against the ship's hull. Jonas suddenly realized they were an easy target.

The small beam of light caught a large body moving rapidly beneath the surface, a flash of white disappearing quickly into the dark water. "Jesus, Doc, what de hell was dat?!"

Jonas looked at Philippe. The big man had fear in his eyes. "What's wrong? What is it?"

"Somet'ing below us, Doc. I can feel it vibrating under de water. Somet'ing very big . . ."

The wooden boat began moving, slowly at first, revolving in a counterclockwise direction. They were spinning in a whirlpool, caught within a fast-moving current originating far below the surface. The two men hung on to the side for support as the craft began picking up speed.

Philippe had his six-shooter out, pointing into the water. "De devil hisself down dere!"

The horizon swirled about them. Jonas looked down and felt the hair on the back of his neck stand on end. Something large and white was hurtling toward the surface!

Both men screamed as the massive white abdomen exploded out of the water. Philippe raised the gun, pumping six rounds into the belly of the dead orca. Seconds later, the twelve-foot tiger shark tore at the twenty-eight-foot carcass of the dead whale, sending gouts of blood straight into the air.

The boat stopped spinning, coming to a rest. Jonas shone his flashlight across the dead creature's stomach. That's when he and Philippe saw it—the huge bite mark, several feet deep, nearly ten feet across.

"Mother of God! What de hell did dat?!" Before Jonas could answer, Philippe slammed the outboard motor into the water and started the engine.

"No—wait!" Jonas shouted.

Too late. The engine roared to life, Philippe steering the boat in a sharp turn back toward shore.

"No nuthin', Dr. Jonas! Dat a monster down dere, somet'ing *real* big! No fish I ever seen coulda killed an orca wit one bite like dat! You chasin' de devil, mon. Keep yo' damn money—we goin' in now!"

THE MEETING

Terry Tanaka entered the Aura naval hospital and glanced at her watch—8:40 A.M. That gave her exactly twenty minutes to get Jonas to Commander McGovern's office, assuming he was in any condition to travel. She walked down the empty hallway, curious why the Navy MP no longer stood on duty. In fact, Jonas's door was ajar.

Inside, a woman with bright blond hair was ransacking a chest of drawers. The bed was empty. Jonas was gone.

"Can I help you, miss?" Terry asked.

Maggie jumped and nearly dropped the clothes she was carrying. "Yes, you can help me. For starters, where's my fucking husband?"

"Your hus . . . You're Maggie?"

Maggie's eyes narrowed. "I'm *Mrs.* Taylor. Who the hell are you?"

"Terry Tanaka."

Maggie eyed her up and down. "Well, well . . ."

"I'm a *friend*. I stopped by to drive Dr. Taylor to the naval base."

Maggie's disposition suddenly changed. "Naval base? What does the Navy want with Jonas?"

"He has a meeting scheduled with Commander McGovern to discuss the Meg—" Terry hesitated, wondering if she'd said too much.

Maggie smiled, her eyes full of venom. "Well, it appears that you're too late. He's gone. When you see him"—she pushed past Terry abruptly—"tell him his *wife* needs to speak with him—if he's not too busy."

Maggie marched down the hallway, her heels clacking on the tile floor.

Terry could only turn and stare at the empty bed.

Terry arrived alone at the naval base at 9:05, only to learn that the meeting had been moved to Warehouse D on the far side of the grounds. By the time she got there, the meeting was already in progress.

Warehouse D contained a refrigerated storage area used to "hold" the bodies of deceased soldiers awaiting transport back to the States. Under three sets of mobile surgical lights lay the remains of the Megalodon. An MP handed Terry a white coat as she entered the cooler.

A conference table had been set up adjacent to the carcass. Heller, DeMarco, and Commander Bryce McGovern sat on one side. Terry didn't recognize the two men seated across the table or the two Japanese examining the enormous jaws of the shark.

"Where's Taylor?" Frank Heller barked across the room at her.

"I don't know. He must have left the hospital."

"That figures."

DeMarco pulled a chair out for her. "Terry, I think you've met Commander McGovern."

"Ms. Tanaka, we're all sorry about what happened to your brother. This is Mr. André Dupont of the Cousteau Society, and over by the carcass are Dr. Tsukamoto and Dr. Simidu from the Japan Marine Science Technology Center." Terry shook hands with Dupont. "And this gentleman is Mr. David Adashek. He's been asked to cover this story on behalf of the local government."

Terry shook hands warily with the bushy-eyebrowed reporter. "I've seen you before, Mr. Adashek. Where have we met?"

David smiled. "I'm not sure, Ms. Tanaka. I spend a lot of time in Hawaii, perhaps . . ."

"No, not Hawaii." She continued staring at him.

"All right, gentlemen . . . and Ms. Tanaka," announced Commander McGovern, "if we can all take a seat, I'd like to get started. The United States Navy has assigned me to investigate the incident that occurred in the Mariana Trench. My rules are simple: I'm going to ask the questions and you people are going to give me the answers. First"—he pointed toward the carcass— "would somebody please tell me what that *thing* is over there?"

Dr. Simidu, the younger of the two Japanese, was the first to speak. "Commander, JAMSTEC has examined the teeth of the creature and have compared it with those of *Carcharodon carcharius,* the great white shark, and its extinct predecessor, *Carcharodon megalodon.* The presence of a chevron or scar above the root indicates that this is definitely a Megalodon. Its existence in the Mariana Trench is shocking, to say the least."

"Not to us, Dr. Simidu," replied André Dupont. "The disappearance of the Megalodon has always been a mystery, but the *Challenger I*'s discovery in 1873 of several ten-thousand-year-old fossilized teeth over the Mariana Trench made it clear that some members of the species may have managed to survive."

"What the Navy wants to know is whether there are any more

of these creatures alive and whether any others have surfaced," McGovern stated. "Dr. Heller?"

All heads turned to Frank Heller. "Commander, the shark you see here attacked and killed the pilot of one of our deep-sea submersibles seven miles down, then apparently got itself entangled in our cable and was attacked by another one of its kind. These creatures have been trapped in a tropical layer at the bottom of the trench below six miles of freezing temperatures for God knows how many millions of years. The only reason you even see this specimen before you is because we accidentally hauled it up to the surface."

"So you're telling me at least one more of these . . . these Megalodons exists, but it's trapped at the bottom of the trench."

"That's correct."

"You're wrong, Frank." Jonas Taylor entered the room, holding a white coat in one hand and a newspaper in the other. Masao Tanaka followed closely behind.

"Taylor, what do you think you're—"

"Frank," Masao interrupted, "sit down and listen to what Jonas has to say." Terry stood to greet her father, who hugged her tightly for a long moment, then took an empty seat beside her, still holding her hand.

Jonas approached the head of the table. "Late last night I hired a local fisherman to take me out to an area where a humpback whale had recently been killed. I wanted to examine the carcass to see if the Megalodon could have possibly killed it. While we were out there, the remains of a slaughtered twenty-eight-foot orca surfaced alongside our boat with a wound that was definitely the result of a shark attack. The bite radius was no less than ten feet in diameter."

"That proves nothing," Heller said.

"There's more. Here's this morning's paper. Wake Island residents report that whale carcasses have been washing up along their northern beaches all night. Commander, the second Megalodon not only managed to surface, it's now adapted to shallower waters!"

"Ridiculous!" retorted Heller.

"Dr. Heller, please sit down," McGovern commanded. "Dr. Taylor, since you seem to be the closest thing to an expert on these creatures and you were present in the trench, perhaps you can tell me how this monster managed to surface. Dr. Heller seems to believe these creatures were trapped below six miles of frigid water."

"They were. But I witnessed the second shark attacking the first down in the trench. The first Meg was bleeding badly, and the second was gorging itself on its innards, ascending while within the dense blood stream. As I explained yesterday to Terry, if the Megalodons are like their cousins, the great whites, their blood temperatures will be about twelve degrees higher than the surrounding ocean water, or, as in the case of the hydrothermal layer of the trench, about ninety-two degrees. The *Kiku* hauled the first Meg topside and the female followed the bait straight up to our warmer surface waters, protected by a river of hot blood streaming out of its mate!"

"The female?" André Dupont looked perplexed. "How do you know the second Megalodon is a female?"

"Because I saw her. She passed over my sub when I was in the trench. And she's much larger than this first shark."

McGovern didn't like what he was hearing. "What else can you tell us about this . . . female, Doctor?"

"Well, like its mate, it's totally white, actually luminescent. This is a common genetic adaptation to its deep-water environment, where no light exists. Its eyes will be extremely sensitive to light. Consequently, it won't surface by day." He turned to Terry. "That's why no one on board the *Kiku* saw her rise. She would have stayed deep enough to avoid the light. And now that the shark has adapted to our surface waters, I think she's going to be very aggressive."

"Why do you say that?" Dr. Tsukamoto spoke for the first time.

"The deep waters of the Mariana Trench are poorly oxygenated compared with our surface waters. The higher the oxygen content, the more efficiently the Megalodon's system will function. In its new highly oxygenated environment, the creature will be able to process and generate greater outputs of energy. In order to accommodate these increases in energy, the Meg will have to consume greater quantities of food. And, I don't need to tell you, sufficient food sources are readily available."

McGovern's face darkened. "Our coastal populations could be attacked."

"No, Commander, these creatures are too large to venture into shallow waters. So far, the female has attacked smaller sharks and now whales. My concern is that her mere presence among the whale pods may affect the cetacean's migration patterns."

"How so?"

"Please understand that *Carcharodon megalodon* is the greatest predator, the greatest killing machine in the history of our planet. As it develops its taste for warm-blooded whales, it will go on a feeding frenzy. Our modern-day whales have never come across anything like this creature before. This female is aggressive and as large as most whales. Her mere presence could very well cause a cetacean . . . stampede, if you will. Even a slight change in the migration patterns among whale pods now coming south from the Bering Sea could create an ecological disaster. For instance, if the whale populations that currently inhabit the coastal waters off Hawaii were to suddenly flee into Japan's coastal waters in an attempt to avoid the Megalodon, the area's entire marine food chain would be affected. The additional presence of several thousand whales would cause an imbalance among those species that share the same diets as these mammals. The competition among marine life for plankton, krill and shrimp could drastically reduce the populations among other species of fish. The inadequate food supply would change breeding patterns, severely affecting the fishing industry in that locale for years to come."

Dr. Simidu and Dr. Tsukamoto whispered to each other in Japanese. Heller, Adashek, and Dupont simultaneously fired questions at Jonas.

"Gentlemen, gentlemen!" McGovern stood up, regaining control of the conference. "As I said before, I'll ask the questions. Dr. Taylor, I want to be sure that I understand our situation correctly. Essentially, it is your belief that we have an aggressive sixty-foot version of a great white shark on the loose, the mere presence of which could indirectly affect the fishing industry of some coastal nation. Does that about sum it up?"

"Yes, sir."

Heller stood up. "Masao, I'm leaving. I've had enough of this nonsense. A cetacean *stampede*? No disrespect intended, Commander, but you're taking advice from a guy whose overreaction to this creature seven years ago got two of your officers killed. Let's go, DeMarco. You can take me back to the boat."

DeMarco stood up, excused himself, then followed his shipmate out the door. Jonas sat, stunned by Heller's words, while David Adashek turned away, scribbling furiously on his notepad. As the two men walked to the door, Masao whispered in his daughter's ear. Terry nodded and kissed her father's cheek, then followed the men out of the warehouse.

"Commander"—Jonas cleared his throat—"let me assure you that—"

"Dr. Taylor, I don't want your assurances. What I need is options. So perhaps you could tell me what the hell the United States Navy is supposed to do about this?"

OPTIONS

"Commander, why must you do anything?" André Dupont spoke up first. "Since when does the United States Navy concern itself with the behavioral patterns of a fish?"

"And what if this 'fish' starts devouring small boats or scuba divers? What then, Mr. Dupont?"

"Dr. Taylor," said Dr. Tsukamoto, "if this creature's presence alters the migration patterns of whales around Japan, our entire fishing industry could suffer a major setback. Theoretically, JAMSTEC and the Tanaka Institute could be held legally responsible. The UNIS program has already been suspended, and we can't afford any more financial setbacks. JAMSTEC therefore officially recommends that this creature be found and destroyed."

"Dr. Taylor," said McGovern, "I happen to agree with Dr. Tsukamoto. I don't think nature intended to release this monster from the abyss. That was your doing. Despite your assurances, I can't take the chance that this Megalodon might venture into populated waters. We already have one dead"—McGovern paused—"and I'd rather not wait for a body count before we act.

Therefore, I'm going to take the recommendation from one of my senior officers in Hawaii and assign the *Nautilus* to track the female down and kill her."

"And the Cousteau Society will have every animal rights group picketing your naval base in Oahu starting tomorrow," Dupont said.

"Jonas." Masao was a voice of reason. "In your opinion, in which direction will this Megalodon head?"

"Difficult to predict. She'll follow the food, that's for sure. Problem is, there are four distinct whale migration patterns occurring at this time of year in this hemisphere. West toward the coast of Japan, east and west of the Hawaiian Islands, and far east, along the coast of California. At this juncture, it appears the female is heading east, toward Hawaii. I'm guessing she'll continue east, eventually ending up in California waters . . . Wait a minute!"

"What is it, Taylor?" McGovern asked.

"Maybe there's another option. Masao, how close to completion is the Tanaka Lagoon?"

"Two weeks—until JAMSTEC cut off our funding when the UNIS systems went down," said Tanaka. "You're not thinking of capturing this creature?"

"Why not? If the lagoon was designed to study whales in a natural environment, why couldn't we use it to capture the Meg?" Jonas turned to face the JAMSTEC directors. "Gentlemen, consider the opportunity we'd have to study this predator!"

"Tanaka-san," Dr. Simidu asked, "is this option feasible?"

"Simidu-san, *hai,* it is possible, assuming we can locate the beast to begin with." Masao reflected for a moment. "Of course, the lagoon would have to be finished quickly, the *Kiku* refitted. If we could locate the creature, perhaps we could tranquilize it, then drag it in."

"Masao," Jonas interrupted, "if we're going to attempt this, we'll need to rig some type of buoyant harness to drag the Meg. Remember, unlike a whale, the shark will not float. Once we tranquilize her, she'll sink and drown."

"Ah, excuse me," interrupted Adashek. "Exactly *why* don't sharks float?"

Jonas looked at the reporter for the first time. "Sharks are inherently heavier than seawater. If they stop swimming they'll sink." Jonas looked at Commander McGovern. "Why is this man here?"

"About an hour ago, I received a call from several local officials who were concerned about the presence of another Megalodon in their coastal waters. One official requested I allow Mr. Adashek to be present during these discussions. In order to maintain good relations, I agreed to the request."

The two representatives of JAMSTEC had been talking among themselves. "Tanaka-san," said Dr. Tsukamoto, "you have already lost a son to these creatures. With respect, if you so desire to capture this female, we will agree to underwrite the project and allow you to complete the lagoon. Of course, assuming you are successful, JAMSTEC will expect full access to the captured Megalodon, as well as our agreed-upon financial share of the lagoon's tourism trade."

Masao paused, tears welling in his eyes. "Yes . . . yes, I think D.J. would have wanted this. My son dedicated his life to the advancement of science. The last thing he'd want would be for us to destroy this unique species. Jonas, we must attempt to capture the Megalodon."

McGovern rejoined the conversation. "Mr. Tanaka, Doctors . . . just so we understand each other, the Navy cannot support your efforts. The *Nautilus* will be assigned to track down this creature and protect the lives of Americans. If you manage to capture the shark first, so be it. Personally, I hope you're successful. Officially, however, the Navy cannot recognize this course of action as being a viable option." McGovern stood up, signaling an end to the meeting.

"By the way, Dr. Taylor"—the commander turned to face Jonas—"what makes you think this shark will travel all the way into California waters?"

"Because, Commander, as we speak, over twenty thousand whales are migrating from the Bering Sea south toward the peninsula of Baja, Mexico, and the Megalodon can literally sense the beating of their hearts."

Twenty minutes later, David Adashek was at a pay phone outside the naval base, dialing the number of a local hotel room. He waited until the female voice answered.

"Maggie, it's me. Yeah, I got into the meeting. Tell Bud he did good. Yes, I got exactly what you were looking for."

"Capture the Meg?" Frank Heller was livid. "Masao, listen to what you're saying! This creature killed D.J.! It's a menace. Trying to capture it would be a tragic mistake. It should be destroyed. How many more innocent people have to die?"

Masao turned his back to Heller, facing the sun as it melted into the Pacific. He breathed in the salt air, closing his eyes in meditation.

Heller turned to face Jonas. "This is your fault, Taylor! D.J. died because of your incompetence, and now you're gonna kill all of us!"

"Frank!" Masao swung around, his eyes burning into the man's face. "This is my project, my ship, and I have made my decision. You either support the team's efforts, or I'll have you dropped off in Hawaii. Is that clear?"

Heller glared at Jonas, then looked at Masao. "You and I go

back sixteen years, Masao. I think you're making a big mistake listening to this nut. But I'd like to stay on board and help if I can, out of respect for you and Terry."

"If you stay, you'll be working with Jonas. I've decided to name him group leader to capture the Megalodon. So tell me now if you two can work together."

Heller focused on the deck. "I'll work with him." He looked at Jonas. "I'll do all I can to protect the lives of this crew."

"Good." Masao turned to Jonas. "When is your meeting?"

"Fifteen minutes. In the dining room."

The dining room had been converted into a war room. Jonas had attached to one wall a large map illustrating the migration patterns of the whales, along with red pins marking the locations where whale carcasses had recently been spotted. A pattern was apparent: the female looked to be headed to the northeast, toward the Hawaiian Islands. Next to the whale map hung a large diagram illustrating the internal anatomy of the great white shark.

Terry and Masao sat next to each other, while DeMarco and Mac Mackreides stood before the whale map. Heller was the last to arrive.

"Mac," asked Jonas, "have you met everyone here?"

"Yeah. Hello, Frank. It's been a while." They shook hands.

"Mac. Didn't know you were gonna be mixed up in this shark business."

"You know me, Frank, always looking to make a quick buck."

Jonas addressed the group. "Mac and I will be flying together in his copter, trying to spot the Meg. Since the tranquilizer harpoons and harness are being readied in Honolulu over the next few days, our first objective is to see if we can tag her with a homing device."

"How the hell are you gonna find one fish in all this ocean?" smirked Heller.

Jonas pointed to the map. "As you can see, this map illustrates the locations of the winter breeding grounds of whales currently migrating south from the Bering Sea. The Megalodon can detect the massive vibrations produced by these whale populations to the east and west of Guam. Based on recent kills, she seems to be heading east, toward the whale populations located along the coastal waters off Hawaii."

Jonas looked at Masao. "It's not going to be easy to locate her, but we know that her eyes are too sensitive to surface during the day. That means she'll do the majority of her feeding at night, attacking whale pods close to the surface. Mac's helicopter has been equipped with a thermal imager and monitor, which will assist us in spotting both the Megalodon and the whale pods in the dark. I'll be riding shotgun, using a pair of night-vision binoculars. The Meg's hide is fluorescent, she should be easy to locate at night from above, so that helps." Jonas looked around the room. "Once the female begins hunting, we'll have a fairly dense trail of blood and debris floating along the surface to spot."

Jonas held up one of the homing darts. It was attached to an electronic device roughly the size of a pocket flashlight. "This transmitter fits into the barrel of a high-powered rifle. If we can inject this homing dart close to the Megalodon's heart, we'll not only be able to track her, we should also be able to monitor her pulse rate."

"What good will that do?" asked DeMarco.

"Once we tranquilize the Meg, knowing her heart rate could be vital to our own safety as well as to the Meg's survival. The harpoons will contain a mixture of pentobarbital and ketamine. The pentobarbital will depress the Meg's cerebral oxygen consumption, which concerns me a bit. The ketamine is more of a nonbarbiturate general anesthetic. The Meg's heart should slow significantly once the combination of drugs take effect. I've estimated the dosages based on the female's size. I'm just a little concerned about the potential side effects of the tranquilizers."

Heller looked up. "What side effects?"

"The pentobarbital could cause some initial excitement in the Meg."

"What the hell does that mean?"

"It means she's going to be mighty pissed off just before she falls asleep."

"Masao, are you listening to—?"

"Let him finish, Frank." Masao looked at Jonas. "Once we manage to tranquilize this creature, how do you expect to drag it to the lagoon?"

"That's the tricky part. The harpoon gun will be positioned at the *Kiku*'s stern. We'll use the steel cable that's wrapped around the big winch as its line. The harpoon won't remain fastened very long in the Meg's hide, so it's important that we get the harness around her as quickly as possible. The harness itself is basically a thick two-hundred-foot fishing net with flotation buoys attached every twenty feet to its perimeter. The net will help keep her afloat while we drag her into the lagoon. The harpoon should remain attached to the Megalodon's hide long enough for the *Kiku* to drag her forward until the net's secured. That's extremely important. If we don't keep circulating water through her mouth, her gills will cease functioning and the Meg will drown."

"And how do you propose we secure the net?" asked DeMarco.

"One end of the net will remain attached to the stern of the *Kiku*. I'll be using the AG I to run the other end beneath the female."

Terry looked at Jonas. "You're going to put yourself back in the water with that monster?"

"Terry, listen . . ."

"No, you listen! This reeks of macho bullshit. Risking your life to capture this monster . . . I've already lost a brother, I don't . . ." She stopped herself in midsentence, afraid of what might come out next. "Sorry, Dad, I'm not up to this."

Masao watched his daughter leave the room. "It's D.J.'s death. None of us has really had time to mourn." Masao rose from his seat. "I must go and speak with her. But, Jonas, tell me, is there any danger to yourself while in the AG?"

"We'll be monitoring the Megalodon's heart rate and I'll be in constant communication with the *Kiku*. If the Meg begins to wake, her pulse rate will increase rapidly as a warning. The AG I's a fast sub, I'll have no problems getting out of harm's way. Believe me, Masao, I have no desire to play hero. The Meg will be knocked out long before I enter the water in the AG I."

Masao nodded, then left the room to locate his daughter.

"Hey, I have a question." Mac walked up to the diagram of the great white's internal organs. "You say we gotta implant this little dart near the shark's heart. Where the hell is that?"

Jonas pointed to the great white's mouth. "If you follow the path into the mouth and through the esophagus, the heart should be located just below the point where the esophagus connects with the stomach. Of course, this is the anatomy of a great white shark—no one knows for sure how the internal organs of a Megalodon are laid out. We have to assume that the two species are not only physically similar but anatomically as well. If we can shoot the tracking dart about here"—Jonas pointed to a location along the underbelly of the shark between its gill slits and pectoral fins— "I think we'll be okay."

Mac shook his head. "And if we miss?"

ATTACK

The full moon reflected off the windshield of the helicopter, illuminating the interior of the small compartment. For nearly four hours, Mac had flown his chopper along a thirty-mile semicircular patch of ocean, hovering two hundred feet above the black Pacific. They had located nearly two dozen pods of whales without seeing a trace of the Megalodon, and the initial excitement Jonas had felt was quickly fading into boredom as he realized just how difficult their task was going to be.

"This is crazy, Jonas!" Mac shouted over the noise of the rotors.

"How are we set for fuel?"

"Another fifteen minutes and we'll have to turn back."

"Okay. Look ahead, Mac, about eleven o'clock. There's another pod of humpbacks. Let's follow them a while, then we'll turn back."

"You're the boss." Mac changed course to intercept the pod.

Jonas focused on the Pacific with the his ITT Night Mariner Gen III binoculars. The bifocal night glasses penetrated the dark, improving light amplification by using a coating of gallium arsenide on the photocathode of the intensifier. The black sea now appeared a pale shade of gray, revealing the quickly moving behemoths as they rose up and down along the surface of the Pacific.

Mac had "borrowed" the Agema Thermovision 1000 infrared thermal imager from the Coast Guard. Mounted below the helicopter was a small gyrostabilized platform which held the thermal imager pod in place. Inside the cabin was a television monitor, attached to a video recorder. The thermal imager was designed to detect objects in the water by the electromagnetic radiation the object emitted. The internal temperature of a warm body would appear on the monitor as a hot spot against the image of the cold sea. The warm-blooded whales were easily detected; the Megalodon's internal temperature would be slightly cooler.

Jonas was worried. It was vital that the Megalodon be located quickly. With each hour that passed, the circumference of the female's predicted course would extend an additional twenty miles. Soon there would simply be too much ocean to cover, even with their sophisticated tracking equipment.

Jonas was exhausted. He felt himself becoming mesmerized by the moonlight dancing across the ocean, barely noticing the white blur streak across his peripheral vision. The moon had illuminated something below the surface. For a moment it had seemed to glow.

"See something, Doc?"

"Not sure. Where's that pod?"

"Just ahead, three hundred yards."

Jonas located the spouts, then focused with the night glasses. "I can make out two bulls, a cow and her calf . . . no, make that two cows, five whales total. Get us on top of them, Mac."

The helicopter hovered above the pod, keeping pace as the whales changed direction, turning north.

"What's goin' on, Doc?"

Jonas concentrated on the black water. "There!"

To the south a white glow appeared, streaking beneath the surface like a giant luminescent torpedo.

Mac saw her on the monitor. "Holy shit, I can't believe it. You actually found her. Good job. What's she doing?"

Jonas looked at Mac. "I think she's stalking the calf."

One hundred feet below the black Pacific, a deadly game of cat and mouse was taking place. The humpbacks' sonar had detected the hunter's presence miles back, the mammals altering their course to avoid a confrontation. As the albino predator closed to intercept, the two cows moved to surround the calf, the larger bulls taking positions at the front and rear of the pod.

The Megalodon slowed, circling to the right of her quarry. The warm-blooded creatures were larger than the female, their close formation preventing a direct attack. The humpbacks remained close to the surface, continuously breaching, nervously observing their unwanted guest. The Megalodon circled once more, sizing up her prey, marking the position of the calf.

As the predator crossed in front of the leader, the forty-ton bull broke from the group and made a run at the Meg. Although the humpback whale possessed baleen instead of teeth, it was still quite dangerous, able to ram the female with its enormous head. The male humpback's charge was sudden, but the Meg was too quick, accelerating away from the pod, then returning in a wide arc.

"What do you see?"

Jonas was peering through the night glasses. "Looks like the lead bull is chasing the Megalodon away from the pod."

"Wait a minute, did you say the whale's chasing the Meg?"

Mac chuckled. "I thought this Megalodon of yours was supposed to be fearsome?"

Jonas loaded the tracking dart, snapping it into the custom-designed barrel of his rifle. "Don't be fooled, Mac. Don't be fooled."

The pod once again altered its course, heading southeast to lose the hunter. But the Meg's wide circular path intersected that of the two cows. The lead bull again turned to intercept, and this time the Meg retreated to the rear, leading the bull farther away from the safety of the pod's numbers.

As the male humpback turned to rejoin the others, the predator circled quickly, intercepting the isolated bull along its flank. With a frightening burst of speed and power, the Megalodon launched her 42,000 pounds of muscle and teeth at the retreating humpback. Her upper jaw hyperextended away from her mouth, her bite radius expanding to its full nine feet, sinking into the helpless humpback's huge fluke. In a fraction of a second, the razor-sharp upper rows of teeth sliced through the muscular tail of the whale before the mammal knew what had happened.

So large and powerful was the bite that it completely amputated the fluke from the apex of the whale's tail. The bull writhed in a violent contortion as the Megalodon swallowed its prize whole. An agonizing, high-pitched moan reverberated from the bleeding beast.

"What the hell was that?"

"I can't be sure," said Jonas, the night glasses pressed against his eyes, "but I think the Meg just tore off the humpback's fluke."

"What?"

"Forget the pod, Mac. Stay with the bull."

Warm blood gushed from the gaping wound as the crippled humpback feebly attempted to propel itself forward with its massive lateral flippers. The Megalodon's second attack came from the front and was even more devastating than the first. Seizing the baleen-fringed edges of the dying creature's mouth within its nine-inch fangs, the Meg ripped and tore apart an entire section of the humpback's throat, whipping its enormous head to and fro as a long strip of grooved hide and blubber peeled away from the mammal's body like the husk from an ear of corn.

Helplessly drifting in the ocean swells, the tortured humpback wailed a death song of agony. Fleeing in panic, the rest of the pod propelled themselves as one body away from the carnage. The Megalodon did not pursue, but instead continued to feast on the soft flesh of her prey, swallowing thousands of pounds of warm blood and blubber, obsessed with her kill, oblivious to all else.

And then the Meg sensed the rapid vibrations from above.

"What's happening, Jonas?"

"It's hard to tell, Mac, there's so much blood. What's your thermal imager picking up?"

"No good, Doc. The blood's spreading out over the surface and it's so warm that it's camouflaging any objects the imager could pick up. I'll have to bring us closer."

"Not too close, Mac. There's no predicting what the Meg might do."

"Relax. You want to get a good shot, don't you?" Mac descended to fifty feet. "Can you see any better now?"

Jonas looked through the night glasses. Yes, now he could just make out the Megalodon's white hide, her glow minimized by the warm blood pooling along the surface.

Then, as Jonas watched, she simply disappeared.

"Damn."

"What?"

"She went deep. I wonder if the vibrations of the copter scared her off. Or maybe she feels threatened by our presence around her kill."

Jonas searched the sea below. He could see the dark shadow of the dead humpback floating in its entrails. Where was the Meg?

"Mac, I've got a bad feeling about this. Take us higher."

"Higher?"

"Goddamnit, Mac, higher—now!"

The Megalodon launched straight out of the sea like an intercontinental ballistic missile, flying at the hovering helicopter faster than Mac could increase his altitude. Jonas slid out of his seat, his right foot losing its grip on the floor as the G force of the copter's climb pushed him toward the open door. Only the seat belt kept his body from falling into the night where the garage-sized head closed quickly, its bloodied fangs—now only five feet away—reaching for him. As if in slow motion, Jonas watched the upper jaw jut forward of the mouth, revealing crimson gums and white teeth, so close he could have kicked them with his dangling right leg. But he couldn't move, paralyzed with fear, his body dangling out of the open copter door. Somehow he held on, whipping his leg back into the cockpit as the jaws slammed together in the spot his limb had been. The vision of white death was still rising.

The copter reached sixty feet just as the broad snout connected from below, sending the airship sideways and out of control. The cabin began spinning.

"Come on, goddamnit!" Mac clutched his control stick with both hands.

The copter was slicing toward the sea at a thirty-degree angle when the mighty rotors finally caught air. Mac pulled the chopper out of its nosedive seconds short of plunging into the Pacific. The pilot groaned with relief as his airship soared above the waves, making its getaway.

"Gawd-damn, Jonas, I think I just shit in my pants!"

Jonas fought to catch his breath. His limbs were quivering, his voice abandoning him. After a good minute, he forced the words out of his parched throat. "She's . . . she's a lot bigger than I thought." He tried to swallow. "Mac, how high . . . how high were we when she hit us?"

"About sixty feet. Shee-it, look at me, I'm still quivering like a little girl. Did you get a shot off?"

Jonas looked at the rifle, still held tightly in his right hand. "No, she caught me off-guard. Do we have enough fuel to circle back?"

"Negative. I'll radio the *Kiku* to rendezvous, then we'll follow the trail." They flew without speaking for several minutes.

"Tell me something," asked Mac, finally ending the silence. "That monster . . . is that what you saw coming at you in the Mariana Trench seven years ago?"

Jonas looked at his friend. "Yeah, Mac, that's what I saw."

NETWORK

Maggie leaned forward uncomfortably in the high-backed leather chair, afraid to relax, knowing how easy it would be to simply lie back on the soft cushion and doze off. She had taken a late night flight in from Guam, Bud picking her up in his limo at the airport. She had come straight to the television station and now felt her blood pressure rising as she waited impatiently for Fred Henderson to get off his phone. Finally, she stood up over his desk and snatched the receiver out of his hand. "He'll have to call you back," she said into the mouthpiece, and hung up the phone.

"Maggie, what the hell do you think you're doing? That was an important call—"

"Important my ass, you were talking to your goddamn accountant. You want to make some money, listen to what I have to say." For the next thirty minutes, she briefed her station manager about the Megalodon story.

"Damn . . . this really *is* big. You're absolutely sure about David Adashek's information?"

"I've been paying Adashek to follow Jonas over the last few weeks. He's reliable."

Henderson leaned back in his leather chair. "And how can we be sure that your husband really knows where this monster is headed?"

"Listen, Fred, if there's one subject my soon-to-be ex-husband knows about, it's these damn mega-sharks. Christ, he's spent more time studying them over the last seven years than being with me. This is the biggest story to hit this century. Every news agency in the world is headed toward Guam. Let me run with this, Fred, and I'll get you an exclusive that will rocket this station to the top."

Henderson was sold. "Okay, Maggie, I'm going to call the network. You've got carte blanche. Now, tell me what you need."

Bud was reading the paper when Maggie rapped on the back window of the limousine an hour and a half later. When he unlocked the door, she ripped it open, climbed onto his lap, and planted a huge kiss on his lips.

"We got it, Bud! He loves it!! The network agreed to back me up on everything!" She kissed him again, pushing her tongue into his mouth, then came up for air and leaned her forehead against his.

"Bud," she whispered, "this is really the one, the story that makes me an international star. And you'll be there with me. Bud Harris, executive producer. Right now, though, I really need your help."

Bud smiled, enjoying the con. "Okay, darling, just tell me what you need."

"For starters, we'll need the *Magnate*. And a skeleton crew. I've already spoken with three cameramen and a sound guy who have underwater experience. We'll all be meeting on board the *Magnate* tomorrow morning. Fred's spoken with a Plexiglas company that can have something for us in two days."

"Plexiglas"

"The real challenge is the bait. That's where I'm really gonna need your help, baby . . ."

PEARL HARBOR

The *Kiku* was anchored next to the USS *John Hancock,* the 563 foot Spruance class destroyer that had arrived in port earlier that morning. Commander McGovern had personally granted Masao Tanaka the berth; now a harpoon gun was being mounted at the stern of the ship by Captain Barre's men.

On deck, Jonas and Mac watched DeMarco check and double-check the battery system on the Abyss Glider I. The AG I was a smaller, sleeker version of the deep-sea sub used in the Mariana Trench. Designed for speed, the one-man torpedo-shaped sub weighed a mere 462 pounds, with the majority of that weight located in the instrument panels in the Lexan nose cone.

"Looks like a miniature jet fighter," said Mac.

"Handles like one too."

"Is this what the kid was attacked in?"

"No," said Jonas, "the AG II was bigger, the hull thicker and much heavier. The AG I was the prototype. It was designed for depths only to four thousand meters. The hull is made of pure aluminum oxide, extremely sturdy, but positively buoyant. This baby can move fast, turn on a dime, even leap straight out of the water."

"Yeah? Can it outleap the monster we saw last night?"

Jonas looked at his friend. "It would take a rocket to outjump that fish."

"You've got one," DeMarco said, overhearing their conversation. Jonas walked over to the sub. "Here, Taylor. See this lever? Turn it a half-turn counterclockwise, pull it toward you, and it'll ignite a small tank of hydrogen installed in the tail. Never used it to launch the AG straight out of the water, but it would free up the sub in case you ever got stuck in the muck at the bottom."

"How much of a burn would you estimate?"

"Not much—a good fifteen, maybe twenty seconds tops. Once the sub's freed up, she'll float topside anyway, assuming you've lost power." DeMarco grabbed a wrench. "Course, you already know that."

"Jonas, take a look." Mac was at the port-side rail, pointing at two tugboats that were busy pushing the *Nautilus* into her berth. The black vessel looked ominous, a dozen of her crew on deck, proudly standing by with ropes to tie the ship off. As the world's first nuclear-powered sub approached the *Kiku,* Jonas could clearly see the faces of the two officers who stood on the conning tower.

"Christ, Mac, it's Danielson. Can you believe this?"

"Your former CO? Yeah, in fact, I already knew. A Navy friend stationed on Guam told me Danielson volunteered when he heard you were involved. In fact, it was his suggestion to Mc-Govern to use that old tin can coming at us."

As the *Nautilus* passed, United States Navy captain Richard Danielson, his gray eyes squinting in the sunlight, spotted his former deep-sea pilot aboard the *Kiku.*

"Hi, Dick, how's it hanging?" muttered Mac, a smile plastered on his face.

"He probably heard you."

"Who cares? Danielson can kiss my tattooed lovin' ass. I thought you told me this guy made a career out of destroying your reputation. How many months in the loony bin did you have to put up with before your ol' buddy Mac here saved your sorry butt? Two months? Or was it three?"

"Three. Probably would have been easier if I had just said I imagined the Megalodon. You know, psychosis of the deep, temporary insanity brought on by fatigue."

"Would have been a lie, pal. Now that these sharks have surfaced, looks like you're vindicated."

"You think Danielson's here to apologize? Megalodon or not, the guy blames me for killing two of his men."

"Fuck him. No man on this planet would have done any different if they had seen what we saw come at us last night. And I told that to Heller."

"Yeah, what'd he say?"

"Heller's an asshole. If he'd have been with me in Nam, I'd have had to shoot him. Screw him and Danielson." Mac looked toward the stern. "When's that net due in?"

"This afternoon. Damn, Mac, I should've tagged her last night."

"If memory serves, you were busy holding your sorry ass inside the copter. What were you gonna pull the trigger with? Your johnson?"

"You don't get it. Our window of opportunity is closing quickly. Within a few days, the female could start a panic among the whale pods. Once they run, the Meg will abandon the area, going God knows where. Tracking down the Megalodon in coastal waters by following the bloody carcasses of whales is one thing, but locating this monster once it heads out into open seas will be impossible. Period."

"Hold it. I thought you told everyone this female's gonna head into California waters."

144

"I said eventually. It could take weeks, maybe years. No one can predict what a predator like this will do." Jonas paused, pointing to the horizon. "Damn . . . check out those clouds, Mac. What do you think?"

Mac looked to the west, where dark storm clouds had gathered. "Well, looks like the chopper's out. No hunting tonight, I'd say."

Jonas looked at him. "Hope the Meg agrees with you."

Frank Heller stood on the pier, watching as two crewmen secured the thick white ropes, carefully lining the slack up along the deck of the *Nautilus*. Moments later, Captain Richard Danielson emerged from the forward section of the hull. He smiled at Heller, slapping the "571" painted in white along the black conning tower.

"So, Frank, what'd you think of my new command?"

Heller shook his head. "I'm just amazed this old barge still floats. Why the hell would McGovern assign a forty-year-old decommissioned sub to hunt down this shark?"

Danielson strode across the open gangway. "It was my idea, Frank. McGovern's in a tough position. The publicity's killing him. He can't very well assign a Los Angeles class sub to destroy this fish. Hell, he's already got the Cousteau Society, Greenpeace, and every animal rights activist and their mother putting pressure on the Navy. But the *Nautilus,* she's a different story. The public loves this old boat. She's like an aging war hero, going out with one last victory. McGovern loved the idea—"

"I don't. You have no concept of what you're even dealing with, Captain."

"I read the reports, Doctor. Don't forget, I tracked Russian Alphas for five years. This mission is nothing. One tube in the water and this overgrown shark is fish food."

Frank was about to respond when he saw a tall officer exit the sub, a big smile planted on his face.

"Denny?"

"Frank!" Chief Engineer Dennis Heller came bounding down the ramp and bear-hugged his older brother.

"Denny," chuckled Frank, "what in the hell are you doing aboard this rusty tin can?"

Dennis smiled at his brother, then glanced at Danielson. "You know I'm due to retire this year. Turns out I'm thirty hours shy on active duty. I figured, why not serve them aboard the *Nautilus* with my first CO. Besides, shore leave in Honolulu beats the hell out of Bayonne, New Jersey."

"Sorry to disappoint you, Chief," interrupted Danielson, "but all shore leaves are canceled until we fry this Megala . . . whatever Taylor calls it. By the way, Frank, I saw him on board your ship this afternoon. Honestly, I can't stomach the man."

"Let it go, Danielson. Turns out he was right. Why not just leave it alone—"

"So he was right. So fucking what! His actions still killed two of my crew, or did you forget? Shaffer and Prestis. Both men had families. I still write their widows twice a year. Shaffer's boy was only three years old when—"

"It's our fault too." Heller lowered his voice to his former commanding officer. "I should never have allowed you to talk me into certifying him as medically fit for that last dive."

"He was fine—"

"He was exhausted. Like him or not, Jonas Taylor was one of the best deep-sea pilots in the business. If he wasn't, the Navy would have used one of their own on the mission. Had he been allowed adequate recovery time from his first two descents, maybe he would have slowed his ascent—"

"You're out of line, Doctor." Danielson's neck was turning red.

"Hey, hey . . . Frank, Captain, what's done is done." Dennis stood between them now. "Come on, Frank, I'll take you out for a quick bite before it begins to pour out here. Captain, I'll be back at sixteen-thirty hours."

Danielson stood in silence as the two men headed into town, the first drops of rain echoing against the outer steel casing of the *Nautilus*.

NORTHSHORE

The towering, thirty-foot swells rolled into Oahu's Sunset Beach, carrying large chunks of whale blubber and debris that littered the sand. The two hundred-odd tourists didn't seem to mind. They'd been gathering all day to watch local surfers brave the most dangerous waves on earth, where wiping out could mean crashing into the sharp coral reef below.

Eighteen-year-old Zach Richards had been cutting waves on Oahu's Northshore since he was twelve. His younger brother Jim had only recently begun training on the mammoth waves that rolled in each winter from Alaska and Siberia. The afternoon swells had been rising steadily with the incoming tide. Now, as evening approached, the waves were reaching heights of twenty-five feet or more. The bloody chunks of whale carcass were more than a nuisance . . . shark fins had been spotted sporadically all day. Still, the surfers had an audience, mostly girls, and to Zach and Jim that alone was worth the risk.

Jim was still pulling on his black wet suit when Zach and two of his surfer buddies, Scott and Ryan, caught their first set of waves. Glancing back at Marie McGuire, he gave a quick wave. When the brunette waved back, he almost tripped on his board in his hurry to get in the surf and join the group.

Michael Barnes, a twenty-two-year-old with a tattoo on every muscle, had caught a twenty-footer. Spotting the paddling surfer, he cut across the wave to intercept. Jim looked up at the last moment to see Barnes's surfboard on a collision course with his head! Quickly, he rolled off his own board and braced his head between both hands, tucking his chin. The concussion of the incoming wave plowed into his stomach, driving him toward bottom, then tossing and dragging him thirty feet in to shore. Coughing up salt water, Jim rose to the surface in time to see Barnes riding the wave out, laughing as he glanced back.

"You're an asshole, Barnes!" Jim yelled, but the surfer was too far away to hear. Jim's leash had kept his board close, and he squirmed back on and paddled out to his brother. Zach was waiting just beyond the break point, straddling his own board.

"You okay, Jimmy?"

"What's that guy's problem, man?"

"Barnes was born an asshole and he'll die an asshole," said Scott.

"Yeah, well I hope it's soon."

"Try to stay out of his way," Scott warned. "He's not worth dealing with."

"C'mon Jim," said his brother. "Let's ride some waves. Remember, just go, don't hesitate. Put your head down and paddle as hard as you can. You'll feel the wave take you, just aim for the bottom, make a turn, and ride it out. When you kick out, your legs'll probably be shaking. If you go down, tuck tight, stay away from the bottom, the coral will . . ."

"Slice me up. I know, Mom."

"Hey, girls," Scott teased, "enough yapping. Let's go . . ."

Jim fell on his stomach, paddled hard, and raced toward the

break. All three surfers caught the swell, a massive twenty-eight-footer that broke to the right. Jim bounced onto his feet gracefully, but took the descent at too great an angle. Unable to hold his balance, he plunged headfirst into the water. The force of the breaking wave tossed him around and around as if he was in a giant washing machine.

"Hah, look at that faggot! My grandmother surfs better than that!" Barnes was on the beach, squeezing himself between Marie and her girlfriend, Carmen.

"Why don't you show us how it's done," said Carol-Ann, hoping Barnes would leave.

Barnes stared at the girl, then looked at Marie. "I will," he said. "But not for you, Carmen. This ride's for Marie!" Barnes grabbed his board and ran into the ocean like an excited twelve-year-old.

Moments later, all five surfers were straddling their boards, waiting. They were a good half mile out, in water over ninety feet deep.

In just seventy-two hours, the female had attacked eighteen different pods of whales, killing and feeding off fourteen of the mammals while mortally wounding three more. Haunting calls from the humpback and gray whales reverberated through miles of ocean. Almost as one, the pods began altering their migratory course, skirting west, away from the coastal waters of Hawaii. By morning of the third day, not a whale could be seen off the islands.

The Megalodon sensed the departure of its prey, but did not give chase. In the waters surrounding the island chain it detected new stimuli. Gliding effortlessly through the thermocline, the boundary between sun-warmed waters and the ocean depths, it moved its head in a continuous lateral back-and-forth motion as it swam. Beneath the thick conical snout, water passed through the creature's nostrils to the nasal capsule. The independently directional nostrils were capable of sampling water on both sides of the head, enabling the Megalodon to determine the direction of a particular scent. By late afternoon, the predator had followed the scent of man to Waialua Bay, in the northern coastal waters of Oahu.

"Where the hell are the waves?" yelled Barnes. The five surfers had been sitting on their boards for nearly fifteen minutes. The sun was going down, the air had turned chilly, and Barnes was losing his audience as the beachgoers began heading in.

"Hey, I just felt a swell pass under me," said Scott.

"Me too," said Zach.

In unison, the five surfers went prone and began paddling frantically toward shore. Maneuvering his board, Barnes grabbed Jim's leash from behind and yanked back hard, propelling himself forward and halting Jim's momentum. The four surfers caught the thirty-foot swell just as it broke, leaving Jim Richards behind.

"Goddamnit, I hate that guy!" He sat erect and sculled backward to prepare for his next approach.

Sixty yards ahead, a mountainous white dorsal fin surfaced momentarily in the fading swell, then dived beneath the wave.

"Jeez, oh shit!" Jim whispered to himself. Silently, he pulled his dangling legs back onto the surfboard and froze.

The monster's upper torso exploded straight out of the surf without warning and into the pack of surfers. Zach, Ryan, and Scott, near the bottom of the wave, remained completely unaware of what was happening behind them.

Barnes had just made his turn when a massive white wall emerged in front of him out of nowhere, leaving no time or room to maneuver around it. The nose of the surfboard, driven by the force of the wave, plowed into the Megalodon's five-foot-long gill slits as Barnes's face and chest simultaneously smashed into the towering object. The sudden impact sent Barnes flipping backward into the breaking wave, the raw power of which drove the semiconscious surfer toward the coral reef below.

Weak and disoriented, Barnes managed to get his head above water. His board was still attached to his ankle by its leash and he held on to it with both hands. His nose was broken and bleeding from both nostrils. His chest burned painfully. Barnes cursed under his breath and looked for the reckless sailboat he thought he had just hit. "I'll kill that asshole," he mumbled to himself.

He tried to hoist his bruised body onto the board, but fell back into the water in agony. At least two ribs were broken, but the worst pain came from his chest. Looking down in the fading light, he was shocked to see that most of his tan skin had been sheared off, the subcutaneous tissue clearly exposed, blood seeping from the wound.

"What the fuck," he muttered, then looked back and saw another swell approaching rapidly, rising as it blotted out the darkening red horizon. Gingerly, he inched onto the board, supporting his weight with his elbows and knees.

Seconds before the twenty-five-foot swell reached the surfer, the Megalodon's nine-foot maw rose from the dark sea beneath him, engulfing Barnes and his surfboard and lifting both twenty feet into the air. As the wave crashed into its exposed girth, the monster slammed its mouth on surfer and board like a steel bear trap, exerting more than 40,000 pounds per square inch of brute force. Blood and froth shot upward as the Meg shook its head back and forth instinctively, shredding the remains of the carcass still dangling from its jaws, sending chunks of pink flesh and fiberglass cascading outward in a thousand directions. Then it was gone.

High-pitched screams of terror filled the beach. Almost every remaining bather and observer had witnessed the attack. Dozens of people were standing at the edge of the water, trying to see into the advancing darkness. Ryan, Scott, and Zach had ended their ride and now walked through the surf toward the screaming crowd.

"What's up with them, man?" asked Scott, confused.

"They must want more," laughed Ryan.

"No, assholes. They want us to come in. Hey, where's Jim?"

Still hungry, the female circled the spreading blood from the kill, gnashing her teeth as she swam, searching the area for vibrations. Beneath her thick skin, along her lateral line, a canal extended the entire length of her body. The upper section of this canal held sensory cells called neuromasts. Mucus contained in the lower half of the canals transmitted vibrations from the seawater to the sensitive neuromasts, giving the predator spectacular "vision" of its surroundings through echolocation.

Jim Richards shivered from cold and absolute fear. He had witnessed the massacre and now could only watch as the monster circled less than thirty yards in front of him. Small bits of bloody flesh clung to his surfboard. He felt vomit rising in his throat and swallowed hard to keep it down. The break point lay a good ten yards ahead, but Jim dared not paddle for it. He knew from watching the Discovery Channel that the slightest vibrations would attract sharks. He looked around in all directions—still no rescue boats or copters in sight.

Quietly, Jim slipped the leash from his ankle. Somehow, the enormous great white seemed to detect the inaudible disturbance. The towering white dorsal fin swung around, gliding forward to investigate! Jim froze, willing his muscles and nerves to be still, but looking down, he saw his board was quivering in the water.

The Megalodon rose to the surface, its six-foot dorsal fin parting the water before it. The sheer mass of the Meg moving through the sea created an undertow, the momentum of which pulled the surfboard and its passenger back and sideways another ten feet. The crescent tail fin, rising higher in the water than Jim's head, flicked by inches from the teenager's face.

Jim felt something lifting him. His heart fluttered, anticipating the bloody mouth and rows of fangs. But the shark was still swimming away from Jim's position; the pressure had been caused by a swell. The next set was coming in. The first wave rose under Jim's board, pushing it forward six feet. The break point was still a good fifteen feet ahead, the monster thirty feet behind.

Now or never . . . Jim rolled quietly onto his stomach, pulling water slowly, tentatively. Ten feet to go, still no swell. He looked back, feeling his heart explode from his chest.

The Megalodon had turned, detecting the new vibrations. A white snout broke the surface fifteen feet behind him.

Without hesitating, Jim slammed his face against the board, simultaneously gripping the outer edges with his ankles as he plunged his arms into the water, double-stroking furiously.

Jim registered the monster's teeth on the soles of his bare feet as the wave caught the surfboard. He exploded forward, out of the Megalodon's open mouth, rising way out over the crest, plunging down in total darkness. Popping up at the last moment on his exhausted legs, feet wide, crouching low, Jim reached his right hand below the board as he plummeted blind to the bottom of the thirty-foot swell. Miraculously surviving the drop, Jim turned into the furious curl, feeling its power, a gust of salty air at his back. He hesitated, then allowed his right hand to reach back and brush against the moving wall of water, creating a backlash of froth.

The Megalodon was seconds away from taking its prey from below when it detected the new vibrations originating from the boy's hand. The stimulus convinced the predator to alter its angle of attack. Rising from beneath the wave, the creature burst through the curl just as the surfer cut back against the current.

Jim shot a quick glance over his right shoulder and saw jaws wider than a school bus snap shut, catching nothing but water. As the Meg's torso plunged headfirst and down into the wave, the surfer cut again hard to his right, accelerating in the dark, shooting past the last place he'd seen the luminescent white monster.

Jim knew he had only seconds before the creature would relocate him. As the wave sputtered out, he launched his body forward in a racing dive and swam for his life. A good hundred yards still lay between him and shallow water.

The sea floor was rising quickly, the water now only thirty feet deep, but the Megalodon ignored the danger. Homing in on her escaping target and speeding toward shore, she reached her fleeing prey in seconds flat. The predator opened her powerful jaws and closed them on her victim, crushing it like a carton of eggs in a giant trash compactor. The fiberglass board shattered into tiny fragments within her dripping maw.

Jim Richards screamed as the lifeguards grabbed him. He had spanned the final fifty yards with his head down and eyes squeezed tight. The beach was lit by tiki torches, a crowd of over a hundred having gathered on the shore. They were chanting, "Jim, Jim, Jim . . ."

Zach was hugging him now, slapping him on the back and telling him what a great job he had done. He was exhausted, shaking with fear, the burst of adrenaline nearly forcing him to puke. He caught himself as Marie appeared, a huge smile stretched across her face.

"Are you okay?" she asked. "You scared the shit out of me."

Jim cleared his throat and took a breath. "Yeah, no problem." Then, seeing his opening, he gave Marie a crooked smile and said, "So, you doing anything tonight?"

BATTLE AT SEA

Moments after Jim Richards had been pulled from the surf, the Coast Guard Air Rescue arrived, hovering two hundred feet above the breaking swells. Spotting the predator's glow, the chopper followed the female as she headed out to sea, radioing their position to the naval base at Pearl Harbor. Within minutes, both the *Nautilus* and the *Kiku* had put to sea, racing north past Mamala Bay. By the time the *Kiku* reached Kaena Point, the incoming storm had reached gale-force proportions, the raging night fully upon them.

Jonas and Terry were in the pilothouse as the door leading to the deck tore open against the howling wind. Mac slipped into the dry compartment, slamming the hatch closed behind him, his yellow slicker dripping all over the floor.

"Copter's secured. So's the net and harpoon gun. We're in for a rough one, Jonas."

"This may be our only chance. Our last report indicated most of the whale pods have left these coastal waters. If we don't at least tag the female before she heads into open waters, we may lose her for good."

The three entered the CIC, where Masao was standing over a crewman seated at the sonar console. He looked grim. "The Coast Guard broke off their pursuit because of the weather." Masao turned to the crewman. "Anything on sonar yet, Pasquale?"

Without looking up, the Italian shook his head. "Just the *Nautilus*." He hung on to his console as a twenty-foot swell lifted and tossed the research vessel from one side to the other.

Captain Barre stood at the helm, his sea legs giving naturally with the roll of his vessel. "Hope nobody had a big dinner. This storm is gonna be a bitch."

Life on board the world's first nuclear-powered submarine was relatively calm as the ship entered Waimea Bay one hundred feet below the raging storm. Originally commissioned in the summer of 1954, the sub possessed a single nuclear reactor that created the superheated steam necessary to power its twin turbines and two shafts. Although the vessel had set many records for undersea voyages, none would match her historic journey to the North Pole in 1958. Decommissioned in 1980, the sub was originally scheduled to return to Groton, Connecticut, where she was built, until Commander McGovern petitioned the Navy to bring her to Pearl Harbor as a tourist attraction.

When he learned of the Megalodon attack in the Mariana Trench, McGovern knew the crisis required naval intervention. But he also knew he could not justify the use of a Los Angeles class submarine to locate a prehistoric shark. Danielson's suggestion to use the *Nautilus* made sense, and so the submarine returned to duty after seventeen years of inactivity.

"Anything on the sonar, Ensign?"

The sonar man was listening with his headphones while watching his console screen. The screen was designed to give a visual representation of the difference between the background noise and a particular bearing. Any object within range would appear as a light line against the green background. "Lots of surface activity from this storm. Nothing else, sir."

"Very well, keep me informed. Chief of the watch, what's our weapons status?"

Chief Engineer Dennis Heller, six years younger than his brother Frank, yet still one of the oldest members of the sub's makeshift crew, looked up from his console. "Two Mark 48 AD-CAP torpedoes ready to fire on your command, sir. Torpedoes set for close range, as per your orders. A bit tight, if you don't mind my saying, sir."

"Has to be, Chief. There's nothing to lock on to here. When sonar locates this monster, we'll need to be as close as possible to ensure an accurate solution."

"Captain Danielson!" The radioman leaned back from his console. "I'm receiving a distress call from a Japanese whaler. Hard to make out, sir, but it sounded as if they're being attacked!"

"Navigator, plot an intercept course, ten degrees up on the fair-weather planes. If this is our friend, I want to kill it and be back at Pearl in time for last call at Grady's."

The Japanese whaler *Tsunami* rolled with the massive swells, rain and wind pelting her crew mercilessly. The vessel's hold was dangerously overloaded with its illegal catch: the carcasses of eight gray whales. Two more had been lashed to the port side of the ship with a cargo net.

Two lookouts held on to their precarious perch and strained their eyes in weather and darkness. The two mates had been assigned the hazardous duty of making sure the valuable blubber remained firmly secured during the storm. Unfortunately for the exhausted men, their searchlight hardly penetrated the maelstrom.

Sporadic flashes of lightning afforded the only real vision of their precious cargo.

Flash. The ocean dropped from view as the ship rolled to starboard, the cargo net groaning with its keep. The sailors hung on as the *Tsunami* rolled to port. *Flash.* The sea threatened to suck them under, the net actually disappearing momentarily beneath the waves. *Flash.* The vessel rolled back to starboard, the net reappearing. The men gasped—a massive white triangular head had risen from the sea with the cargo!

Darkness. The *Tsunami* rolled, its lookouts blind in the storm. Silent seconds passed. Then, *flash,* a fork of lightning lit the sky and the horrible head reappeared, its mouth bristling razor-sharp teeth.

The mates screamed, but the storm muted the sound. The senior mate signaled to the other that he would find the captain. *Flash.* The unimaginably large jaws were tearing at the carcass now, the head leaning sideways against the rolling vessel, gnashing at the whale blubber.

The ship rolled to starboard once more. The senior mate struggled to make it down to the wooden deck, squeezing his eyes shut against the gale and holding tight to the rope ladder. He could lower himself only a rung at a time as the ship listed to port . . . and kept rolling! He opened his eyes, felt his stomach churn. *Flash.* The sea kept coming, the triangular head gone. But something was pulling the *Tsunami* onto its side and into the water.

"Captain, the whaler is two hundred yards ahead."

"Thank you, Chief. Take us to periscope depth."

"Periscope depth, aye, sir."

The sub rose as Danielson pressed his face against the rubber housing of the periscope and stared into darkness. The night scope turned the blackness topside into shades of gray, but the storm and rolling waves severely reduced visibility. *Flash*. The raging Pacific was illuminated, and for an instant Danielson caught a silhouette of the whaler lying on its side.

He pulled back. "Contact the Coast Guard," he ordered. "Where's their nearest cutter?"

"Sir," responded the radioman, "the only surface ship within twenty miles is the *Kiku*."

"Captain, you'd better look at this, sir." The sonar man stood. His fluorescent screen showed the position of the downed whaler . . . and something else, circling the vessel.

Pasquale held the headset tightly against his ears, verifying the message once more. "Captain, we're receiving an emergency call from the *Nautilus*." All heads in the control room turned. "A Japanese whaler is down, twelve nautical miles to the east. They say there may be survivors in the water, but no other surface ships are in the area. They're requesting assistance."

Masao looked at Jonas. "The Meg?"

"If it is, we don't have much time," said Jonas. "The whales have vacated the area and she's tasted human blood now. She'll be hungry."

"Get us there quickly, Captain," ordered Masao.

The *Tsunami* lay on her port side, refusing to sink, instead rising and falling with the twenty-foot swells. Within the bowels of the vessel, eleven men strove in total darkness to escape a chamber of death in which they could not tell which way was up. The cold ocean hissed from all directions, inexorably filling the ship.

Below the waves the frenzied Megalodon pushed upward on the sinking ship, tearing at the remaining whale meat in the cargo net. It was her physical presence, in great part, that supported the vessel from below, keeping the dying ship afloat.

The senior lookout had been slammed underwater as the ship fell. But somehow he managed to maintain a grip on the rope ladder, and now he struggled against the waves, making his way toward the *Tsunami*'s vertical deck. Treading water, he located the open cabin door and clung to its frame. From within, he heard the screams of his shipmates. He shone his flashlight inside just as four crew members poured out of the wrecked cabin. Together, they wrapped ice-cold arms against the rigging of the wooden mast and held on.

"Captain, I can hear shouts," said the sonar man. "Men are in the water now."

"Damn. How far away is the *Kiku*?"

"Six minutes, tops," Chief Heller called out.

Danielson tried to think. What could he do to distract the Megalodon, keep the monster from the survivors? "Chief, start pinging, loud as you can. Sonar, watch the creature, tell me what happens."

"Continuous ping, aye, sir."

Ping . . . ping . . . ping. The metallic gongs rattled through the hull of the *Nautilus,* radiating acoustically through the seawater like sirens cutting the night air.

The first pings reached the female's lateral line in seconds. The shrill sound waves overloaded her senses, sending her into an instinctive rage. An unknown creature was challenging the female for her kill. Abandoning the last scraps of whale meat entangled within the net, the Megalodon circled below the sinking *Tsunami,* shook her throbbing head twice, then homed in on the *Nautilus.*

. . .

"Captain, I've got a bearing. Signal's registering three hertz. It's got to be that monster. You've definitely got its attention!" said the sonar man. "Two hundred yards and closing."

"Chief?"

"I've got a temporary solution, sir, but the explosion will kill the crew of that whaler."

"One hundred yards, sir!"

"Helm, change course to zero-two-five, twenty degrees down-angle on the planes, take us to twelve hundred feet, make your speed fifteen knots. Let's see if she'll chase us. I want some ocean between this fish and that whaler."

The sub accelerated in a shallow descent with the Megalodon in pursuit. The female measured less than half the *Nautilus*'s length. The submarine, at 3,000 tons, easily outweighed her. But the Meg could swim and change course faster than her adversary; moreover, no adult Megalodon would allow a challenge to its rule go unanswered. Approaching from above, the female accelerated at the sub's steel hull like a berserk sixty-foot locomotive.

"Brace for impact!" yelled the sonar man, ripping off his headset. *BOOM!!* The *Nautilus* jerked sideways, her crew hurtling from their posts. The power died, darkness enveloping the crew, as steel plates groaned all around them. Moments later, the red emergency lights flickered on. All engines had stopped, the sub now drifting, listing at a forty-five-degree angle.

The Megalodon circled, carefully measuring her challenge. The collision had caused a painful throbbing in her snout. The female shook her head, several teeth falling out. They would be replaced almost immediately by those beneath them lying in reserve.

Captain Danielson felt warmth dripping into his right eye. "All stations report!" he yelled, wiping the blood from his forehead.

Chief Heller was the first to call out. "Engine room reports flooding in three compartments, sir. Reactor is off-line."

"Radiation?"

"No leaks found."

"Batteries?"

"Batteries appear functional and are on-line, Captain, but the stern planes are not responding. We got hit just above the keel."

"Son of a bitch." Danielson was fuming—how could he have allowed a fish to cripple his boat! "Where's the Meg?"

"Circling, sir. Very close," reported sonar.

"Captain," said the Chief. "Damage control says one screw is out, the other should be on-line within ten minutes. Emergency batteries only, sir."

"Torpedoes?"

"Still ready, sir."

"Flood torpedo tubes one and two, Chief. Sonar, I want to know when we have a firing solution."

The hull plates groaned again. Seawater suddenly sprayed into the control room.

"Sonar . . ."

"Sir?" the sonar man looked pale. "I think the Megalodon's attempting to bite through our hull!"

The *Kiku* arrived at the last known coordinates of the whaler; but without the support of the Meg, pushing from below, the *Tsunami* had gone under without a fight.

Jonas and Heller, dressed in life jackets and secured to the ship by lines around their waists, stood at the bow. Heller guided the searchlight. Jonas held the rifle loaded with the tracking dart in one hand, a life ring in his other. The *Kiku* rose wildly and fell, swells crashing over her bow, threatening to send both men into the sea.

"There!" Jonas pointed to starboard. Two men clung to what was left of the whaler's mast.

Heller aimed the light, then called Barre on his walkie-talkie. The bow swung hard to the right.

Jonas handed the rifle to Heller, held on to the rail, and threw the life ring toward the men. With the sea breaking in peaks and valleys and the *Kiku* bucking Jonas like a wild bronco, he could not tell whether the men could even see the flotation device, let alone reach it.

"Forget it, Taylor!" Heller yelled. "You'll never reach them!"

Jonas continued scanning the water as the bow dropped thirty feet, another swell rising ten yards away. The bow rose again and Jonas saw the light flash on the men. One was waving.

"Get some men as my rope's anchor!" Jonas screamed.

"What!"

The bow dropped and Jonas placed one foot onto the rail. As the ship rose again, he leaped into the maelstrom with all his strength. Propelled by the rising deck, Jonas flew into the sea, over and beyond the incoming swell. The icy water shocked his body, driving the breath from his chest, sapping his strength. He rose with the next wave, unable to see anything, and swam as hard as he could in the direction he prayed was correct.

Without warning, Jonas found himself plunging again in mid-air, then dropping into the sea. Swimming was not an option: he was being hurled up and down mountains of water. And then his head smashed into a hard object, blacking his vision.

The Meg couldn't tell if the creature was alive. The piercing sound impulses had ceased. The strange fish seemed too large to grip in her mouth; her senses told her it was inedible. She circled again, occasionally trying to wrap her hyperextended jaws around

164

the object, but the creature was simply too large. And then the Meg detected familiar vibrations along the surface.

"It's moving off, Captain!" The radar man pointed to his screen.

"Affirmative, sir," confirmed sonar. "She's headed back to the surface."

"Engines back on-line, Captain," reported Chief Heller. As if in response, the *Nautilus* leveled.

"That's my girl. Helm, bring us around, make your course zero-five-zero, up ten degrees on the planes, take us to one thousand feet. Chief, I want a firing solution on that monster. On my command, you start pinging again. When she descends to attack, I want to hit her with both torpedoes!"

Heller looked worried. "Sir, engineering says the ship cannot withstand another collision. I strongly suggest we return to Pearl—"

"Negative, Mr. Heller. We end this *now*."

A hand grabbed Jonas by his collar and hung on. The senior lookout sputtered something in Japanese, obviously grateful. Jonas tried to look around. The second sailor was gone. He felt a strong tug on his waist. Heller and his men were pulling him back.

"Hold on!" Taylor grabbed the sailor from behind, and the two were dragged backward toward the *Kiku*.

The Meg locked in on the vibrations, rising fast at its prey. One hundred feet from its next meal, she heard the pinging again. The female could smell the warm blood, but the aggressive challenge of the vibrations overwhelmed her hunger. She wheeled around in a fluid motion, a white blur on course with its challenger.

165

"Six thousand yards and closing quickly, Captain," screamed sonar.

"Chief Heller, do we have a firing solution?"

"Yes, sir!"

"On my command . . ."

"Two thousand feet . . ."

"Steady, gentlemen."

"One thousand feet, sir!"

"Let her come in . . ."

"Sir, she's changed course!" Dennis Heller looked up frantically. "I lost her!"

Danielson ran to the console, sweat and thickening blood dripping down his face. "What happened?"

Sonar was bent over, cupping his ears, trying to hear. "Sir, she went deep. I can barely hear her. . . . Wait, four thousand feet . . . Oh shit, she's below us!"

"Full speed ahead!" ordered Danielson.

The crippled forty-year-old submarine lurched forward, struggling to reach a speed over ten knots. The Megalodon rose from below, homing again on what it perceived to be the creature's tail. Her snout impacted the steel plates at over thirty-five knots, puncturing the already stressed hull. This time, the casing gave, opening a ten-foot gap between the steel plates. The entire engine room was immediately vented to the sea.

The collision also ruptured the submarine's aft ballast tanks. As the keel of the *Nautilus* filled with seawater, the crew's environment shifted to a forty-five-degree tilt. The engine room was hardest hit. Assistant Engineer David Freyman tumbled backward in the dark. His head slammed hard against a control panel, knocking him unconscious. Lieutenant Artie Krawitz found himself pinned under a collapsed bulkhead, his left ankle shattered. As the engine room filled with water, he managed to free himself and crawl upward into the next compartment, sealing the watertight door seconds before the sea could rush in.

"Damage report!" commanded Danielson.

"Engine room flooded," said Chief Engineer Heller. "I can't—"

A loud wail and flashing red sirens cut Heller off.

"Core breach!" he yelled. "Someone's got to shut it down."

"Helm, high-pressure air into the ballast tanks, put us on the ceiling. Heller, get down to the reactor room—"

"On my way!"

The *Nautilus* rose, still listing to starboard as she climbed at a forty-five-degree angle. Heller ran through a maze of absolute chaos. In every compartment, crew members attended to the wounded while attempting to staunch the flow of seawater spraying from a thousand leaks. At least half of the electrical consoles looked down.

Lieutenant Krawitz was frantically throwing switches, shutting down the nuclear reactor, when Heller entered the compartment. The chief finished the last three, then shut off the alarm.

"Report, Lieutenant."

"Four dead in here, a whole section of pipe collapsed on impact. Everyone and everything aft of the engine room is underwater."

"Radiation?"

The officer looked at his chief engineer. "Denny, this ship's over forty years old. We've lost the integrity of the hull, the steel plates are falling off like shingles. We'll drown before any radiation kills us."

Jonas was hauled on deck and carried into the pilothouse. A moment later, Frank Heller and his men dragged in the Japanese seaman.

"Taylor, are you insane?" screamed Heller.

"Frank, quiet," said DeMarco. "We're receiving a distress call from the *Nautilus*."

Heller strode into the command center. "Well?"

Bob Pasquale cupped his ears, trying to hear. "They're surfacing. No power. They need our assistance immediately!"

Captain Barre barked his orders to change course. The *Kiku* turned, fighting against the relentless twenty-foot swells.

David Freyman had regained consciousness, his face pressed hard against the watertight door where a small pocket of air remained. The chamber was bathed in a red light. Blood gushed from his forehead.

As the *Nautilus* rose, debris began seeping out of the gap in the hull and into the Pacific. The Megalodon rose with the sub, snapping its jaws at anything that moved. The predator smelled the blood.

Driving her enormous head into the opening, the Meg began separating the already loose steel plates, enlarging the gap in the hull significantly. Her white glow suddenly illuminated the flooded compartment from below. The engineer put his face underwater, looked down . . . and screamed! The monster's nine-foot-wide jaws filled the entire compartment, the upper jaw pushed forward away from the head like something out of a 3-D horror film. The hideous triangular teeth were less than five feet away. Freyman felt his body being sucked into the vortex. He tore at the door, his screams muffled by the sea. Unable to stop his descent, he ducked his head down, inhaling the salt water deep into his lungs, struggling to kill himself before the nine-inch daggers reached him.

The female sucked his body into her mouth, crushing and swallowing it in one gulp. The warm blood sent her into a renewed frenzy. She shook her head, freeing herself from the opening, then circled again as the *Nautilus* burst through the surface waters.

"Abandon ship! All hands, abandon ship!" Captain Danielson barked his orders as the *Nautilus* tossed hard to starboard against the incoming swells.

Three hatches exploded open, water pouring into the hull, pink phosphorescent flares piercing the blackness. Three yellow rafts, eight feet in diameter, sprang to life. Minutes later, the survivors were aboard, struggling to maintain their balance against the raging sea. The *Kiku* was close, her spotlight now guiding the rafts.

Danielson was in the last raft. Bolts of lightning lit the seascape as he looked back at the *Nautilus*. Within seconds, the submarine was overcome by the sea. Her once-mighty bow rose out of the ocean, then another swell drove the ship toward her final resting place below the Pacific.

Flash. The first raft reached the *Kiku*, fifteen men scrambling up a cargo net along her starboard side. A swell slammed against the ship, lifting it high, then dropping it thirty feet. *Flash.* The force of the wave had pulled some of Danielson's crew back into the sea.

Jonas aimed the spotlight into the swell, locating a seaman. It was Dennis Heller. Frank saw his younger brother struggling to stay afloat less than fifteen feet from the *Kiku* and tossed the ring buoy as the second raft closed from behind.

Dennis grabbed at the life preserver and held on as his brother pulled him toward the *Kiku*. The crew from the second raft had climbed aboard, the last group now within ten feet of the ship. Dennis reached the net and began climbing. He was halfway up when his shipmates from the last raft joined him.

The *Kiku* rose straight up, the climbers holding on tightly as a mammoth wave lifted them with the ship. Frank Heller lay prone on deck beneath the rail, one hand holding the metal pipe, the other extending toward his brother, now only three feet away.

"Denny, give me your hand!" They touched momentarily.

Flash. The white tower rose straight out of the swell, grasping Dennis Heller in its jaws. Frank froze in place, unable to react as the tip of the snout passed less than a foot from his face. The Meg seemed to hang in midair, suspended in time. And then the monster slid back into the sea, dragging Dennis Heller backward with her.

"No, no, nooooo!" Frank screamed, helpless. He stared at the sea, waiting for the Meg to return with his brother.

Danielson and the others had witnessed the scene. Petrified, they scrambled up the cargo net like insects, climbing for their lives with reckless abandon.

The Meg rose again, the bloody remains of Dennis Heller still shredded within its fangs. Danielson turned and screamed, flattening himself against the cargo net.

Jonas grabbed the searchlight, spinning it toward the Meg with his left hand as he raised the rifle with his right. He was close, a mere thirty feet. Without aiming, he pulled the trigger. The dart exploded out of the barrel, burying itself within the thick white hide as the device attached itself firmly behind the female's right pectoral fin.

The searchlight's powerful beam blazed into the right eye of the nocturnal predator, burning the sensitive tissue like a laser. The excruciating pain sent the monster reeling backward into the sea, repelling her attack only feet from Danielson's back. The Meg slammed its wounded eye into the swell below, then disappeared.

Danielson and his men collapsed onto the deck and were pulled, one by one, inside the shelter of the pilothouse. Jonas grabbed Frank, tugging him backward, but he refused to let go of the rail.

"You're dead, bitch, you hear me?!" Heller screamed into the night, his words deadened by the wind. "This isn't over. You're fucking dead!"

OPENING DAY

At precisely noon, in front of a crowd of nearly six hundred on-lookers, including the governor of California, several members of the 49ers football team, a high school marching band, and four television networks, the giant sliding doors of the D. J. Tanaka Memorial Lagoon opened to the sea. Millions of gallons of ocean water rushed into the valley to fill the world's largest swimming pool.

Jonas stood next to Terry Tanaka on the lower observation deck, admiring yet another extraordinary example of human inge-nuity. Using designs and technology developed during the build-ing of the great dams, the Tanaka team had constructed an artifi-cial lake connected to the Pacific Ocean by an access canal large enough to allow a pod of whales to enter and exit uninhibited. Once inside, the mammals could be observed through twenty-two-foot-high acrylic windows that lined the lagoon and from smaller observation posts constructed beneath the floor of the fa-cility.

Nearly two weeks had passed since the disaster at sea. Twenty-nine members of the *Nautilus*'s crew had perished, as had fourteen from the *Tsunami*. A ceremony honoring the dead had taken place at Pearl Harbor. Two days later, Captain Richard Danielson retired from the Navy.

Commander Bryce McGovern was on the hot seat. Who had authorized the United States Navy to hunt the Megalodon? Why had McGovern selected the *Nautilus* to complete the mission, knowing the forty-year-old submarine was far from battle-worthy? The families of the deceased were outraged, and an internal investigation was ordered by the Pentagon. Many believed Commander McGovern would be the next naval officer to retire.

Frank Heller, on the other hand, was a raging bull. His brother Dennis had been his only family, following the death of their mother three years earlier. Now Heller's hatred for the Megalodon threatened to become all-consuming and burn out of control. He informed Masao that he flatly refused to be a part of any more insane attempts to capture the monster, stating that he had his own plans for the white devil. After the ceremony in Oahu, he flew home to California.

Thanks to David Adashek, the Tanaka Institute's plans to capture the Megalodon appeared on the front page of *The New York Times* and *The Washington Post* within twenty-four hours of the *Nautilus* disaster. From that moment on, the hunt for the Megalodon turned into a media circus. JAMSTEC was secretly delighted at the publicity, as it stood to share in the proceeds from the captive Megalodon display. Construction crews had worked around the clock to complete the lagoon. Now everyone wanted to know one thing: when would the guest of honor be appearing?

Twelve days, Jonas thought, and not a sign of the female. For six consecutive nights following the attack on the *Nautilus,* he and Mac had flown over Hawaii's coastal waters in search of the Megalodon. The homing device had worked, allowing the copter to track the predator as it headed east, the *Kiku* always trailing close behind. But the female, perhaps still in pain, refused to surface, remaining deep. And then, on the seventh day, the signal had simply disappeared.

For two days, the *Kiku* and its helicopter crew circled the area without relocating the signal. Frustrated, Jonas finally recommended to Masao that the *Kiku* should return to Monterey, guessing the Meg would head for the California coast and the migrating whale pods. Now, one week later, there was still no sign of the female. The question was: where had she gone?

THE CANYON

Situated less than two hundred yards offshore from the Tanaka Lagoon's western wall lies the deep waters of Monterey Bay Canyon. Created by the subduction of the North American plate over millions of years, the massive underwater gorge traverses over sixty miles of sea floor, plunging more than a mile below the ocean's surface. There, the canyon meets the ocean bottom, eventually dropping another 12,000 feet in depth.

The Monterey Bay Canyon is the heart of the Monterey Bay National Marine Sanctuary, the nation's largest marine wildlife preserve. Similar to a national park, the sanctuary consists of federally protected waters, encompassing an area roughly the size of Connecticut. The marine park extends from the Farallon Islands just west of San Francisco, south for more than three hundred miles, to just off Cambria, California. Home to 27 species of marine mammals, 345 different types of fish, 450 kinds of algae, and 22 endangered species, the sanctuary also serves as the winter breeding ground for 20,000 whales.

· · ·

Moving north along the sheer canyon wall at a speed just under five knots was the largest creature ever to inhabit the planet. Ninety-six feet long, weighing almost one hundred tons, the female adult blue whale glided in six hundred feet of water, catching tiny particles of plankton in her baleen grooves as she swam. Directly above the gentle giant, rising to the surface for air, was her six-month-old calf. The adult mammal required only three to five breaths per hour, but her calf had to return to the surface once every four to five minutes. This meant mother and calf had to separate from each other every few minutes as they fed.

Five miles to the south, traveling in total darkness, a fluorescent white glow slowly cruised above the canyon's rocky seafloor. Having deserted the coastal waters of the Hawaiian Islands in search of whales, the Megalodon had come across a warm undercurrent flowing along the equator to the southeast. Riding the huge river of water just as a Boeing 747 rides an airstream, the female had traveled across the Pacific Ocean, arriving in the tropical waters off the Galápagos Islands. From there, she had migrated north along the coast of Central America, hunting gray whales and their newborn calves.

And then, as she approached the waters off Baja, her senses had become overwhelmed by the pounding of tens of thousands of beating hearts and moving muscles. The female went into a frenzy, her predatory instincts driving her to the north, into the Monterey Canyon.

The hydrothermal vents along the floor of the canyon seemed familiar. The turbidity currents and temperatures of the gorge approximated those of the Mariana Trench. Territorial by nature, the sixty-foot female claimed the area as her new home, an expanse of ocean awarded by her mere presence as supreme hunter. Her senses indicated that no other adult Megalodons were in the area to challenge her rule. The territory therefore became hers to defend.

For three hours, the predator had been stalking the blue whale and its calf. Vibrations detected by the Megalodon's lateral line indicated that the smaller creature would be vulnerable to an attack. Still, the female waited, preferring to keep her distance. Now totally blind in her right eye, she would not risk surfacing while any traces of daylight remained.

And so she trailed her prey, waiting impatiently for nightfall in order to surface, and feed again.

RED TRIANGLE

Anchored in six hundred feet of water, the *Magnate* bobbed gently as the last golden flecks of sunlight reflected from the sea. On the main deck of the yacht, her weary crew watched as thousands of California seals and sea lions stretched out upon the rocky, uninhabited landmass of the Farallons.

When Maggie learned that Jonas had predicted the Megalodon would eventually end up in California waters, she wasted no time in organizing her expedition to the Farallon Islands. The Farallons were the center point of an expanse of ocean known as the Red Triangle. Of all the documented attacks by great whites worldwide, over half occurred here. If Jonas's prediction proved accurate, Maggie figured that the Megalodon would waste little time in coming to the center of the Red Triangle to hunt sea lions, the preferred prey of the great white shark.

For five straight days, the film crew had waited impatiently for the Megalodon to show itself. Underwater video cameras, audio equipment, and special underwater lights littered the ship's deck, along with cigarette butts and candy wrappers. A community laundry line had been hung along the upper deck, dangling swimsuits, underwear, and shorts.

Now the long hours of boredom, the constant sun, and the occasional nausea associated with seasickness had finally gotten to the crew. Miles of chum had been ladled into the sea, attracting the several smaller sharks, preventing the *Magnate*'s passengers from even cooling off with a quick dip. And yet, even these conditions would have been tolerable had it not been for the overwhelming stench that hung thick in the November air.

Trailing the yacht on a thirty-foot steel cable floated the rotting carcass of a male humpback whale. The pungent smell seemed to hover over the *Magnate* as if to mark the crime, for killing a whale in the Monterey Bay Sanctuary was indeed a criminal act. No matter: with his financial influence, Bud had made a deal with two local fisherman to locate and deliver a whale carcass to their location, no questions asked. But now, after nearly thirty-eight hours of the wicked stench, the *Magnate*'s crew were ready to mutiny.

"Maggie, Maggie, listen to me," begged her director, Rodney Miller. "You've gotta give us a break here. Twenty-four hours of shore leave, that's all I'm requesting. It could be weeks, months before this Megalodon even ventures into these waters. All of us need a break, even a fresh shower would be heaven. Just get us off this smelly barge."

"Rod, listen to me. This is the story of the decade, and I'm not about to blow it because you and your cronies feel the need to get drunk in some sleazy hotel bar."

"Come on, Maggie—"

"No, Rod. Have you any idea how difficult it was to organize all of this? The cameras? The shark tube? Not to mention that hunk of whale blubber floating behind us?"

"Yeah, don't mention it," he said sarcastically. "What ever happened to your campaign for protecting the whales? Gee, I would have sworn that was you I saw onstage accepting a Golden Eagle on behalf of the Save the Whales Foundation."

"Christ, Rod, grow up, will you? I didn't kill the fucking whale. I'm just using its carcass as bait. Look around you: there are thousands of the goddamn things migrating into the sanctuary, as if you hadn't noticed. Get real. Can't you see that this may be the biggest story of the decade?" She shook her head, her blond hair sticking to her bare shoulders.

"Maggs." Rod lowered his voice. "You're grasping at straws. Honestly, what're the chances of the Megalodon actually showing up in the Red Triangle? No one's even reported seeing the thing in the last two weeks."

"Listen, Rod, if there's one subject my good-for-nothing husband knows about, it's these Megalodons. The Meg will show, believe me, and we'll be the ones to get the exclusive pictures."

"In what, that piece of plastic. Christ, Maggie, you'd have to be suicidal—"

"That plastic is three-inch-thick Plexiglas. Its diameter is too wide for even the Meg to get its mouth on." Maggie laughed. "I'll probably be safer in there than you guys will be on the *Magnate*."

"There's a comforting thought."

Maggie ran her fingers across her director's sweaty chest. She knew Bud was still in bed, sleeping off another hangover.

"Rod, you and I have worked very hard together on these projects. Hell, look how much good our whale documentary did for those beasts."

Rod smirked. "Tell that one to your dead humpback."

"Forget that already, damnit." She grabbed his oily shoulders in her hands. "Rod, don't you get it? This is the one! This is the story that puts both of us on top. Both of us. How does executive producer sound to you?"

Miller thought for a moment, then smiled. "Sounds good."

"It's yours. Now, can we forget about the dead whale for a moment?"

"I guess so. But listen, as your executive producer I highly recommend we do something to create a little diversion, because your film crew's losing patience."

"I agree, and I've got an idea. I've been wanting to do a test run on the shark tube. What do you say we get it into the water and I'll shoot some footage this evening."

"Hmmm, now that's not a bad idea. That'll give me a chance to position the underwater lights." He smiled. "Maybe you'll be able to get some nice footage of a great white. That alone could be worth the trip."

Maggie shook her head. "See, that's your problem, Rodney my love. It's why you'd better stick with me if you ever want to get anywhere in this business." She gave him a motherly pat on the cheek. "You think way too small."

Bending over to pick up her wet suit, she rewarded Miller with a glimpse of her tanned, thonged behind. "One other thing, Rod. Do me a favor and don't mention anything to Bud about being my executive producer." She smiled sweetly. "He gets jealous."

LIFE AND DEATH

As the thousands of beating hearts and pulsing fins continued to overload the Megalodon's sensory array, the albino creature gently ascended to the surface. Darkness had finally fallen.

The hunter quickly closed the distance to the calf. The mother blue stopped feeding, detecting the danger approaching rapidly from behind. She rose to the surface and forcefully nudged her young to remain in tight formation. Mother and offspring propelled their bodies faster, less than a mile separating them from the jaws of their pursuer.

Minutes later, the female had closed to within striking distance. Jaws agape, the Meg aimed for the smaller fluke, careful not to venture too close to the larger mammal's tail. And then, just as she was about to strike, something happened.

The Megalodon shook wildly, her back arching in an uncontrollable spasm. She abandoned her prey, descending rapidly to the canyon floor. Her muscular body quivered and she began swimming in tight circles, her internal organs twitching out of control.

And then, with a mighty shudder that shook her entire frame, a fully developed Megalodon pup emerged from its mother's left oviduct.

It was a male, pure white and eight feet long, already weighing fifteen hundred pounds. The teeth were smaller but sharper than its mother's. With its senses fully developed, the newborn was fully capable of hunting and surviving on its own. It hovered momentarily, icy-blue eyes focused on the adult, instinct warning the pup of imminent danger. With a burst of speed, it glided south along the canyon floor.

Still circling in convulsions, the female shuddered again, expelling a second pup, tail-first, out of its womb. This time a female, larger than its sibling by three feet. The pup shot past its mother, barely avoiding a mortal, reflexive bite from the jaws of its uncaring parent.

With one last convulsion, the Meg birthed her final pup in a cloud of blood and embryonic fluid. The runt of the litter, the seven-and-a-half-foot male twisted toward the bottom, righted itself, then shook its head to clear its vision.

With a flick of her caudal fin, the Meg pounced upon her newborn from behind, severing its entire caudal fin and genitals as she snapped her jaws shut. Convulsing wildly and trailing a stream of blood, the dying pup writhed to the bottom, out of control. Giving immediate chase, the female finished her offspring in one last bite.

The Megalodon hovered near the bottom, exhausted from the efforts of labor. Opening her mouth, she permitted the canyon's current to circulate through her mouth and over her body, allowing her gills to breathe. Slowly, the head rotated from side to side, nostrils flaring, channeling water. Now the predator could "see" the sanctuary through her olfactory senses.

Once again, the female detected the maddening vibrations of

the migrating whales, and something else—blood! The Megalodon swung her caudal fin back and forth, regaining her momentum and rising. She resumed her northerly movement, passing within thirty feet of the concrete canal entrance that connected the Tanaka Lagoon with the Pacific Ocean.

VISITORS

They came without warning, catching the disgruntled crew of the *Magnate* completely by surprise. Captain Talbott spotted the lead-gray dorsal fin first, slicing through the dark waters of the Pacific twenty feet off the starboard side of the yacht. Within several minutes, two more fins appeared, cutting back and forth through the slick of bloody chum.

Rod Miller found Maggie already pulling on her luminescent white wet suit for the night dive.

"Okay, Maggie, you wanted some action. How about a test dive with three great whites?"

"Relax, Rodney." Maggie was smiling. "Is everyone ready?"

"Both remotes are in the water, underwater lights are on, and the plastic tube is all set for you. Oh yeah, Bud's still asleep."

"Sounds good. Now remember, I want it to look like I'm all alone in the water with the sharks. How much cable is attached to my tube?"

Rod thought. "I'm guessing you've got about sixty or seventy feet of line, but we'll keep you in around forty feet or you'll lose the light."

"Okay, I'm ready," she announced. "Grab my camera, Rod, I want to be in the water before Bud wakes up."

Maggie and Rod hurried to the starboard side where the plastic shark cylinder awaited. Ten feet long, twelve feet in diameter, the container had been custom-made for Maggie from a design originally developed in Australia. Unlike a steel-mesh shark cage, the shark tube could not be bitten or bent. It would maintain positive buoyancy at forty feet, and it afforded the photographer an unobstructed view. The cylinder was attached by steel cable to a winch on board the *Magnate*.

Secured to the *Magnate*'s hull were two remote-controlled underwater cameras that would be operated on deck. While Maggie was filming the Megalodon, the crew would be filming Maggie. If the lighting worked properly, the shark tube would remain invisible in the water, giving the terrifying appearance of Maggie exposed and alone in the water with the sharks.

Maggie positioned her face mask, checking to make sure she was receiving an adequate supply of oxygen. She had been diving for ten years now, though rarely at night. The practice would do her good.

The tube was already overboard, its vent holes allowing water to fill and sink the container. Stepping on top of the tube with her right flipper, holding the steel cable with her right hand for support, she took a quick glance around to confirm the location of her subjects. Satisfied she was not about to be attacked, Maggie pulled her other leg over the guardrail. Squatting on the edge of the tube, she reached back to receive the forty-pound camera from Rod. Allowing the bulky casing to drop through the opening first, Maggie slipped into the water, pulled the hatch closed above her, and sank into the center of the plastic tube.

The current was moving away from the yacht. Miller and another crewman let out the steel cable slowly, watching as the tube slipped underwater and drifted out to sea.

"Stop it at forty feet, Joseph," instructed Miller. "Peter, how're your remotes functioning?"

Peter Arnold looked up from his dual monitors. "Remote A is a little sluggish, but we'll get by. Remote B is perfect. I can zoom right up on her—too bad she didn't wear her thong."

Maggie shivered from the potent combination of adrenaline and fifty-eight-degree water. Her world was now shades of grays and blacks, visibility poor. She glanced behind, locating the two remotes and their set of lights, and as she did, they activated, lighting her plastic refuge and the surrounding waters for fifteen to twenty feet in every direction. Moments later, the first predator entered her arena.

It was a male, seventeen feet from snout to tail, going a full ton. It circled the plastic tube warily, and Maggie rotated to compensate. Her eyes detected movement from below as a fifteen-foot female rose out of the shadows, catching Maggie totally off-guard. Forgetting she was in a protective tube, she panicked, frantically kicking her fins in an effort to get away. The shark's snout banged into the bottom of the tube just as Maggie's head collided with the closed hatch above. She smiled in relief and embarrassment at her own stupidity.

Peter Arnold was also smiling. The footage was incredible, and scary as hell. Maggie appeared totally alone in the water with the three killers, and the artificial lighting combined with the white dive suit worked perfectly. The viewer would not be able to detect the protective tube.

"Rod, this is great stuff," he announced. "Our audience'll be squirming in their seats. I gotta admit it, Maggie really has a knack for the work."

Rod watched as the great whites began tearing at the humpback carcass. "Film everything, Pete. Maybe we'll be able to convince her to quit before this Megalodon actually shows up."

But Miller had a hard time believing that himself.

Jonas held the night binoculars with two hands, steadying them against the herky-jerky motion of the helicopter. They were following the coast southward, at an altitude of one thousand feet.

"Mac, I can't recall ever seeing so many whales in one place," yelled Jonas.

"Who cares, Doc." Mac stared at Jonas with a burnt-out look. "We're wasting our time, and you know it. The batteries in that homing transmitter ran out days ago. The Meg could be a million miles from here."

Jonas turned back to face the ocean. He knew Mac was thinking about calling it quits, and would have days ago if it hadn't been for their friendship. He couldn't blame him. If the female were feeding in these waters, there would be traces of whale carcasses to be found. But they had come across nothing, and now Jonas was beginning to doubt himself. Without the homing signal, they were searching for a needle in a haystack.

Mac's right, Jonas thought to himself, and for the first time in years, he felt truly alone. How many years of my life have I wasted chasing this monster? What do I have to show for it? A marriage that fell apart years ago, a struggle to make ends meet . . .

"Hey!" He hadn't been paying attention, though he'd been looking right at it.

"Doc, what is it? The Meg?"

"No . . . maybe. Look below. The pods, Mac—notice anything different?"

Mac looked down. "They look just like they did five minutes ago. . . . No, wait a second! They're changing course."

Jonas smiled. "They were all heading due south, but see, the pods below are veering sharply to the west."

"You think they're changing course to avoid something." Mac shook his head. "You're grasping at straws again, Doc."

"You're probably right. But just humor me one last time."

Mac looked down on the whales again from the thermal imager. If the Meg was heading north along the coast, it would be logical for the pods to avoid her.

"Okay, Doc, one last time." The helicopter spun around, changing course.

Maggie checked her camera, noting that she had plenty of film left and another twenty minutes of air. The shark tube was suspended just below the humpback carcass, allowing for a spectacular view. But Maggie knew footage of great whites feeding had become commonplace. She was after much more.

I'm wasting film, she thought. She turned to signal the *Magnate* to pull her in, then noticed something very troublesome.

The three great whites had all vanished.

Bud Harris kicked the silk sheets off his naked body and reached for the bottle of Jack Daniel's. Empty.

"Damnit!" He sat up, his head pounding. It had been two days and still he couldn't get rid of the nagging headache. "It's that damn whale," he said out loud. "The smell's killing me."

Bud staggered to the bathroom, picked up the bottle of aspirin, and struggled to get the childproof cap lined up correctly. "Fuck this," he yelled, and threw the bottle into the empty toilet. He looked at himself in the mirror. "You're miserable, Bud Harris," he said to his reflection. "Millionaires aren't supposed to be miserable. Talk to me, pal. Tell me why you feel this way."

His head ached even worse and he felt nauseated. "Why do I let her talk me into these things? Enough's enough!" He grabbed a pair of swim trunks and his bathrobe and headed up on deck.

"Where's Maggie?" he demanded.

Abby Schwartz sat on deck, monitoring the audio track. "She's in the tube, Bud. Hey, we're getting some great—"

"We're leaving. Rodney!"

Rod Miller looked up. "Really? That's the best news I've heard all week. When?"

"Now. Pull Maggie in and cut that damn whale loose before the Coast Guard arrests us."

"Wait!" Peter Arnold held up his hand. "Something's happening out there. Look at my monitor. It's getting brighter."

Maggie saw the glow first, illuminating what remained of the humpback carcass. Then the head appeared, as big as her mother's mobile home and totally white. She felt her heart pounding in her ears, unable to comprehend the size of the creature that was casually approaching the bait. The snout rubbed against the offering first, testing it. Then the jaws opened. The first bite separated a six-foot chunk of blubber from the carcass; the second swallowed it whole, the movement of the powerful jaws sending quivers across the gill slits, vibrating the flesh along its stomach.

Maggie felt herself drifting to the bottom of the shark tube. She couldn't move. She was in total awe of the Megalodon, its power, its nobility and grace. She raised her camera slowly, afraid she might alert the creature. It continued feeding.

"Christ, pull her back in!" Bud ordered.

"Bud, this is what we came here for." Rodney was excited. "What a monster! Goddamn, this is amazing footage!"

"Pull her back in now, Miller." Bud sounded irritated, and more. He had seen the size of the Meg on the monitor. Maggie was in danger.

"She's gonna be mighty pissed off," said Peter Arnold.

"Listen to me, both of you," demanded Bud. "This is my yacht. I'm paying for everything. Get her in, now!"

Rod started the winch, the steel cable snapping to attention as it began dragging the shark cylinder through the water.

The Meg stopped feeding, her senses alerted to the sudden movement. Being plastic, the shark tube had not given off any electronic vibrations, and so the predator had ignored it. Now the Meg abandoned the carcass, sculling forward to examine the new stimulus.

Maggie watched the Megalodon approach. It rubbed its snout along the curvature of the shark tube, confused. Now it turned, focusing with its left eye.

It sees me, she realized.

The tube continued moving toward the *Magnate.*

These idiots are going to get me killed, Maggie thought, bracing her legs against the inside of the tube for support.

The Meg kept moving its mouth, almost as if it was speaking to her. Then it opened its jaws wider, attempting to wrap its mouth around the tube. Without any leverage to gain a hold, the Meg kept losing the plastic cylinder as it slid off her teeth.

Maggie smiled. "Too big for ya, huh." Regaining her nerve, she repositioned the camera, filming the cavernous mouth only a few feet away. This is my Academy Award, she thought.

The tube was only twenty feet from the *Magnate* when the Meg turned. Maggie caught a flicker of its caudal fin before it disappeared into the gray mist. She took a breath, all smiles.

"It moved off," said Peter Arnold.

"Thank God," said Bud. "Get her out of there before it comes back."

"Ohhhh shit!" yelled Arnold. He scurried backward on all fours away from the edge of the rail.

The Meg had circled, accelerating at the tube. Maggie screamed, biting into her regulator as the 42,000-pound monster slammed its hyperextended jaws onto the cylinder. Maggie's body smashed into the interior wall of the tube, her head spinning from a concussion wave that would have shattered her skull had she not been underwater. The cylinder impacted the *Magnate,* propelled from behind by the Megalodon. Even hyperextended, the creature's jaws still could not wrap around its prey. But the tips of a few of the Megalodon's teeth managed to catch on to the cylinder's drainage holes. The Meg had established a grip, although, try as it might, the creature could not generate enough leverage with its jaws to crush the tube.

Frustrated, the beast rose to the surface in a mad frenzy, the plastic cylinder still locked in its bite. The Meg turned away from the *Magnate,* plowing the tube ahead of its open mouth, creating a ten-foot wake along the surface. At the end of its length, the steel cable snapped. The Megalodon rose vertically out of the sea, and in an unfathomable display of brute strength, lifted the shark tube above the waves and, as if in slow motion, shook it back and forth, water streaming out of the tube's vent holes.

Maggie squeezed her eyes shut as she slid downward, her oxygen tanks colliding with the base of the tube. A moment later she tumbled backward in the opposite direction, each collision bringing her closer to unconsciousness.

The effort of supporting the shark tube and its passenger quickly wore down the Megalodon. The female released her death grip on the cylinder, circling it as it sank swiftly beneath the waves.

CAT AND MOUSE

"Mac, I can see a chum slick," yelled Jonas. Through his night glasses he saw a grayish haze appear over the darker Pacific.

Mac glanced at the thermal imaging monitor. "I can see it too."

"Mac, where are we?"

"Twenty-six miles due west of San Francisco. You should be able to see the Farallon Islands." Mac noticed a new hot spot on the monitor, the heat of twin engines showing clearly. "Hey, what's that yacht doing out here?"

"Can you take us down?"

The copter dropped to five hundred feet.

Jonas looked through the night binoculars, zooming up onto the deck of the ship. "Wait a minute . . . I know that yacht. The *Magnate*! It's Bud Harris's ship."

"The guy you told me is bangin your wife?" Mac circled the yacht. "How 'bout I see if I can hit his deck with my tool chest from this height. So what's Mr. Moneybags doin' out here, chumming blood off of his twenty-million-dollar yacht?"

Jonas pulled the glasses away from his face. "Maggie."

Chaos reigned on board the *Magnate*. Captain Talbott had started the engines, then shut them down, afraid the noise would attract the Meg. Rod was excited, yelling to everyone that they needed to continue filming, but Bud was in a state of shock, kneeling on deck, head in hands. When the helicopter appeared, he had panicked, thinking it was the Coast Guard, afraid the authorities had come to arrest him because of the humpback carcass.

"Bud," yelled Abby, "some guy in that helicopter wants to speak with you. Says his name is Jonas."

"Did you say Jonas?" Bud jumped to his feet and ran into the control room.

"Jonas, it's not my fault. You know Maggie, she does whatever she wants!"

"Bud, calm down," commanded Jonas. "What're you talking about?"

"The Meg. It took her. She's trapped in that damn shark tube. It wasn't my fault!"

Mac spotted the Megalodon, pointing to the slowly circling hot spot on the monitor. She was circling in fifty feet of water, three hundred yards off the *Magnate*'s bow. "I'm not getting a thermal reading on Maggie. She must be wearing a wet suit."

Jonas focused with the night glasses. "I think I see her," he said, barely able to distinguish the outline of her fluorescent white wet suit. He picked up the radio's mike. "Bud, how much oxygen does she have left?"

Rod Miller grabbed the radio. "Jonas, this is Rodney. I'm guessing no more than five minutes. If we can distract the Meg, we could get her out of there."

Jonas tried to think. What would draw the monster's attention away from Maggie? The copter? Then Jonas noticed the Zodiac.

"Bud, the Zodiac, is it working?"

"The Zodiac? Yeah, it works fine."

"Get it ready to launch," ordered Jonas. "I'm coming aboard."

Maggie fought to stay awake. Everything hurt, but the pain was good, it kept her conscious. Her face mask had a hairline crack leaking water into her eyes. Her ears were ringing, and it hurt to breathe. The Megalodon continued circling counterclockwise, watching her with its functional left eye. The glow from its hide cast an eerie light, illuminating Maggie's wet suit. She checked her oxygen supply: three minutes of air left.

I've gotta make a break for it, she told herself. She grabbed the video cam tightly to her chest, refusing to leave it behind.

Jonas hung on a cable from the chopper's winch, the dart gun strapped across his back, earphones around his neck. "Remember, Mac," he yelled, "wait until I say before you hit her with the beam."

Mac looked at the spotlight to his left. "Don't worry about me, Doc. Just don't get eaten."

Jonas gave the thumbs-up, and Mac lowered him to the deck of the *Magnate.*

Bud and Rodney grabbed him by the waist. He slipped out of the harness. "Ready?"

Bud pointed to the starboard rail. "Zodiac's in the water. What do you want us to do?"

"I'm going to distract the Meg. Once she follows me, get your yacht over to Maggie's location and get her the hell out of there, fast."

Bud helped Jonas over the rail. He stepped into the center of the yellow rubber raft. The Johnson motor read "65 horsepower." He started the engine, looking up at Bud.

"Wait for Mac to signal you that the Meg has moved off. Then get Maggie, okay?"

Bud nodded in agreement, watching the Zodiac take off.

The rubber raft skimmed across the surface, its engine a high-pitched whine. "Mac, can you hear me?"

The helicopter was hovering two hundred feet above the Zodiac. "Barely, pal. Fifty yards, not too close . . . Jonas, you're getting too close, she's coming up!"

Jonas veered hard to his right as the dorsal fin broke the surface fifteen feet in front of him. He raced into open waters. "How am I doing?"

"Hard left," screamed Mac. The Zodiac turned, just as the Meg's jaws snapped shut in midair.

"Doc, quit yapping and keep zigzagging, and don't stop! Can't you go faster? She's right under you!"

Jonas sat low in the raft, gunning the engine, cutting hard against the wake. He couldn't see the Megalodon, but knew it was close. "Mac, tell Bud to get moving!"

The *Magnate* sprang to life, her twin engines spewing out blue smoke as the yacht moved ahead. Maggie was already out of the cylinder, her gear left behind. She struggled to the surface with the underwater camera, kicking hard with her flippers.

"Jonas," yelled Mac, "she's gone."

"Huh? Say again?"

Mac focused below. The Megalodon had given up the chase.

. . .

196

Maggie struggled in the darkness, heart pounding in her ears. And then her head broke the surface ten feet from the *Magnate*. She took a deep breath, hearing the cheers from her production crew.

"Way to go, champ," yelled Peter.

"Maggie, get in the fucking boat!" screamed Bud.

Exhausted, she released the heavy oxygen tanks and kicked, moving herself next to the yacht. "Bud, grab the camera." She struggled to lift it, but the forty-pound device was too heavy to lift from the water.

Bud was hanging over the side, reaching down. There was no ladder close. "Damnit, Maggie, I can't reach it."

Maggie felt a wave of dizziness. "Take the fucking camera, Bud!" she screamed with her last bit of energy.

He had no choice. Bud swung over the rail, holding tight with his left hand, reaching down with the right. He grabbed the camera, hefting it and swinging it back to Rodney, who took it—and screamed!

Maggie was rising out of the sea, levitated from below by the monster's open maw. The Megalodon's head continued rising, elevating Maggie, who had fallen into a dream state, imagining she was looking down on the upper deck of the yacht.

Abby was standing by the rail, on the upper deck, clutching her mouth, an expression of horror on her face. I'm warm, Maggie thought, registering the slightly higher temperature of the creature's mouth, still unable to grasp where she was or what was happening.

The white mammoth fell back into the water, jaws closing slowly, squeezing the breath from Maggie's lungs. As the triangular daggers punctured her rib cage, the pain jolted her to attention. She screamed a high-pitched wail, which ended as her head passed underwater.

Bud was hyperventilating, his limbs no longer his to control. The underwater hull lights were on, illuminating the monster's head. Bud couldn't move, staring at the face of the devil that looked back at him, hovering ten feet underwater. The creature appeared to be smiling, while Maggie, thrashing about, attempted to scream as she drowned in its grasp. The Megalodon seemed to be toying with her, Maggie's upper torso dangling from its jaws. Bud saw blood pour from his lover's open mouth as she struggled one last time in agony.

The predator turned its gaze upon Bud. And then the hideous mouth opened, creating a vacuum that sucked Maggie into its black vortex and out of sight. Bud screamed. A bloody bubble rose, breaking the surface.

Bud was in shock, unable to move. He closed his eyes and waited to die. As if beckoned, the monster rose again from the sea for its next meal, its jaws open.

The bolt of light from above smashed through the darkness as if guided by the hand of God. It burned into the functional left eye of the Megalodon, permanently blinding the creature, sending a white-hot wave of stabbing pain into the optic lobe. The monster twisted sideways in convulsions as Jonas Taylor stood in the Zodiac, firing the dart at point-blank range into the creature's exposed abdomen.

The Megalodon spun backward into the sea, the wake flipping Jonas out of the raft. He surfaced, climbing quickly up and over the rail of the yacht.

His insides were quivering. The world was spinning out of control. He collapsed to the deck on all fours and vomited.

MORNING, MOURNING

There was no moon, no stars. Not a wave stirred. Bud stood at the rail and waited, the underwater lights of the *Magnate* illuminating the hull and surrounding sea. And then the whispers came, tickling his ear.

"Bud . . . baby, where are you?"

"Maggie? Maggie, is that you?" Bud leaned over the rail, searching the black sea. I'm losing it, he thought.

"Bud, my love, please help me." The whispers cooed into his ear.

"Oh God, Maggie, where are you?" Hot tears rolled down his cheeks. He watched a droplet fall into the ocean.

Bud waited. He felt its aura rising. Then the glow, followed by the snout, still hovering below the surface. The jaws opened, revealing blackness. The words came again, tearing at Bud's heart . . . *"Bud, please, I don't want to die."*

"MAGGIE!"

The nurse ran in, grabbed his arm.

"Maggie! Maggie, no . . ." The monster slowly turned, disappearing into blackness. Bud screamed a bloodcurdling howl.

The orderly held him down, the hypodermic releasing its serum. "It's okay, Mr. Harris," the nurse soothed. "It's okay." The orderly strapped him down, bound his wrists and ankles.

Bud fell backward in slow motion onto the *Magnate*'s deck and watched the sky, helpless, as the gray haze of dawn approached.

Jonas passed out as the sun rose, the birds chirping permission to sleep. The sea was gray, the swells bobbing the AG I up and down along the surf. He saw the swimmer, black hair, almond eyes. It was D.J.

The sub was inverted, no power. Jonas hung suspended upside down, waiting for D.J. to pull him out. He looked down into the mist.

The surreal glow appeared, then the immense mouth, the serrated teeth. She rose slowly. Jonas couldn't move, paralyzed with fear. He glanced at . . . Terry! Not D.J. D.J. was dead.

"Terry, get away!" he screamed. She smiled, waving at Jonas. The monster opened its mouth.

"Terry, nooooo!"

The knock bolted him upright. "Terry?"

Three more knocks.

Jonas rolled off the sofa, spilling the shot of Jack Daniel's onto the carpet. Staggering, he opened the door.

"Masao." The bright daylight burned into Jonas's eyes.

"Jonas, you look like hell. Let me in."

200

Jonas stood aside.

"You have coffee?" Masao went into the kitchen.

"Ah, yeah, Mas, um, one of the upper shelves, I think."

Masao made coffee, handed it to Jonas. "Here, drink this, my friend. It's three o'clock. Morning is over."

Jonas shook his head, taking a seat at the kitchen table. "I can't. I'm sorry, Masao, I can't anymore."

"Can't?" Masao Tanaka stood over his friend, eyeball to eyeball. "What can't you do?"

Jonas looked down. "There's been too much death. I can't do this anymore."

Masao sat down. "Jonas, we have a responsibility. I feel it. I know you do as well."

"I've lost my desire to keep chasing this monster." Jonas looked into Tanaka's eyes.

"Hmm." Masao was quiet. "Jonas?"

"Yes, Mas."

"You are familiar with Sun Tzu?"

"No."

"Sun Tzu wrote *The Art of War* over twenty-five hundred years ago. He said, if you know neither the enemy nor yourself, you will succumb in every battle. If you know yourself but not the enemy, for every victory gained you will also suffer a defeat. But if you know the enemy and know yourself, you need not fear the result of a hundred battles. Do you understand?"

"I don't know, Masao. I can't think right now."

Masao placed his hand on Jonas's shoulder. "Jonas, who knows this creature better than you?"

"Masao, this is different."

Masao shook his head. "The enemy is the enemy." He stood. "But if you will not face our foe, then my daughter will."

Jonas jumped up. "No, Masao. Not Terry!"

"Terry can pilot the AG I. My daughter knows her responsibility. She is not afraid."

"Forget it, I'm going!"

"No, my friend. As you say, this is different. D.J.'s death must not be a meaningless one. The Tanaka clan will finish this business ourselves."

"Give me five minutes to get dressed." Jonas ran into the bedroom. The television was still on, channel 9 Action News. They were showing the underwater footage, Maggie's footage, taken from the cylinder.

"*. . . amazing footage taken just before she died in the creature's jaws. Maggie Taylor gave her life to her profession, leaving these incredible scenes as her lasting legacy. A public service was held yesterday, and Channel 9 will be presenting a two-hour special tonight at eight honoring Ms. Taylor.*

"*In a related story, a federal judge ruled today that the Megalodon has been officially listed as a protected species of the Monterey Bay Sanctuary. We bring you live to the steps of the Federal Court Building.*"

Jonas sat on the edge of the bed and turned up the volume.

"*. . . hope to speak with him. Here he comes. . . . Mr. Dupont, Mr. Dupont, were you surprised today how quickly the judge ruled in favor of protecting the Megalodon, especially in light of the recent attacks?*"

André Dupont of the Cousteau Society stood next to his attorney, several microphones pressed to his face.

"No, we weren't surprised. The Monterey Sanctuary is a federally protected marine park designed to protect all species, from the smallest otter to the largest whale. There are other marine predators in the park, orcas, great whites. Each year, we see isolated attacks by great white sharks on divers or surfers, but these are isolated attacks only. Studies have shown that the great white sometimes mistakes a surfer for a seal. Humans are not the staple of the great white's diet, and we certainly are not the preferred food source of the sixty-foot Megalodon. Of greater importance will be our effort to immediately place Carcharodon megalodon on the Endangered Species list, so it is protected in international waters as well."

"Mr. Dupont, what is the Cousteau Society's opinion of the Tanaka Institute's plan to capture the Megalodon?"

"The Cousteau Society believes that all creatures have a right to survive and thrive in their natural habitat. However, we are dealing with a species that was never intended to interact with man. The Tanaka Lagoon is certainly large enough to accommodate a creature of this size, so we agree that it would be in the best interest of all parties to have the Megalodon captured."

The Channel 9 anchor reappeared.

"We had our field reporter, David Adashek, conduct an unofficial street poll to see what the public's opinion is. David?"

"Field reporter?" Jonas stood up, feeling the blood drain from his face. "This guy works for Maggie's network? Jesus, Maggie . . ."

". . . opinions seem to favor capturing the monster that destroyed the lives of so many gallant people, including my close friend Maggie

Taylor. Personally, I feel the creature is a menace, and I've spoken to several biologists who believe that the monster has acquired a taste for humans. This means that we can expect more gruesome deaths, especially in light of today's federal court ruling. This is David Adashek reporting, Channel 9 News."

Jonas hit the power button on the remote, turning off the set. He sat motionless on the edge of the bed, trying to piece together everything he had just learned.

God, Maggie, he thought, what did I do to ever make you so bitter, so unhappy. But Jonas knew in his heart: the long hours, the traveling, the long nights alone in his study, writing his books. Tears rolled down his cheeks. "I really am sorry, Maggie, so sorry." At that moment, Jonas felt more love for his wife than he had over the last two years.

The noise of the car horn forced him to move. He washed the tears from his face, then grabbed his duffel bag and shoved a few days' worth of clothing inside. He pulled out his workout bag, already loaded with his wet suit. Jonas looked inside, verifying that his good-luck charm was packed. He took a moment to examine the blackened seven-inch fossil, as wide and as large as the palm of his hand. He felt its sharp serrated edges as he ran the tooth across his fingers.

"Fifteen million years old, and still sharp as any knife." He replaced the tooth in its leather pouch, dropped it in the gym bag, and slung the two carry-ons over his shoulder.

He looked in the mirror. "Okay, Dr. Taylor. Mourning's over. Time to get on with your life."

When he walked out the front door, Masao Tanaka was waiting.

WHALE WATCHERS

For two long days and nights, the *Kiku,* her helicopter, and three Coast Guard cutters cruised the Monterey Bay Sanctuary, attempting to locate the homing signal of the transmitter. The device implanted in the hide of the Megalodon possessed a range of up to three miles, gaining strength as the receiver got close. But after combing four hundred miles of coastal ocean, no signal could be detected.

Hundreds of whales continued migrating south through the sanctuary without any noticeable changes of direction among the pods. On the third day, the Coast Guard gave up the search, theorizing that either the Megalodon had left the California coast or the transmitter had malfunctioned.

Two more days passed, and even the crew of the *Kiku* began to lose hope.

Rick and Naomi Morton were celebrating their tenth anniversary in San Francisco, glad to momentarily escape the cold weather of

Pittsburgh and their three children. They had never actually seen a real whale, so the idea of spending the day whale watching seemed exciting. Dressed in a yellow slicker, loaded with camcorder, binoculars, and his trusty 35 mm, Rick followed his wife on board *Captain Jack's Whale Watcher,* a forty-two-foot sightseeing boat docked at the Monterey Bay wharf. The couple found an empty spot along the stern, then waited impatiently for the twenty-seven other passengers to take their seats among the wooden benches.

The presence of the Megalodon had initially hurt business among Monterey's whale-watching tours. But the tourists gradually began returning, mostly because the predator had not been seen in almost a week, and surfaced only at night. For their part, tour-boat owners unanimously chose to cancel all sunset excursions rather than risk a confrontation with the Meg.

"Ladies and gentlemen," announced a beautiful redhead decked out in a white sailor outfit, "Welcome on board *Captain Jack's Whale Watcher.* You folks are in for a real treat today. The humpbacks have been putting on a great show all morning for us, so get your camcorders ready!"

The boat chugged ahead, a film of blue exhaust choking those passengers seated in the stern.

A male voice boomed over the PA system. "Folks, this is really exciting! On our left is an unusually large pod of orcas." Everyone shifted toward the port side of the boat, cameras poised. "The orcas, also known as killer whales, are extremely intelligent hunters, able to kill whales many times larger than themselves. It looks like we're catching these orcas in the middle of a hunt."

Rick focused his binoculars on the pack of towering black dorsal fins moving parallel with the boat, now less than two hundred yards away. There were at least thirty orcas, ten of which were converging on a smaller object, the rest racing along the perimeter for their turn at the prey. Rick watched, fascinated by the battle tactics. And then he saw the shark, totally white, its three-foot dorsal fin half bitten off as the wolf pack tore at its hide.

The male Megalodon pup raced along the surface, prevented from submerging by the attackers below. A pod of six orcas had initially tracked the male as it hunted along the Farallon Islands. Since then, the six had been joined by two larger groups. The mammals' motivation was simple: the Megalodon pup could not be permitted to live.

With frightening speed and power, the orca males launched themselves upon the pup, the sharp teeth of the attackers tearing mouthfuls of flesh out of the smaller Meg. The pup retaliated with its own bite, catching one orca along its pectoral fin, tearing the fin in half. And then the battle ended as twelve orca males, each well over twenty-five feet, converged as one upon the pup, ripping apart its carcass, prematurely ending the reign of the future king of the sea.

Bud Harris gathered his belongings and stuffed them into a brown paper bag provided by the orderly. Unshaven, badly in need of a shower, the once-proud entrepreneur had been reduced to a feeble shell of his former self. Deeply depressed after having witnessed his lover's death, Bud was also suffering from exhaustion brought on by a lack of REM sleep. Memories of his awful experience were now manifesting themselves in his subconscious mind in the form of night terrors. More frightening than the worst nightmare, the night terrors were violent surreal dreams of death. For the last five nights, Bud had let out bloodcurdling cries that rocked the west wing of the hospital's fourth floor. Even after the frantic nurses had managed to wake him, he would still be screaming, blindly flinging his fists into the air. After the second episode, the orderlies had to strap his wrists and ankles to the bed while he slept.

Bud Harris no longer cared whether he lived or died. He felt alone and in pain, uninterested in eating and afraid to sleep. Extremely worried, his doctors brought in a psychiatrist, who decided that a change in environment might do the patient some good. And so it was decided that Bud would be discharged.

The nurse arrived to escort her patient out of the hospital with the traditional wheelchair ride. "Mr. Harris, is anyone meeting you downstairs?" she asked.

"No."

"Well, sir, I'm really not supposed to discharge you unless someone is here to meet you."

"We're here to meet Mr. Harris." The elderly man strode into the room, followed by his younger counterpart. "Mr. Harris, it's a privilege to meet you, sir. My name is Dr. Frank Heller, and this is my associate, retired naval captain Richard Danielson." Heller held out his hand.

Bud ignored it. He looked up at the nurse. "I don't know who these guys are, and to tell you the truth, I don't give a rat's ass. Get me the hell outta here." The nurse began wheeling Bud out, with Danielson and Heller in pursuit.

"Wait, Mr. Harris, we're here to discuss some important business." Heller walked ahead of the wheelchair, stopping it head-on. "Hold on a second, Mr. Harris. I understand that your friend Maggie Taylor was killed by the Megalodon. My brother Dennis was butchered by the same monster."

Bud looked up. "I'm sorry for your loss, but right now, I'm kind of fucked up myself, so if you'll excuse me . . ."

"Hey," said Danielson, "this *thing* has killed a lot of people, and we need your help to kill it. Now, it was our feeling that maybe you'd want to be involved in a little payback." Danielson looked at Heller. "Maybe we were wrong."

The thought of killing the Megalodon seemed to set off a spark in Bud. He focused his eyes on Danielson for the first time. "Listen, pal, that monster ruined my life. It took the only person I ever cared for, tortured her right in front of my eyes. If you're serious about killing this thing, then I'm in."

"Good," said Heller. "Listen, we're going to need your boat."

Bud shook his head. "That's how I got into this fucking mess in the first place."

The male humpback leapt out of the water, twisting its 82,000-pound torso in midair, then slammed its back upon the surface of the blue Pacific with a thundering splash. Two hundred yards away, the whale watchers clapped with enthusiastic approval.

"Wow! Rick, did you get that one on tape?" asked Naomi.

"Got it."

"Get some more still shots, okay?"

"Naomi, I've got two full rolls already. Give me a break."

For several minutes, no other whales appeared. And then the sea began swirling, the swells lifting the boat, slapping it up and down.

"Something's coming up," announced the tour guide. "Get your cameras ready!" Twenty camcorders rose in unison.

The mammal surfaced, flopped onto its stomach, and lay motionless in the water. Silence. Nothing moved, the whale still floating. And then the torso rolled, revealing a twelve-foot bloody gash along its stomach.

The whale watchers gasped as one.

"Is it dead?"

"What killed it?"

"Is that a bite mark?"

Something was rising from beneath the humpback. The carcass lifted several feet and then the entire forty-one-ton mammal disappeared, dragged underwater.

Screams rose from the whale watchers.

The carcass resurfaced. Blood gushed from another crater-sized wound along the dorsal side of the dead humpback. The sea turned crimson red.

The captain of the whale-watching boat panicked. As he revved his engines and swung around hard, the momentum knocked half of his passengers out of their seats. The tourists screamed, unsure of what was happening.

Fifty feet below, the predator felt the sudden vibrations.

The *Kiku* was anchored eight miles due west of the Tanaka Institute. Most of her crew were still asleep from the previous night's patrol. Terry Tanaka, clad only in a white string bikini, lay on a lounge chair on the upper deck facing the sun. The suntan oil glistened off her dark skin. Jonas sat in the shade, attempting to read his newspaper, his eyes constantly returning to the woman.

"Aren't you cold, Terry?"

She smiled. "It's warm in the sun. You should try it. You'd look good with a tan."

"When this is all over, I'll take a vacation, get away somewhere. Maybe a tropical island." Jonas smiled at the thought. "Want to come?"

Terry sat up. "Yeah, okay."

Jonas could see the girl was serious. His tone changed. "You'd want to come?"

Terry sat up. Pulling off her sunglasses, she looked Jonas square in the eyes. "Try me, Jonas. You won't be disappointed."

"Jonas Taylor, report to the CIC immediately." The metallic announcement boomed over the ship.

210

Jonas stood up, unsure of what to say to Terry.

"Hey, wait for me," she said, pulling on a sweat suit over the bikini. They headed down the stairwell. "So, where are we going to stay in Hawaii," Jonas heard Terry call out over her shoulder.

DeMarco was waiting for him in the pilothouse. "Jonas," he said, "we just picked up a distress call from a whale-watching boat not far from here. Looks like the Meg's back!"

"In broad daylight? How?" The answer popped into the paleontologist's head almost as quickly as he asked the question. "Wait a minute . . . she's blind! It doesn't matter anymore. Damn, how could I have been so stupid."

"The monster's blind?" asked Terry.

"Yes and no, Terry. Her eyesight may be—"

"Jonas, Masao needs you right away in the CIC," commanded DeMarco.

Jonas and Terry followed the engineer into the dark information center as the *Kiku* weighed anchor, her twin screws churning water.

Masao was standing over his sonar man, watching the fluorescent green screen intently. "Where is she?" Masao asked Pasquale for the fourth time in the last fifteen minutes.

"Sir, I'm sorry, we're still not within range of the transmitter."

"How much farther?"

The sonar man pinched the bridge of his nose, calming himself. "We're still approximately twelve miles southeast of the distress call. Like I said earlier, sir, the signal only has a three-mile range. But I've increased our tow array to five thousand feet."

"Jonas!" Masao's exhaustion over the last few weeks was showing. "Jonas, what's happening here? You said this monster only surfaces at night."

"Masao, it's my fault. I didn't take into account that the Megalodon may have been totally blinded. I knew Mac's spotlight had damaged one eye. I didn't realize that I may have blinded her in her other eye during the night of the storm."

"So the monster's blind. That's good," said Masao, smiling. "Isn't it?"

"Not really," said Jonas. "If the Meg really has surfaced, it means she's not only blind but has overcome her fear of ultraviolet light. But a Megalodon losing its sight is a lot different than you or me going blind. You have to realize this creature possesses seven other sensory organs that are extraordinarily efficient. She can hear low frequencies, especially splashing noises, at a distance of at least several miles. She can smell one drop of blood, sweat, or urine in a hundred million parts of water fifty miles away from the source. Her nostrils are directional, meaning the Meg will head in the direction of the nostril receiving the strongest olfactory impulse. Her lateral line and ampullae of Lorenzini can detect electronic impulses and vibrations. She can home in on a signal better than our most advanced torpedo. And she has acute senses of touch and taste as well. Considering the fact that this female spent most of her life in complete darkness, losing her eyesight is probably a minor inconvenience at best.

"In other words," said Jonas, "we're still dealing with the most formidable predator ever designed by nature, and she's no longer limited to surfacing at night.

"I'd say things just got worse."

FIGHT OR FLIGHT

"Sir, I've got a visual on sonar," announced Pasquale excitedly. Jonas, DeMarco, and Masao converged on the sonar man. "She's this line right here, very faint. Wait, I can hear her now." He cupped the earpiece with his hand. "Yes, louder now . . . there it is, on my other console." He pointed to another computer screen. The red blip appeared as the fluorescent green wave band circled counterclockwise across the monitor.

"Where's she headed, Pasquale?" Captain Barre stood over the screen, watching.

"Looks like she's moving away from us, about two miles due east," responded the sonar man.

"Good job, stay on her." Barre slapped the man on his back. "Helm, change course five degrees to starboard, slow to ten knots. Where's your flyboy, Dr. Taylor?"

"I'm here." Mac came stumbling in, still half asleep.

"Mac, we've located the Megalodon. Are you ready to go?" asked Jonas.

Mac rubbed his eyes. "Sure, Doc, just give me thirty seconds to pour some coffee into my eyes."

"Jonas, Alphonse, get to your stations," ordered Masao. "Mac—"

"I'm leaving." Mac headed out through the pilothouse. Moments later, the helicopter lifted off the deck of the *Kiku*.

The whale watchers could now see land clearly, still a good two miles away. The tour guide sat dejectedly in her chair, her red hair soaked with salt water from the captain's steering.

"Miss, why are we going in?" asked Naomi. "Will we get a refund?"

"Ma'am, I'm not sure what's . . ."

WHUMPPP. The collision knocked the redhead off her stool and hard on the deck. Passengers screamed. Naomi grabbed Rick's arm and held on with both hands, her nails digging into his flesh.

The female had tasted her prey, pushing her snout hard against the hull of the moving boat. Her senses told her that this was not food. The Meg cut toward open water, circling back to the remains of her kill. The large creature was no threat.

The captain knew his boat was under attack. He grabbed the wheel and began zigzagging violently. The boat's bow slammed back and forth against the sea's three-foot swells.

The Megalodon slowed. These new vibrations were different. The creature was wounded. Instinct took over, and the female banked sharply, rising to the surface as she homed in on her prey once more.

"Jonas, you read me?"

"Go ahead, Mac," yelled Jonas into the walkie-talkie. He and

DeMarco were positioned at the stern, ready at the deck-mounted harpoon gun.

"I'm about two hundred feet above the boat. It's difficult to see because of the reflection along the surface. Stand by, I'm changing my angle." Mac turned the airship south, hovering to the right of the boat, the thermal imager rendered useless during the day. "Oh shit, there she is!"

"Where, Mac?"

"Right behind the whale watcher's keel. Christ, she's gotta be twice the size of that boat!"

The *Kiku* was now following the tourist boat's wake, bearing down on the smaller vessel.

"DeMarco," Jonas yelled into the wind, "have Barre take us alongside. I can't risk firing at this angle. I might miss and take out a passenger."

DeMarco yelled into the internal phone that connected directly with the pilothouse. The *Kiku* swung hard to starboard, then began overtaking the smaller boat.

Jonas spun the harpoon gun counterclockwise on its base and focused through its sight. The *Kiku*'s draft was a good twenty-five feet higher than that of the smaller boat. He released the safety just as the whale watcher began zigzagging.

"Mac, where is she?" he yelled into the headset.

"She's coming up fast. Stay ready." The *Kiku* raced alongside the sightseeing boat, twenty feet away.

Rick Morton watched the former Navy frigate approach the tourist boat from his seat at the rear of the ship. The *Kiku*'s white bow dwarfed the smaller boat, rising high out of the sea, plowing a four-foot wake against the *Captain Jack*.

"Naomi, let go of my arm, I want to get a shot of this ship."

Naomi released his arm and grabbed her husband's waist as the boat zigzagged again.

As he lifted the camcorder, a different object appeared in his eyepiece. At first glance, Rick thought he must have focused on the frigate's towering bow, white and triangular. Then his autofocus adjusted and he dropped the camera.

Naomi screamed. Others turned and joined her cry. Rising fifteen feet above the *Captain Jack,* the Megalodon's head and lower jaw crashed down upon the stern. The twin propeller shafts snapped like twigs, the transom shattering into a thousand splinters of fiberglass.

Rick and his wife were tossed sideways into the Pacific, thrown in the opposite direction from the *Kiku*. The cold waters took their breath away and bit painfully into their flesh as the *Kiku*'s wake roared over their submerged heads.

Rick dragged his wife upward, their heads breaking the surface. Lacking propulsion, the tourist boat had slowed to nearly a standstill. The couple watched in horror as the monster rolled off the vessel, turning its snout toward them!

Naomi screamed. Rick hugged her tight, closing his eyes.

Jonas fired. The harpoon exploded out of the cannon, trailing smoke and steel cable. The projectile struck home, burying itself four feet deep into the Megalodon's thick hide, inches from the dorsal fin. The monster spasmed, arching its back and whipping its head sideways into the moving *Kiku*. The ship lurched to starboard. DeMarco, caught off-balance, felt himself flying in midair, his torso lifted out and over the rail. Jonas lunged after him, catching his right ankle with both hands just before it disappeared over the rail. He held on, feeling his own feet slide beneath him along the deck.

The rail broke Jonas's slide abruptly. He pulled DeMarco upward, twisting the man around so the back of his knees could lock on to the rail. One of DeMarco's hands appeared, gripping the rail, pulling upward.

His face was flushed purple, his eyes bugged out. "God-damn." He coughed. "Good catch."

WHAMMM. The Meg rammed its head into the *Kiku*'s port-side hull, bending steel plates. Jonas and DeMarco fell to the deck.

"Hard to starboard," growled Captain Barre, picking himself up off the control-room floor. "Masao, when the hell is this shark gonna fall asleep?"

"I don't know, Leon. Just get us away from that tourist boat."

"You heard the man," yelled Barre. "Take us out to sea!"

Rick scissor-kicked hard, dragging his wife toward the crippled tourist boat. A passenger grabbed his wrist, and Naomi and he were hauled on board. Blankets were thrown over the shivering couple as they held on to each other close.

Three hundred feet above the Pacific, Mac watched as the *Kiku* raced to open waters. The Meg followed, submerging, the slack of the steel cable still floating momentarily along the surface before being dragged below. The triangular head rose once more, slam-ming against the frigate's bow.

"Jonas, you guys okay?"

"Yeah, Mac, but we're taking a beating."

"I radioed the Coast Guard to pick up those tourists. I suggest you continue leading the Meg out to sea."

"Okay. Can you still see her?" Jonas asked.

Silence.

"Mac, you still there?"

"Jonas, she disappeared."

Jonas ran to the control room, DeMarco staying with the winch. "Pasquale, where is she?" yelled Jonas.

The sonar man listened intently to the signal coming from his headphones. "I think she went deep."

Jonas checked the cardiac monitor that was receiving data directly from the transmitter, still implanted in the Meg's belly. "Damn, two hundred and twelve beats per minute. I think she's having a bad reaction to the drugs." He picked up the internal phone.

"DeMarco, how much cable has she taken?"

"About two thousand feet. Should I start the—"

"She's coming up!" cried the sonar man. "Hold on!"

Seconds passed in silence.

BOOM!! The *Kiku* was blasted from below, rising and then dropping in a sickening lurch.

"I think she's a bit pissed off," whispered Jonas.

"She's gonna tear my ship apart!" yelled Barre, picking up his phone. "Engine room—"

"Captain, we've got problems," reported his engineer. "Can you come below?"

"On my way." Barre signaled to one of his crew to take the helm, then paused to give Jonas a nasty look before disappearing down the stairwell.

"Jonas." Terry emerged from below, squeezing past the captain. "Are those drugs ever going to take effect?"

Jonas was watching the monitor. "I think they just did."

The Megalodon's brain was on fire, her blood boiling, her heart racing out of control. The predator's sensory system was overloaded by the madness brought on by the large dosage of pentobarbital. The female could only follow her last instinct: attack her enemy.

Plunging to a depth of fifteen hundred feet, the Meg spun and raced back toward the surface. The crescent tail whipped back and forth, the monster a white blur streaking upward. Feeling the vibrations of the *Kiku*'s bow cutting the surface, the Megalodon adjusted her line of attack and rammed into her enemy, smashing the forward compartment of the ship's hull.

Had the Megalodon connected with the *Kiku*'s flat keel, the ship would surely have sunk within minutes. But the attack occurred near the bow and the force of the impact dispersed outward. The force of the blow knocked the giant predator senseless, slowing her pulse enough for the pentobarbital and ketamine to take effect, shutting down the creature's central nervous system.

"Heart rate just plummeted to eighty-three beats per minute," reported Jonas. "I can't say for certain whether that's normal, but the drugs have definitely taken effect." He stood up. "We don't have much time." He picked up the receiver of the internal phone.

"What needs to be done, Jonas?" asked DeMarco.

"Take up the slack right away. The Meg is losing consciousness. The *Kiku* has to tow her before she sinks and drowns. Terry, release the net along the stern. I'll take the AG I and secure it beneath the Meg."

Terry looked worried. "Jonas, how can you be sure—?"

"Terry, we don't have much time." He held her shoulders and looked her squarely in the eye. "I'll be fine. Come on."

Terry followed him onto the deck.

. . .

The female was losing feeling in her tail. She slowed, barely moving, hovering almost twelve hundred feet below the *Kiku*.

DeMarco and his assistant, Steve Tabor, stood at the stern, watching closely as the *Kiku*'s winch gathered in the steel cable.

"Slow her down at one thousand feet, Tabor," instructed DeMarco. "Once we get some resistance, secure the line and we'll tow this bitch in." DeMarco looked to his right. The AG I was secured in its saddle. Jonas, in his wet suit, stood ready to climb inside.

"Jonas." Terry moved close, pulling him toward her, whispering in his ear. "Don't forget about our vacation, okay?"

Jonas smiled at her, then crawled into the submersible, lying prone in its one-man chamber. He moved forward, his head appearing within the clear Lexan nose cone. He slipped into the pilot's harness, feeling the sub lift off the deck, swing over the side, then drop into the Pacific. Jonas strapped himself in, absentmindedly thinking of Terry in her bikini.

"Snap out of it, asshole," he growled to himself.

As the AG I slipped from its saddle, Jonas pushed the joystick forward and down. The sub responded, accelerating into the vast blue world.

"Jonas, can you hear me?" Masao's voice broke into his thoughts.

"Yes, Masao, loud and clear. I'm at five hundred feet. Visibility's poor."

"Can you see the Meg?"

Jonas focused hard. Something was below. He could see a slight glow, but not as big as expected. "Nothing yet. Stand by." Jonas accelerated the submersible, descending at a forty-five-degree angle. He felt the interior temperature drop. He checked the depth gauge again. Eight hundred sixty feet. Then he saw the Meg.

She was suspended face-up, tail dropping out of sight at a sharp angle, unmoving.

"Masao, the Meg's out cold. She's gonna drown if we don't get water circulating through her mouth. You've got to tow her immediately. Do you copy?"

"Yes, Jonas. Stand by." The *Kiku*'s engines restarted and a metallic, grinding sound reverberated all around Jonas. The line grew taut, and the Megalodon jerked upward at the sub.

Jonas momentarily panicked, having foolishly positioned the AG above the unconscious creature. He circled her quickly, watching as she leveled off. Jonas drew his submersible parallel with the Megalodon's gills and focused his attention upon the five vertical slits. They were closed, not moving. And then, as she moved forward, they gradually began to flutter, flapping gently. The Meg was breathing again, water passing through her mouth and out through the gills.

"Good job, Masao, she's breathing. I'm going to secure the harness, but the Meg's too deep to secure within the net. Have DeMarco take in another five hundred feet of line, very slowly. Let's be careful not to pull the harpoon free."

"Stand by, Jonas."

Moments passed and the Meg began rising slowly, pulled from above by the winch. Jonas followed her up, marveling at the size of the creature, her beauty, her savage grace. The paleontologist found himself appreciating the Megalodon for what she was, a product of evolution, perfected by nature over seventy million years. It was the true master of the oceans, and Jonas felt glad they were saving rather than destroying her.

The Meg stopped rising at two hundred and thirty feet. Jonas continued to the surface, locating the net that would serve as the Meg's harness floating adjacent to the *Kiku*'s keel. He extended the retractable arm of the sub, catching the edge of the net with the claw. Slowly, so as not to tangle the line, he submerged, trailing the harness beneath his sub, spreading out from behind.

The harness was simply a weighted cargo net, designed to sink uniformly in order to haul in tuna. Jonas had ordered flotation buoys attached along its perimeter. The devices were designed so they could be inflated or deflated from aboard the *Kiku*. In this way, the Megalodon could be released safely once secured inside the lagoon, with the net simply dropping away as the devices were deflated.

Jonas brought the AG I to eight hundred feet, moving well below the dormant monster. Satisfied, he accelerated forward, moving beyond the creature's caudal fin. "Masao, I'm in position. Inflate the harness."

"Here we go, Jonas." The net sprang to life, rising upward, conforming to the contours of the Megalodon. The 42,000-pound monster rose, releasing most of the tension from the harpoon.

"That's good, that's enough," yelled Jonas. "Excellent, Masao. We don't want her too shallow. I'm coming aboard."

"Wait, Jonas, before you surface. Captain Barre is requesting you check the damage to the ship's hull."

"No problem. Stand by." Jonas released the claw's grip on the net, retracted the mechanical arm, then accelerated in a tight circle below and around the captive female. He was feeling giddy, extremely pleased with his plans, anxious to get back on board and talk with Terry.

And then he saw the hull.

DUSK

"It's about eight to nine feet wide," explained Jonas, describing the hole created by the Megalodon's collision with the *Kiku*. The ship had taken on a tremendous amount of water, and was now listing at a fifteen-degree angle to starboard.

"That's only the beginning, Masao," said Leon Barre. "We sealed off the forward compartment but the damn port screw's all bent outta shape."

"Will we sink?" asked Masao.

Barre contemplated the question. "No, watertight compartments will keep the damage isolated for now, but we don't wanna push her. Pulling that monster out there, that's a lot of drag, lots of work for one screw. The *Kiku*'s gonna have to crawl home."

"How long until we arrive at the lagoon, Leon?" asked DeMarco.

"Hmmm, let me see. It's just after seven. I'd say we make it back tomorrow morning, just before dawn."

DeMarco looked at Barre, then back at Jonas. "Christ, Jonas, will the Meg stay unconscious that long?"

"Honestly, I don't know. There's no way of telling. I gave her what I thought was a sufficient dosage to keep her under twelve to sixteen hours."

"Can we inject her again?" asked Masao. "Maybe wait until she's been under a good ten hours, then shoot her up?"

"She'll die," said Jonas matter-of-factly. "You can't keep an animal this size under for so long without permanent damage to her nervous system. She'll need to come around and breathe on her own or she'll never regain consciousness."

Masao scratched his head, unsure. "Not many options here. Captain, how many crew members do you need to run the ship? Maybe we can evacuate some of the men—"

"Forget it, Masao. With the damage to the screw and the sea knocking on the door, I need every man I got, plus some. We leave this ship, we're all gonna leave together."

"Masao, let me make a suggestion," offered Jonas. "The cardiac monitor should warn us if the Meg is coming around. But just in case, let me go back down in the AG I and keep a watch on our friend. If she appears to be waking up, we'll release the line and get out of here. If we're not already in the lagoon, we'll be damn close. Without the additional weight of the Meg, we should be able to make it in fairly quickly."

"What happens when the Megalodon wakes up?" asked Masao.

"She'll have a bad hangover and she'll be pissed off. I wouldn't be surprised if she followed us right into the lagoon."

"Chased us is more like it," added DeMarco.

"And what about you?" asked Terry.

"In the AG I," Jonas said, smiling, "I'll probably be safer than you guys."

Masao thought it over. "Okay, Jonas, you'll take the Abyss Glider out in the early morning and keep an eye on our fish. DeMarco, you take the first watch on the cardiac monitor. Any changes, you call Jonas right away." Masao stopped, listening to the thunder rumbling in the distance. "Is that a storm moving in?"

Mac stepped into the CIC, his copter having just landed on deck. "No, Masao. That's the sound of helicopters. News choppers, five of 'em to be exact, with more coming. I'd say it's gonna be mighty crowded around here by dawn."

Frank Heller paused from his work, looking up at the television for the fourth time in the last hour to watch the latest news update:

". . . two hundred feet below us, lying in a comatose state is the sixty-foot prehistoric Megalodon, a monster that is responsible for at least two dozen gruesome deaths over the last thirty days. From our view, one can clearly see the creature's snowy-white hide, skin glowing under the reflection of the full moon.

At her present speed, the heavily damaged Kiku is expected to reach the entrance of the Tanaka Lagoon sometime before dawn. Channel 9 News will be keeping a vigil all night, bringing you the latest from this breaking story. This is Tori Hess, Action News, reporting live from the . . ."

"Turn it off already, Frank," said Danielson. They were aboard the *Magnate*, assembling a homemade depth charge in the yacht's exercise room. Danielson was hard at work, busy installing the fuse to the four-by-two-foot steel barrel.

"You've been watching the same story all night."

"You asked me to find out how deep the Meg is," answered

Heller in his defense. "Did you expect me to swim out with a tape measure?"

"Yeah, so tell me." Danielson looked up from his work. "How deep is that bitch?"

"From the camera angle, I'd guess about one hundred and fifty to two hundred feet down. What kind of range will your depth charge have?"

"Plenty. The fuse should have no problem lasting to that depth. As for the charge itself, I've added a generous amount of amatol, which is rather primitive but highly explosive. Believe me, Frank, there's enough power here to fry that fish. The difficult part will be getting close enough to accurately drop the charge onto the monster. We'll have to rely on Harris for that. Where is he anyway?"

"Up on deck," answered Heller. "Have you noticed that the guy doesn't sleep at night?"

"Yeah, I noticed. I'll tell you something, Frank," admitted Danielson. "I haven't been sleeping much at night myself."

Bud Harris was at the starboard rail, staring at the reflection of the moon, perfectly still on the black sea. The *Magnate* was anchored three hundred yards south of the Tanaka Lagoon. Bud could just make out the white concrete wall of the huge canal entrance.

"Maggie," Bud whispered aloud between sips of gin. He watched the small waves lap at the hull. "Maggs, look what you've got me into. Hanging out with a bunch of Navy bozos, playing war against some fucking monster. Can you believe this shit?"

Bud took another sip of gin, draining the glass. "Ahh, Maggs." Hot tears rolled down his cheeks. "Why couldn't you have just dropped the fucking camera?" He flicked the empty glass into the ocean, the ripples dissolving the image of the moon.

"Fuck it. I'm gonna kill that monster tomorrow and cut out

its eyes." He turned, staggering down the circular stairs to the guest bedroom. Bud could no longer sleep in the yacht's master suite. Maggie's perfume still lingered, her presence too vivid. He collapsed onto the queen-size bed, passing out.

Thirty seconds after Bud left the rail, a three-foot fluorescent white dorsal fin sliced the surface, circling the discarded glass as it sank into the black waters of the sanctuary.

Jonas opened his eyes, his internal alarm clock going off moments before his watch. He was still in the lounge chair with Terry snuggled against his chest under the wool blanket, keeping him warm. Gently, he stroked her soft hair with his callused fingertips.

She stirred. "Go back to sleep, Jonas," she mumbled, eyes closed.

"I can't. It's time."

She opened her eyes, twisted around to face him. She stretched, her arm reaching around his neck, hugging him. "I'm too cozy to move, Jonas. Let's just sleep another five minutes."

"Terry, I wish I could stay here all night, but we both know I can't."

"I'm jealous. You'd rather spend time with that other female, huh?"

"Come on. Stand up, girl." He pulled her up. "I have to get into my wet suit. DeMarco's probably already wondering where I am." Jonas checked his watch. Four thirty-three.

"Fine. I'm heading to the galley to grab a bite. You'd better eat something too."

"No, I think I'll pass. My stomach's a little jumpy. Just tell DeMarco to meet me by the sub."

• • •

DeMarco checked his watch again. Where the hell was the man? The cardiac monitor's digital readout remained at eighty-five. The sky was beginning to turn gray, the media helicopters still buzzing overhead.

"Damn press," he muttered.

Terry walked in smiling. "Morning, Al."

"Where the hell is Jonas?"

"Already in the AG I. He's waiting for you to lower him into the water."

"He's waiting? Christ, I've been sitting here for the last nine hours waiting." DeMarco left the CIC, passing through the pilothouse, then walked out on deck to the sub.

Jonas was already inside, lying prone. DeMarco knocked twice on the Lexan cone, the pilot giving the thumbs-up. DeMarco climbed into the crane and sat down.

"Ouch! What the hell?" He picked up the object and examined it.

"A tooth?" It was black with age, but still extremely sharp, at least seven inches long. DeMarco walked back to the submersible. He released the rear latch. "Hey, Jonas, you lose something?"

"What? Oh shit, the Meg tooth! Sorry, Al, can I have it please."

DeMarco passed it forward. "Why the hell do you carry that, of all things?"

Jonas shrugged. "I started doing it about ten years ago. It was a good-luck charm for whenever I piloted a sub. I guess I'm a bit superstitious."

"Yeah, well, I'm a bit annoyed. I just sat on the damn thing," barked DeMarco. "Do me a favor from now on. Keep the blade outta my crane. I'm not the fucking tooth fairy."

"Sorry."

DeMarco slammed the hatch closed, returned to the crane, and lowered the AG I into the Pacific.

. . .

Jonas flicked on the exterior light, descending below the *Kiku's* hull. It looked worse, the ship now listing hard to one side. He accelerated ahead, then dropped to three hundred feet, approaching the dormant creature from the left.

The Megalodon's glow illuminated the black sea for fifty yards in all directions. Schools of fish darted back and forth along her hide. Jellyfish were caught within the netting. Jonas turned his exterior light off. Banking in a tight circle, he maneuvered the AG I next to the creature's head, the cranium measuring nearly three times the length of the sub.

The mouth was opened slightly, allowing water to pass through. Jonas hovered close to the Meg's right eye, the pupil involuntarily rolled backward in the monster's head. Jonas knew this to be a natural response, the Meg's brain automatically positioning the now-useless organ for protection.

"Jonas!"

Jonas jumped forward, his harness pulling hard against his shoulders. "Damnit, Terry, you scared the shit out of me."

Jonas could hear her laughing through the radio. "Sorry." She grew serious. "We're still steady at eighty-five beats per minute. How's the Meg look?"

"Looks okay." Jonas slowed the sub, hovering next to the Meg's five gill slits. "Terry, how close are we now to the lagoon?"

"Less than four miles. Barre says another two hours, tops. Hey, you're about to miss a gorgeous sunrise."

Jonas smiled. "Sounds like the beginning of a great day."

DAWN

They had been waiting all night, anchored close to shore, a congregation of followers gathered as if summoned by the creature itself. Some were scientists, most were tourists and thrill seekers, apprehensive yet prepared to face the risks in order to be a part of history. Their transports varied in size, from wave runners to yachts, from small outboards to larger fishing trawlers. Every whale-watching company within a fifty-mile radius was represented, their rates sufficiently inflated for the event. Over three hundred camcorders, batteries charged and cassettes loaded, stood ready.

André Dupont leaned against the rail of the forty-eight-foot fishing trawler, watching through binoculars as the gray haze of the winter sky grew lighter across the horizon. He could just make out the bow of the *Kiku,* still a good mile northwest of the canal entrance. He walked back toward the cabin.

"Etienne, she's close now," Dupont whispered to his assistant. "How close will our captain bring us?"

Etienne shook his head. "Sorry, André. He refuses to leave the shallows with the monster so close. He won't risk the boat. Family business, *n'est pas?*"

"*Oui.* I do not blame the man." Dupont looked around in all directions, the morning light revealing several hundred boats. Dupont shook his head. "I fear that our other friends will probably not be as cautious."

Frank Heller watched the *Kiku* crawl at its agonizingly slow pace toward the lagoon. He shared none of André Dupont's exhilaration. Rage was building within the man, stomach tense. Limbs beginning to tremble. He felt the side of his neck tighten, throbbing with the rising anger.

"It's time, Mr. Harris," he said, not looking away from the horizon.

Bud engaged the throttle. The *Magnate*'s twin engines jumped to life as the yacht moved quickly to intercept.

The dawn's first light filtered down through the sea. Jonas watched as the creature's entire torso became visible, a lethal dirigible being led toward its new hangar. Jonas brought the AG I's Lexan nose cone within five feet of the female's right eye. The blue-gray pupil was still rolled back into the head, the light exposing only a bloodshot white membrane.

"Jonas." Terry's voice crackled over the radio. "I think something's happening with the Meg."

The shot of adrenaline woke Jonas up. "Talk to me, Terry."

"The female's pulse is climbing very slowly. It's at eighty-seven, now ninety—"

"Jonas, DeMarco here. I've reloaded the harpoon gun as per

Masao's new orders. If your monster wakes up before we enter the lagoon, I'm firing, whether it kills the fish or not. Consider yourself warned."

Jonas thought about arguing, but changed his mind. DeMarco was right. If the Meg regained consciousness before the *Kiku* could get her safely in the lagoon, the ship and its entire crew would be in danger. He stared at the creature's open jaws. Coursing through its DNA was seventy-million-plus years of instinct. The predator could not think or choose; she could only react, each cell atuned to her environment, every response preconditioned. Nature itself had decided that the species would dominate the oceans, commanding it to perpetually hunt in order to survive. Jonas whispered, "We should have left you alone—"

"Jonas!" Terry's voice pierced his thought. "Didn't you hear me?"

"Sorry, I—"

"The *Magnate's* bearing down on us." Terry's voice rose. "Five hundred yards and closing fast!"

"The *Magnate?*"

"Bud, what the hell are you doing now?" wondered Jonas, his mind racing.

DeMarco focused his binoculars upon the yacht, his line of sight finally drifting back toward the activity along the stern. Two men, both supporting a steel drum, balanced their cargo on the transom.

"What the hell?" said the engineer.

Three hundred yards. Two hundred, and then DeMarco caught a face . . . Heller! He refocused on the steel drum and realized.

"Jonas, Jonas!" DeMarco snatched the mike out from Terry's hand. "Depth charge coming right at you! Get deep!"

Jonas leaned hard on the joystick, circling right, then rolled the sub beneath the Meg's upper torso.

Mac pulled back on the joystick, the copter leaping off the frigate's deck. Circling the airship hard to his left, he raced toward the incoming Magnate as if leading an air assault on a North Vietnamese patrol boat.

Bud looked up, the helicopter appearing out of nowhere, bearing down on his yacht on a head-on collision course. The millionaire screamed, yanking the wheel hard to his left seconds before the platform supporting the chopper's thermal imager smashed into the Magnate's radar antenna, ripping it off of its aluminum base.

Debris exploded across the deck, the air raining shrapnel. Reacting as if a grenade had just gone off above their heads, Danielson and Heller dove sideways, abandoning the depth charge. They landed hard on the deck, covering their heads in an attempt to avoid the incoming debris. The maneuver left the five-hundred-pound depth charge balancing precariously on the transom. As the yacht veered hard to the left, the steel drum rolled over the transom, plunging into the ocean. Seawater rushed into the canister's six holes, filling the pistol chamber and sinking the bomb.

Shards of aluminum from the decimated radar tower struck Danielson's and Heller's backs painfully as the yacht pulled away from the Kiku. Heller sat up, looking back to see the helicopter bank sharply, nosedive toward the ocean, then level out. This time, it would make its run from the stern.

"That motherfucker's crazy," yelled Heller.

"Get your head down!" screamed Danielson.

233

Mac pushed down on the joystick, yelling in the wind, "Mac attack!" a smile fixed upon his face.

BOOM!!

The explosion caught the pilot off-guard. He yanked desperately on the joystick as the tail of his copter swung out from behind. With a crunch, the landing gear smashed into the upper deck of the *Magnate,* tearing the roof off the luxurious stateroom, ripping the bottom off his helicopter. The airship spun out of control, the blades unable to regain draft. Before Mac could react, the copter slammed sideways into the ocean.

At three hundred and twelve feet, the depth charge's spring had released, thrusting the percussion detonator against the primer. The crude weapon had imploded, then exploded with a flash and subsonic boom. Although the lethal radius of the bomb measured only twenty-five feet, the resulting shock wave was devastating.

The invisible force of current caught the AG I broadside, rolling the winged craft over and over again. Jonas pitched hard against the Lexan cone, cracking his head against the hard surface, nearly knocking himself out.

On board the *Kiku,* lightbulbs shattered and bodies flew as the ship's fittings loosened with the blast. Captain Barre cried to his crew to seal the engine room, but the roar of the media helicopters drowned his voice.

Terry Tanaka knelt on the deck, her first thoughts of Jonas. She found the radio transmitter. "Jonas. Jonas, come in, please." Static. "Al, I'm not getting a signal—"

"Terry . . ." Masao pulled himself up the stairwell, collapsing on the top step. Terry ran to him.

"Call the doctor!" she screamed, her hands covered with her father's blood.

DeMarco grabbed the microphone to the *Kiku*'s speakers, calling for the ship's physician to report. He failed to notice the *Meg*'s cardiac monitor, the digital display now racing past one hundred.

The chilly Pacific snapped Mac to attention. He opened his eyes, startled to find himself submerged underwater at a forty-five-degree angle. Desperately, he struggled to release the seat belt as the mangled helicopter slipped sideways beneath the waves.

Jonas waited until the aftereffects of the shock wave subsided, then attempted to roll the submersible right-side up. The power was dead. He swore to himself, then began rolling hard against the interior, gradually gaining momentum as the sub twisted counterclockwise. As he completed the maneuver, he could feel the natural buoyancy of the sub taking over as it gradually began to rise, tail-first.

"Terry, come in." The radio, like everything else on the sub, was dead.

A glow loomed on Taylor's right, lighting up the interior. Jonas turned to find himself hovering within three feet of the female's basketball-sized pupil.

The blue-gray eye was open. Blind, it stared directly at Jonas.

CHAOS

Bud Harris dragged himself off the polished wooden floor, unsure of what had just taken place. The *Magnate* was drifting, her twin engines off. He glanced sideways in time to see the helicopter's blades slipping beneath the waves.

"Fuck you," he muttered, then pressed the "on" switch, attempting to restart the engines. Nothing.

"Shit. Danielson, Heller! Where the fuck are you guys?" Bud headed out on deck, locating the men standing by the transom.

"Well? Is the monster dead?"

Danielson and Heller looked at each other. "Gotta be," said Danielson, not sounding very sure of himself.

"You don't seem real confident," questioned Bud.

"Unfortunately," said Danielson, "we had to let the charge go a little early when that lunatic attacked."

"We need to get out of here," said Heller.

"Yes, well, boys, that's gonna be a bit of a problem," said Bud. "The engines are dead. Your damn explosive apparently loosened a connection, and I'm not exactly Mr. Goodwrench."

"Christ, you're telling us we're stuck out here with that Meg?" Heller shook his head, his jaws locked tight.

"Frank, the monster's dead. Trust me," said Danielson. "We'll be watching it float belly-up any second now."

Heller looked at his former CO. "Dick, it's a fucking shark. It's not going to float; if she's really dead she'll sink to the bottom."

At that moment, they heard a splashing sound to their left. The yacht seemed to drop, and then a hand appeared at the ladder, Mac dragging himself on board the *Magnate*.

"Beautiful morning, isn't it, assholes?" he said, collapsing on deck.

Jonas lay on his stomach, head down, his claustrophobia causing shortness of breath. The lifeless Abyss Glider's left midwing had caught on the cargo net, keeping the sub at eye level with the Megalodon. Jonas watched in fascination and horror as the female's blue-gray eye continued focusing involuntarily on the tiny submersible.

She's blind, thought Jonas, but she knows I'm here, she senses a presence.

Now the caudal fin began to swish in heavy, side-to-side movements, propelling the predator slowly forward. The gill slits towered into view, passing quickly. And then the prominent snout suddenly whipped back and forth, freeing the AG I's wing from the net as the most frightening animal on the planet snapped awake.

The submersible continued to rise tail-first. Jonas looked down, watching the Megalodon lurch forward, but the cargo net immediately ensnarled her pectoral fins. Enraged, she rolled once, then twice, twisting and tangling herself tighter in the trap.

The AG I tossed backward in the Meg's wake. With no means

of control, Jonas lost sight of the creature. Then, as the sub's cone drifted downward, he caught a glimpse of the furious Megalodon, completely entwined from her gill slits to her pelvic fin in the cargo net.

"She's going to drown," he whispered to himself.

The myriad of boaters anchored in waiting outside the Tanaka Lagoon had witnessed the super-yacht break from the group to rendezvous with the incoming guest of honor. They had seen the helicopter intercept, and attack the vessel, only to end up crashing into the sea as the depth charge had detonated. Now the onlookers grew anxious, wondering if the explosion had killed the creature they had paid good money to see. Almost as one, several dozen of the larger fishing boats grew daring, gradually moving toward the listless *Kiku,* intent on filming the creature, dead or alive.

Nine media helicopters were hovering above the *Kiku,* perpetually shifting positions in their attempt to gain better camera angles. The underwater explosion created a new twist on the story. The networks ordered their helicopter crews to assess whether the Megalodon had survived.

David Adashek was in the back of the Channel 9 Action News copter, straining to see over his cameraman's shoulder. The white glow of the creature was visible, but whether the shark was dead or alive was impossible to determine. The pilot tapped his arm, motioning him to look toward the opposite side of the copter.

Racing toward the Megalodon was a flotilla of pleasure boats.

From the tip of her snout to the edge of her caudal fin, the Megalodon's skin contained fine, toothlike prickles called dermal denticles, literally "skin teeth." Sharp and sandpaperlike in texture, the denticles were another in the predator's arsenal of natural weapons. As the female twisted insanely within the cargo net, the dermal denticles began sawing through the rope, slowly slicing it to ribbons.

Jonas watched the female shake herself free from her bonds as he desperately checked the sub's fuses. Finally, she turned in his direction, jaw slack, triangular teeth splayed. Desperate, Jonas tried the power switch again—still dead, as the monster propelled itself upward.

Bud and Mac had gone below to the engine room, leaving Danielson and Heller on deck. Frank was leaning across the transom, staring into the green water, when the white mass materialized.

"Son of a . . ."

WHOOSH! The stern exploded, fiberglass splintering in a thousand directions. Danielson and Heller fell back onto the tilting deck, rolling toward the water.

DeMarco manned the harpoon gun, training the barrel on his target. He released the safety as the Meg surfaced. He watched as she swam upside down now along the surface, a river of water passing into her mouth as she exposed her glistening white belly to the world. DeMarco aimed, pulled the trigger.

Click.

"Goddamnit!" The explosion had jammed the gun's inner chamber. The entire crew was on deck now, frantically donning orange life vests. In the pilothouse, the ship's physician tended to Masao, now conscious. Terry and Pasquale stood over them.

"He's fractured his skull, Terry," said the doctor. "We need to get him to a hospital as soon as possible."

She could hear the swarm of media copters hovering above. "Pasquale, get on the radio, try to get one of those news choppers to land on the *Kiku*. Tell 'em we have a serious injury. Doc, stay with my father. I'll be aft."

She ran out of the pilothouse, making her way to the hangar deck.

David Adashek saw her first, waving emphatically on the pad. "I know that girl," he said. "That's Tanaka's daughter. Captain, can you land this bird on the *KIKU*?"

"No problem."

"Hold it," said the cameraman. "My producer's screaming at me in my earphones to get close-ups of the Meg. He'll have my balls for breakfast if you land on that ship."

"Look," said David, "the Meg is attacking the *Kiku*—"

"All the more reason why we're not landing."

"Hey," said the pilot, "I'm getting a distress call from the *Kiku*. They're requesting we transport an injured man to shore. Radioman says it's Masao Tanaka. Looks serious."

"Land the copter," ordered Adashek.

The cameraman looked at him with a scowl. "Fuck you."

Adashek ripped the camera from the man, holding it out of the pilot's open door. "We land or I feed this to the Meg."

Moments later, the helicopter touched down on the pad.

The Megalodon circled madly beneath the *Kiku*. The ship's exposed metal hull, immersed in seawater, generated galvanic currents, electrical impulses that stimulated the female's ampullae of Lorenzini like fingernails on a chalkboard, driving her to attack.

Sweating profusely, Jonas could feel his claustrophobia building as he strained to reach the battery connections at the rear of his sub. Blindly, he groped the terminals inside the rear panels, searching in vain for a loose connection.

A sudden current twisted the AG I around and upward, giving Jonas an unobstructed view of a scene that sent pangs of fear through his heart: the Megalodon plunging her snout into the hull of the *Kiku*.

The collision brought the entire crew to its knees. Metal screamed and a low-pitched moan emanated from below.

"Son of a bitch," swore Captain Barre, "that fucking monster's eating my ship. Man the lifeboats! Pilot, get Masao off this boat. We don't need his blood in the water!"

The pilot of the news copter looked at Adashek and the cameraman. "One of you guys has to get off if we're taking on wounded."

The cameraman looked at Adashek with an evil grin. "Hope you can swim, pal."

David felt butterflies in his stomach as he exited the safety of the chopper, allowing the doctor and Terry Tanaka to load Masao on board. He stood on the lopsided deck and watched the copter fly off toward the mainland. "What the hell did you just get yourself into, David?" he asked himself aloud.

Crumpled against the port rail, Dick Danielson stood painfully, grabbed Heller beneath his armpits, and hoisted him to his feet. "We're sinking!"

"No shit." Heller looked around. "Where are Harris and Mac?"

"Probably dead. If so, they're lucky."

"The Zodiac." Heller pointed at the rubberized raft. "Come on."

The *Magnate* was taking on water rapidly. It began to spin and roll sideways, making it more difficult for the two men to lift and lower the motorized raft over the side. When it dropped to the surface with a splat, Danielson looked at Heller.

"Go ahead."

Heller swung over the rail, followed by his former captain. Danielson brought the sixty-five-horsepower outboard whining to life and gunned the throttle. The raft's lightweight bow rose high in the sea, the Zodiac skimming over the waves, accelerating toward land and the pack of oncoming boats.

"Dick, watch these guys!" yelled Heller, the wind whipping in his ears.

Danielson had little room to maneuver, the stretch of motorboats too wide to circumnavigate. He slowed, attempting to swerve around the first wave of hulls.

The female shot straight upward out of the Pacific, her open mouth missing the Zodiac, catching it instead on her broad back and launching the rubber raft fifteen feet into the air. Heller and Danielson flew like rag dolls into the ocean on either side of the shark.

The Megalodon's sudden appearance started a chain reaction. Two oncoming fishing boats veered sharply into adjacent vessels, creating two separate pileups. Chaos reigned among the other craft as the rules of boating were tossed aside for self-preservation. Screams rent the air as pilots frantically tried to turn back, only to crash into the unwitting boaters behind them.

The remaining eight news helicopters dropped to within fifty feet of the armada, contributing to the confusion.

Danielson surfaced, coughing up seawater. He swam toward the nearest pleasure craft, a thirty-two-foot speedboat overloaded with seventeen passengers and a golden retriever. He clawed at the hull, unable to reach high enough to pull himself aboard. The passengers did not see him, could not hear his cries for help over the thunder of the choppers. Then he saw the ladder, and kicked toward it.

The cavernous maw came without warning from below, pulling Danielson underwater. He struggled in time to catch the ladder in a death grip, feeling the sun-warmed aluminum, refusing to let go. His legs, severed at the knees, slipped out of the monster's mouth, blood pouring from the open wounds, swirling in all directions from the boat's propellers.

The Meg's senses lost her prey. Confused by the churning pool of blood, she submerged, attempting to relocate.

Danielson screamed, still dangling from the ladder. Now the passengers in the stern heard him, reaching down and pulling him up by his wrists, laying him on top of the wide fiberglass transom.

The Megalodon's head levitated straight out of the sea, open jaws rotating sideways against the transom, her teeth gently gripping Danielson, tossing his crippled body up into the air high above her open mouth. Like a dog catching a biscuit, the sixty-foot shark snatched her prey in midair, snapping her jaws closed on Danielson, gulping his remains deep into her gullet. The monster slipped back beneath the waves before the first screams of protest from the petrified witnesses could be uttered.

Circling in a tight formation forty feet above the melee, the pilots of the eight news copters panicked, realizing for the first time how massive the Megalodon actually was. Their first reaction was to immediately achieve a much safer altitude. Eight joysticks were simultaneously yanked backward, eight sets of rotors climbing toward the same airspace.

The pilots were so frightened of the monster below they completely ignored the danger above. Two copters rose at intersecting angles, their rotors slashing against one another, igniting a cataclysmic reaction. The flying shrapnel ricocheted into the paths of the other helicopter blades, violating their airspace. In a matter of seconds, all eight choppers either had careened sideways against each other or had been hit with shrapnel, causing their rotors to shatter. Matching fireballs exploded upward two at a time, raining metal, gasoline, and human body parts across the crowded sea.

Swimming fifty feet below the carnage, the predator circled slowly, snapping at the sinking debris, attempting to isolate food with her powerful senses.

The female was stimulated, ravenous with hunger.

FEEDING FRENZY

The once-mighty United States Navy frigate dipped sideways, her waterlogged hull finally pulling her beneath the waves. The twenty-three crew members, packed into two lifeboats, rowed desperately to escape the swirling currents of the sinking vessel that seemed to reach for them from below. The outboard motors would not be used lest it alert the monster.

Leon Barre, tears in his eyes, watched as the bow of his command slid silently into the Pacific. Terry Tanaka scanned the surf for any sign of Jonas or his Abyss Glider. David Adashek was visibly shaking, praying quietly, as were many of the crew. Next to him, crouched at the ready, DeMarco waited for the albino monster to reappear.

Leon Barre stood above the rowers, scanning the tangle of boats and helicopter wreckage a half mile away. "Son of a bitch," he swore to himself. "Do we start the motors or wait?" He looked into the eyes of his men, seeing their fear. "DeMarco?"

"I don't know. I have to believe those ships have the Meg's attention. How fast can these boats move?"

"Overloaded like we are, maybe it'd take us ten or fifteen minutes to make land." The men looked up at him, nodding their heads.

"Wait." Terry spoke to Barre, then looked to the others. "Jonas said this creature can feel the vibrations of the engines. We should wait, let the Megalodon clear the area."

"And what if she doesn't?" asked Steve Tabor. "I've got a wife and three kids!"

Another crew member spoke. "You expect us to sit here and wait to get eaten alive?"

DeMarco held up his hands. He looked at Terry. "Terry, listen to me. Jonas is dead, and the rest of us might wind up the same way if we just sit back and hope that the Meg won't find us." Murmurs of agreement. "Look what's going on out there. The monster's having lunch. If we stay here, we'll be dessert!"

Eyes turned to the pack of boats. Faint screams came across the water.

Terry felt a lump in her throat. She tried to swallow, holding back tears. Jonas was either injured or dead, and they were going to just leave him. She stared ahead, watching as a cigarette speedboat rose from the water and flipped. Again, screams tore the air. Terry realized they had no choice but to leave.

Both engines jumped to life and Leon Barre's boat took the lead, heading south to skirt around the maze ahead.

Frank Heller had managed to swim toward one of the boats. Exhausted and frightened beyond reason, he remained in the water, clinging to the side of a fishing trawler's tuna net, eyes closed, waiting for death. Minutes passed.

"Hey!"

Frank opened his eyes to a vision of a muscular black man

leaning over the transom. "This ain't no time to be takin' a dip, old man. Get your ass in the boat." A large hand grabbed a hold of Heller's life vest and yanked him on board.

Bud Harris woke, chest-deep in seawater in the listing pilothouse of his yacht. He pulled himself up and almost fainted at the unbearable agony in his head. The *Magnate* somehow remained miraculously afloat. He saw Mac working the ship-to-shore radio.

"What happened?" he asked, holding his head.

"I guess the Meg was a little pissed off from that depth charge of yours," replied Mac. "We were in the engine room when she hit. I dragged your sorry ass topside, but this yacht of yours is sinking fast."

"The Zodiac?"

"Gone. Your pals decided to take it for a spin."

"Assholes. Hope they die in pain." The yacht was equipped with several internal pumps. Bud located the controls, flipping the toggle switch up. The motors churned, vibrating the entire vessel as seawater was expelled overboard.

Mac clicked the pumps off. "Too noisy, way too noisy," he said. "I just spoke with the Coast Guard. We're on their waiting list."

"Waiting list?"

"Look around, pal," said Mac. "That monster's on the rampage."

Bud walked back through the control room, down the stairs to his flooded master suite. The room was almost totally underwater. He held his breath, ducked under, and reemerged gasping thirty seconds later. In his hand was an unopened bottle of Jack Daniel's. He returned to the control room, shaking from the cold. On the far wall was a framed picture of his father. Bud raised and removed it, revealing a small wall safe. He manipulated the combination, opened the door, and pulled out the loaded .44 magnum. He returned to the pilothouse.

Mac saw the gun and chuckled. "Hey, Dirty Harry, you gonna kill the shark with that?"

Bud pointed the gun at Mac's head. "No, flyboy, but I just may kill you."

The powerless Abyss Glider bobbed four feet below the surface, the heavier nose cone of the buoyant sub pointing straight down at the ocean floor. Jonas was drenched in sweat, his breathing becoming increasingly difficult as his air supply diminished. He had found the disconnected electrical cables, reattached them, and bore down with all his strength on the rusty wing nut in an attempt to tighten the connection with nothing but his fingers. The wing nut turned one revolution and stopped.

"That'll have to do." He grunted, twisting his body upside down, sliding back into the pilot's prone position. He felt the blood rush to his head. "Come on, baby, give me some power!"

The AG I flickered to life, blowing cool air on his face from its ventilation system. He pushed forward on the joystick, leveling out the sub, then bringing it to the surface. Taylor looked around.

The *Kiku* was gone. To his right he saw the *Magnate,* crippled but still afloat. And then he spotted the flotilla.

Still bobbing above the Monterey Canyon, in waters adjacent to the Tanaka Lagoon, André Dupont and several hundred other boaters looked on in horror as the Megalodon rose from the sea to wreak havoc among their unfortunate comrades who had risked a peek at the once-sedated beast. Even at a distance of a half mile, the size and ferocity of the monster shocked the camera buffs who had remained behind. The nature of the event had changed: this was no longer a game, people were being slaughtered!

A common thought passed through the group: remaining in the water meant they also could be eaten! Forgetting about their ports of origin, the boaters swung their craft around and raced to land. Without hesitation, they propelled their boats beyond the shallows, beaching their vessels right onto the sandy shores of Monterey Bay.

André Dupont watched the mass exodus. Within minutes, the fishing trawler was the only remaining boat in the water. Etienne walked over to the rail and nudged Dupont. "André, Captain agrees to keep us in the shallows."

Dupont continued to look through his binoculars. "He's not going to beach the boat, like the others?"

Etienne smiled. "Captain says he just painted the hull, doesn't want to scratch it up."

Dupont looked at his assistant. "Those people out there, they are all going to die. We should do something."

"Captain says the Coast Guard is on the way."

The trawler suddenly vibrated, her engines sputtering to life.

Dupont brought the glasses back up to his eyes, locating the *Kiku*'s two lifeboats, which were approaching quickly. "My friend, please ask our captain to turn off his engines, unless he also wants to be eaten."

Jonas accelerated to thirty knots, holding his depth steady at twenty feet. Moments later, he came within view of the massacre.

Three smaller speedboats were in the process of descending to their final resting places, their fiberglass hulls torn apart. Jonas circled. The passengers had either escaped or been eaten. He brought the sub to the surface, afraid of what he was about to see.

The flotilla, once twenty strong, now consisted of a maze of floating fiberglass and the remains of cabins, decks, and broken hulls. Jonas counted eight fishing boats that appeared intact, their decks overloaded with panicked civilians. A Coast Guard rescue chopper hovered overhead, raising a hysterical woman in a harness. Those remaining on board seemed to be yelling, pushing each other in an attempt to be next.

Where was the Megalodon?

Jonas descended to thirty feet, circling the area. Visibility was poor, debris everywhere. He felt his heart pounding, his head moving rapidly in every possible direction.

Then he spotted the caudal fin.

The female was moving quickly away from Jonas, her tail disappearing with a flicker into the gray mist. Jonas surfaced the Abyss Glider, locating the towering dorsal fin as it cut across the surface waves.

She was heading toward land.

The two lifeboats were less than a half mile from land when the six-foot dorsal fin appeared behind the second lifeboat, closing fast. Then it disappeared.

Barre stood up and looked back to the other lifeboat. He pointed at them, then motioned emphatically to the south. He tapped Pasquale, who was steering his boat, and pointed north. The survivors would split up.

Eighty feet down, the Meg shook her head, confused. Her senses had registered one prey, now there were two. She rose to attack.

Terry and DeMarco saw the white glow rise a split second before their worlds spun like a gyroscope, out of control. Explosion, bright blue sky, followed by bodies, then icy-cold water. The boat flipped upside down, its motor dead.

Twelve heads, coughing and moaning, broke the surface. Twelve pairs of hands reached for the capsized lifeboat, its wooden hull glistening in the fading sun. They held on for dear life.

The towering white dorsal fin circled twenty feet away, its owner sizing up her next meal. Forty-two thousand pounds of Megalodon coursed lazily along the surface, her sheer mass creating a current that began to spin the lifeboat and its crew. The creature's head emerged, angled sideways in the water. Her jaws opened slightly and water streamed into her mouth. The crew watched in silence, unable to take their eyes off the monster, as they rotated within her current.

Terry gasped as one of the crewmen lost his grip on the slippery hull. He screamed, his body drifting away from the lifeboat in the Megalodon's riptide. He kicked against the current, stroking with all his might and screaming as he saw the open mouth.

The Meg had stopped, twisting her head around and lifting it from the water as she beckoned her prey to drift out. The crewman felt the undertow ease slightly. He swam harder. Then he heard the others scream. He glanced back.

The triangular tip of the snout blocked out the sun. Mesmerized, the crewman whispered a prayer in Spanish and ducked his head as the gargantuan mouth swallowed him whole.

Like drowning rats, the surviving eleven tried to claw their way up onto the capsized hull. Adashek stepped onto the outboard engine, pulling himself higher. DeMarco's fingers were raw and bleeding, gripping the wooden hull. He knew he couldn't hang on. The hunter circled slowly, her undertow tugging hard once more. This time, DeMarco didn't fight it. He thought of his wife—she'd be waiting in the parking lot for him. He had promised her that this would be his last voyage. She hadn't believed him.

Terry saw DeMarco. She screamed.

"Al! Al, swim!" She pushed away from the boat, stroking hard. She grabbed his arm from behind, pulling him toward her.

"No, Terry, leave me! Get to the boat—"

"No, goddamnit."

"Terry . . . oh God—"

The Meg moved toward them, drifting lazily on the surface like a lethal barge. The head again lay sideways, a river of seawater streaming into her mouth. Terry caught herself focusing on the thick snout, peppered with the black ampullae of Lorenzini. And then the jaws stretched wider, revealing glistening white teeth, human flesh still caught between several fangs.

Terry and DeMarco kicked wildly as the jaws opened wider to accommodate the meal, pink gums exposed, serrated teeth beckoning.

Terry Tanaka looked back, paralyzed. She felt herself losing consciousness, not recognizing the familiar whir of the engine.

Six hundred and fifty pounds of submersible and its pilot leapt straight out of the sea, smashing down upon the exposed upper jaw of the Megalodon. The triangular head lifted in the water, blood oozing from its left eye socket.

The AG I rolled into the sea, accelerating downward, circling behind the female.

"Come on," Jonas yelled at the creature. "Come on, catch me if you can!"

Like a mad bull, the Megalodon plunged below the waves to give chase. Jonas turned, saw the garage-door-sized mouth jump into view ahead of him, and whipped the Abyss Glider hard to port, veering around the open maw.

The Megalodon's jaws closed on seawater as its prey escaped.

The female instantly relocated, a sixty-foot torpedo homing furiously on its target.

Jonas checked his speed—thirty-four knots—and saw the Meg was gaining fast. Where to go? Lead her away from Terry, away from the others. He felt a bump from behind as the Meg rammed his tail fin. He turned hard to starboard, then ascended at a sharp angle.

The AG I shot into the air like a flying fish. Right behind it was the Megalodon, jaws snapping air, her upper torso fully exposed. Jonas's sub slapped hard against the waves. The predator flipped sideways into the ocean behind it, the thunderous splash rivaling that of the largest humpback whale.

Jonas pushed down on the joystick to dive . . . Nothing happened! The landing must have jarred the battery cable loose again. Desperate, he twisted backward in the capsule, felt the connection, and slammed it home. The power engaged.

Taylor knew he had no time. He kicked his left foot back, pushing the throttle down with his toes. The submersible jumped, milliseconds ahead of the nine-foot jaws. He twisted again in the tight capsule, praying the battery connection would hold.

The Megalodon was upon him, jaws almost around the tiny vessel. Jonas whipped the sub to port. The snout passed on his right. A red flicker beckoned from his control panel. The batteries were dying!

Jonas spun the submersible around in a tight circle, unable to locate the Meg. He slowed, feeling the rumble of twin engines in the distance.

It took André Dupont ten minutes to convince the captain of the fishing trawler that his institute would pay for any damages to his vessel. The captain finally relented, and the boat raced to the rescue of the wrecked lifeboat's survivors.

Terry Tanaka was pulled on board by Dupont. She tried to stand, then simply collapsed on deck. Adashek vomited from the stress. DeMarco and several other shipmates fell to their knees, all thanking their maker for sparing their lives.

Rising twenty-five feet out of the Pacific, the Meg grasped the capsized lifeboat in its hyperextended jaws and snapped the wooden hull like kindling. Splinters rained upon the trawler's deck, followed by a ten-foot swell as the monster slammed her upper torso back into the ocean.

André Dupont had no time to react. The wave hit him squarely and swept him into the sea. Terry screamed, then saw the AG I skimming the surface. Thirty feet from the fishing trawler, Jonas's submersible stopped, its engines silent.

Jonas kicked at the batteries, but he knew it was hopeless. The voltmeter read zero. His vessel had no power source. Slowly, the heavier Lexan nose cone settled deeper in the water, making the AG I bob head-down in the water like a cork.

Suspended upside down within the pilot's harness, Jonas peered into the gray mist beneath him. He felt his blood pounding in his temples. Movement to his left—a smallish figure swimming toward the fishing trawler.

"Where are you?" Jonas whispered out loud. "I have to get out of this sub and on board that ship."

She rose slowly out of the depths, sensing her challenger was wounded. At one hundred feet she began accelerating, jaws opening wider, nostrils flaring for the scent.

Jonas saw the white face, the satanic grin, appear out of the darkness. It was seven years ago. He was back on the *Seacliff,* but this time there was no retreat, no escape. I'm going to die, he thought. Strangely, he felt no fear.

And then Masao's words came back to him. *"If you know the*

enemy and know yourself, you need not fear the result of a hundred battles.''

"I know my enemy," he said aloud, the head now fifty feet away, jaws stretching open.

Forty feet.

Thirty. Jonas reached forward with his right hand, grasped the lever, turning it counterclockwise.

Twenty feet. He breathed deeply to calm his skipping heartbeat.

Ten feet! The jaws hyperextended.

Jonas screamed involuntarily, pulling the lever toward him. The fuel ignited, the AG I transformed into a rocket, streaking down through the open jaws of the Megalodon.

The black cavern jumped at Jonas. He aimed the sub into its center, catching a glimpse of the almost Gothic, sweeping arches of the creature's cartilaginous ribs, then absolute blackness as the AG I roared down the predator's tongue, plunging deep into the esophagus.

The Abyss Glider's midwings sliced deeply into the esophageal walls, tearing yards of soft tissue before snapping from the sub's body. The torpedo contour of the sub continued sliding downward, driven by the hydrogen combustion.

Fearing he was about to crash, Jonas pushed the lever back, cutting off the burn, as the AG I thudded into a dark fleshy mass. He let out his breath, realizing he was still alive.

Jonas Taylor had entered the gates of hell.

HELL

The Megalodon exploded from the Pacific, its scythelike caudal fin nearly clearing the water. For a frozen moment, the twenty-ton monster hung in space like a marlin, then plunged back into its liquid realm, mouth open, dying to quench the fire that burned within.

Although the AG I's batteries were dead, the sub's small backup generator could power the life-support systems for almost an hour. Jonas switched on the exterior light.

The Abyss Glider was lodged somewhere in the upper regions of the Megalodon's stomach. Warm seawater steamed the Lexan glass as brownish objects swirled within the tight pink walls. Jonas looked at the external temperature gauge: eighty-nine degrees.

"Amazing," he said aloud, trying hard to keep his mind focused, away from the thoughts that created panic. Thick chunks of mutilated whale blubber slapped across the glass cone. Jonas felt queasy, but couldn't stop himself from looking. He could discern the remains of a porpoise, a rubber boot, and several pieces of wood. Molten globs of partially digested whale blubber slithered along the unseen periphery. And then something different.

It was a human leg, snapped off at the knee. Another figure appeared, an upper torso, badly mangled. The figure had a head, a face, still recognizable . . . Danielson!

Jonas gurgled, his scream cut off by the rising vomit. The walls closed in upon him, and he convulsed in fear. The sub shifted hard to one side, rolling with the gaping stomach, sloshing the remains of Taylor's former commanding officer out of sight as the host hurled itself in and out of the ocean, thrashing in agony.

André Dupont sat on deck, catching his breath and watching in amazement and fear as the greatest creature ever to inhabit the oceans spasmed out of control. Terry stood, her legs quivering, tears streaming down her cheeks. She had seen the fuel ignite, knew what Jonas had done. At that moment, she realized how deep her feelings were for him.

Leon Barre was arguing with the fishing trawler's owner, warning him that the boat's engines would attract the monster. The older man swore at Barre, swore at Dupont, but decided it might be best to cut the engines.

The Megalodon went deep, her insides scorched from the rocket's flames. The shark attempted to regurgitate the object it had swallowed. Two five-foot sections of aluminum oxide along with several bloody chunks of esophageal tissue were expunged, making their way out of the female's mouth. The broken wings of the Abyss Glider floated past the creature's snout. She snapped, engulfing them again along with her own innards, unable to override 70 million years of instinct.

· · ·

Jonas shook uncontrollably, hyperventilating, his nerves trembling amid carnal horror the likes of which could not be imagined. He had not really known claustrophobia, not known fear until now.

Then he remembered Terry. She, of all people, could give him hope. "She's still alive," he grunted out loud. "And so am I. Concentrate, goddamnit! Think. Where are you?"

He forced his mind to recall the clean, clinical diagrams of the great white shark's internal anatomy he knew so well. The submersible had cleared the esophagus. Jonas knew he must be in the upper regions of the stomach. What could he do? Was it possible to kill the Megalodon from within?

Jonas realized that rational thoughts had slowed his breathing. "You're okay," he said, "you're okay." His pulse pounded in his ears, getting louder. He found he could barely hear himself speak.

That's not my pulse, he suddenly realized. The diagram reappeared in his head, the esophagus, the stomach . . . It's her heart! Yes, the two-chambered heart lay behind the gills, forward of the enormous liver. Directly below the stomach!

A calm resolve began to settle over Jonas. He had a plan—a ray of hope. He would see Terry again. He rolled onto his side and located a small compartment below his seat cushion. The compartment held an emergency mask, a regulator, and a small oxygen tank. He removed all three from the compartment, attached the mask, and made sure the oxygen flowed. Satisfied, he searched for the underwater knife.

It was gone. Now what? How could he hope to cut through the thick muscular tissue of the Meg's internal organs? Feeling around the capsule, his fingers found the leather pouch. He removed the fossilized tooth from its protective satchel, tucking it in the belt of his wet suit. He took a flashlight, then secured the small cylinder of oxygen across his chest with the Velcro straps. He was ready.

Jonas unscrewed the escape hatch in the sub's tail. The rubber housing lost its suction with a hiss as he pushed the circular door open. A thick liquid, hot to the touch, began oozing into the sub. Breathing through the regulator, Jonas lifted his head out of the hatch, shining the flashlight into the acid darkness.

The Megalodon's stomach revealed a tightly confined, twisting chamber of muscle, constantly moving, churning debris in a caustic atmosphere of humidity, burning excretions, and seawater. The digestive organ protested his presence, high-pitched gurgling noises alternating with a series low, resonating growls. Beneath it all, the constant *thumpa-thumpa* of the Megalodon's heart vibrated through Jonas's body.

With no discernible top or bottom, the stomach simply appeared to be a pocket of continually collapsing and expanding muscle. Jonas carefully swung his right leg out of the AG I, feeling the submersible shift position as he did so. His right foot touched the stomach lining, giving him the sensation of stepping on a surface of molten putty. A thick liquid oozed from pores in the stomach muscle, squishing between his toes and scalding his foot. Jonas pulled his other leg through the hatch. Without warning, the stomach bulged beneath him, the entire compartment rolling 270 degrees. Both his feet slipped from under him, tossing him blindly onto his back. He could feel the heat of the mucous lining attacking his wet suit. Gagging, he rolled over on all fours and crawled on his hands and knees on the uneven, thickly muscled surface.

His hands began to burn, and the change of temperature started fogging his mask. Holding his breath, he rose to his knees, removed the mask, and spit inside, rubbing the glass clear. He gagged at the acidic smell, which began to burn his eyes.

Jonas sucked hard on the regulator, returning the mask to his face. Yes, that was better. "Stay calm, breathe slowly," he coached himself. Now, which way was the shark's underside? He felt a change in pressure and grabbed the tail wing of the AG I just as he was tossed backward again. The sub nearly slid on top of him. As he dodged it, something moved. He shone his light on an object, no, *two* objects, shiny . . . the AG's broken wings! They slid further into the stomach, guided by the muscular walls of the digestive tract.

Jonas calculated as the Megalodon leveled out once more. He placed his ear to the swollen mass below him, hearing the *thumpa-thumpa* grow louder. Bracing himself against the heavy submersible, he grasped the seven-inch serrated tooth like a prehistoric knife, and plunged the sharp tip into the stomach lining below.

The tooth bounced off the thick, muscular wall, popping out of his hand. Frantic, he felt along the lining, relocating the tooth. A sense of dread shattered his calm. I'm going to die in here, he thought.

On all fours, he held the tooth with both hands, pressing down with his weight, this time using the serrated edges as a saw. The thick fibrous tissue began splitting, but it was slow work, like cutting through raw meat with a butter knife. Jonas traced a four-foot-long incision into the thick tissue, then kept rubbing the edges of the blade against the resilient muscle.

The Megalodon could not feel the laceration Jonas made in her stomach, but the cuts along the upper digestive tract caused the shark to gag repeatedly. Agitated, the predator surfaced to attack.

With his left hand, Bud Harris flipped the toggle switch, re-starting the *Magnate*'s pumps. In his right hand was the magnum, cocked and pointed at Mac's head.

"You're activating the pumps?" asked Mac. "You'll attract the Meg."

"I *want* to attract the Meg. Move." Bud put the barrel of the gun in Mac's mouth, his left hand around his throat, and guided him on deck. The late afternoon sun beat down on the collapsed deck of the yacht.

"That monster destroyed my woman, the one person I truly cared for," cried Bud. "This creature, this albino nightmare, continues to haunt me, preventing me from sleeping, preventing me from living. And you?" Bud pushed his face next to Mac's. "You had to interfere, had to play the hero."

Bud stepped back, motioning for Mac to walk toward the rail. "Go ahead."

"What?" Mac listened for the Coast Guard copter, trying to stall.

Bud fired the magnum, blowing a three-inch hole in the deck. "You wanted to save this monster, now you can feed him." He fired again, this time nicking Mac in his right calf muscle. Mac collapsed onto one leg, blood oozing from the wound.

"The next shot will be at your stomach, so I suggest you jump now."

Mac moved to the rail, climbing over. "You're nuts, pal." Mac jumped in.

Bud watched him swim away from the *Magnate*. "See you in hell."

The female's stomach was on fire, sending spasmodic muscular contractions along her belly and pectoral fins. She needed to feed, needed to quench the flames that burned within. The vibrations from the *Magnate* became a homing beacon, the blood from Mac's wound intoxicating. Accelerating within the thermocline, the female approached the hull of the *Magnate* and rammed it, opening a massive fourteen-foot gash along the stern. Within seconds the yacht began spinning slowly, preparing its descent into the deep waters of the sanctuary.

Bud lay back in his lounge chair facing the bow, the bottle of Jack Daniel's now empty. His head ached, and now the world began spinning around him. "Must be the booze," he rationalized, laying his head back again. The second bump snapped him to attention.

"Ohhh shit." He grabbed the magnum, staggering to sit up.

The stern was flooding quickly, the *Magnate* was turning faster now. Bud fell against the rail, spotting the dorsal fin. He fired, missing by a good ten feet.

"Fuck you, fish. You're not gettin me. No way."

Through Dupont's glasses, Leon Barre saw the dorsal fin surface next to the crippled yacht. "I think we should go now, Captain."

The trawler's twin engines growled to life. Coughing blue smoke, the boat raced to shore. A half mile away, the female whipped her head around, her instincts gone mad. She accelerated in pursuit.

Bud closed his eyes, his world spinning too fast to see. He felt the forward deck rising. Feeling nauseous, he fell to his knees, struggled in his drunken state to take one last look. The boat rotated around him, accelerating into the vortex of the whirlpool. Through intoxicated eyes he could just make out the figure of the monster, its towering white triangular head rising above him. The mouth seemed to be opening, searching for food.

He looked up. "I'm coming, Maggie," he slurred, then searched for the monster. "Fuck you . . . bitch!" Bud put the magnum in his mouth and squeezed the trigger, blowing his brains out the back of his skull.

The triangular white bow of the *Magnate* continued rising as the stern rolled beneath the sea.

The Megalodon was long gone.

Jonas was exhausted. Whale blubber and other debris were compressing in the stomach, pushing hard against his back. He refused to look, afraid to see what, or who, it might be.

The tooth finally sliced through the six-inch-thick lining, and Jonas pushed his head and arms through the slit. Having exited the stomach, he found himself in a totally different environment.

The cardiac chamber was very tight, a fleshy crawl space no more than a foot high. Jonas squeezed his body prone into the space, wedging his back against a layer of striated muscle. It gave. He crawled forward, one hand holding the flashlight, the other gripping the tooth, heading in the direction of the bass drum that pounded louder in his brain.

The chamber began widening, the heartbeat getting stronger, vibrating the fleshy walls around Jonas. And then he saw it in the beam of light, a throbbing five-foot rounded mass of muscle, suspended by thick cords of blood vessels.

The fishing trawler closed to within one hundred yards of the beach as the Megalodon surfaced a mere twenty feet behind. The passengers held on, unable to muster the mental fortitude to survive yet another attack.

With a sickening burst of speed, the female rammed the source of the vibrations, crushing the shafts of the twin engines. The propellers stopped churning and the crippled trawler drifted powerless only fifty yards from shore.

"Son of a bitch!" the captain screamed. "This is your fault, Frenchy. You're gonna pay big time for this!"

The Meg surfaced, circling twenty feet away. She closed, approaching the port side of the trawler and pushing her snout against the hull.

The ship rose out of the water at a thirty-degree angle. DeMarco, Terry, and four crewmen slid along the deck. They had nothing to grab hold of but each other. The Meg continued raising the left side of the ship higher and higher, pushing the vessel back out to sea. Two of the crewmen managed to find purchase on the boat's tuna net, but Terry, Adashek, and the four other crewmen tumbled overboard.

The Meg heard the splash and felt the thrashing vibrations along her lateral line. She stopped pushing, allowing the trawler's hull to collapse back into the water. She circled, spiraling into the Monterey Bay Canyon, the icy depths allowing her to quench the burning sensation within as she prepared to attack once more.

Jonas held tightly to the thick cords of the Megalodon's cardiac blood vessels. He felt the hot liquid coursing through the aorta as the monstrous heart pounded against his chest, growing louder now, beating faster. Suddenly, the Megalodon dived, toppling Jonas forward.

Terry was too exhausted to swim. She hovered in the water, suspended above the waves by her life vest. Adashek was near, attempting to pull her toward the boat.

Circling in fifteen hundred feet of water, the female sensed her prey escaping even as the burning within became tolerable. The Megalodon streaked to the surface, her never-ending hunger compelling her to attack. She opened her jaws to the cold seawater, closing to within a thousand feet of her prey.

Adashek tugged at Terry, drawing her close to the boat. Dupont tossed a ring buoy as the other two men climbed back on board.

Six hundred feet.

Jonas hacked at the aorta, meeting little resistance. Warm blood spurted in a thousand directions, coating the flashlight and his mask. The three-foot-wide chamber went dark and Jonas trembled involuntarily. The walls closed in once more.

Four hundred feet.

Terry and Adashek were close to the side of the trawler now, the hands of several crewmen reaching down to the water, pulling the reporter out first. Terry lifted her arm, straining to reach her rescuers, kicking as best as she could to keep from sinking.

Two hundred feet.

André Dupont looked down into the sea and saw the luminescent glow approach. "Get her out, quickly!" he yelled. Terry looked toward the abyss, saw the fluorescent figure appear against the blackness below. The Meg was rising directly beneath her! A shot of adrenaline coursed through her body, pushing her upward. She stretched her hand higher, grabbing a crewman's wrist.

One hundred feet.

The female's upper jaw, teeth, gums, and connective tissue emerged from under the snout, projecting forward and away from the skull. The eyes, blind, rolled protectively back in the creature's head. The Meg would consume its prey in one gargantuan bite.

Fifty feet.

Terry Tanaka felt her slick palm slide down the crewman's arm. Desperately, she reached up with her other hand, lost her balance, and fell back into the sea.

· · ·

Jonas Taylor could not maintain a grip on the slippery cords. From the angle of the cardiac chamber, he realized the Meg was rising, probably to attack. He thought of Terry. Wrapping the crook of his left arm around the bundle of cords, he braced his bare feet against the soft tissues of the inner chamber walls above him and, inverted, pulled the beating muscle downward with all his might. His right hand tightened its grip on the tooth. With one powerful slash, he cut into the cords.

Twelve feet from the surface, upper jaw hideously hyper-extended, the Megalodon slowed, nocturnal eyes bulging forward, all muscles frozen. The only movements came from her powerful caudal fin, which twitched involuntarily.

In total darkness, Jonas lay on his back, covered in warm blood that continued cascading down upon him in buckets. On his heaving chest, like an enormous tree trunk, lay the detached heart of the 40,000-pound Megalodon. Jonas struggled to breathe steadily into the regulator, hyperventilating from his effort. The drums had stopped, but the chamber was engorged with blood.

Jonas wriggled out from beneath the massive organ and cast about for his flashlight. His fingers felt something hard, yes, the light. He wiped the lens but the beam was barely perceptible. On all fours, inching through a cascade of blood, he began crawling back toward the stomach.

Terry Tanaka had expected to die. When death did not come, she opened her eyes. The Megalodon's mouth hung open below her . . . descending. Blood surfaced in gouts, pooling around Terry's lower body.

"Terry, grab the rope," said DeMarco.

"Al, I'm okay. Throw me a mask, quickly."

Dupont grabbed a snorkel and mask and tossed them to her. She pulled the mask over her head, positioned the mouthpiece, and peered below. Through the scarlet-tinted brine, Terry saw a river of blood pouring out of the Megalodon's mouth as it continued to sink. The caudal fin had stopped moving.

Jonas had relocated the stomach, but he could not find the incision he had made. Panic! He strained to see the small circle of light coming from the flashlight. He banged the base of the light against his palm, making the beam slightly stronger. The claustrophobia sent involuntary muscular tremors rippling through his exhausted body. Finally, he spotted the incision. Jonas pushed his right leg through, followed by his head, and flopped forward, disoriented. Where was the AG I?

He plunged ahead on all fours, the strong stomach acids scorching his exposed hands and feet. The flashlight was useless now. Jonas had expected to see the sub's external light. He prayed the sub had not slipped into the intestines.

The angle of the internal anatomy was too great now, the lining too slippery. Jonas lost his balance and plummeted into a mass of debris at the lower end of the stomach. His head struck something solid—the tail section of the Glider.

The submersible's nose had passed through the entrance of the intestines, but the tail section was too large to follow. Grabbing hold of the rear hatch with both hands, Jonas jerked his body backward, the vessel giving slightly. He dug his toes in, adrenal glands pumping, and flung his weight backward again. The nose of the sub miraculously slid out of the blocked intestinal opening, expulsed in part by hundreds of gallons of partially digested food, backing up through the digestive tract.

The exterior light from the AG I cast an eerie luminescent glow in the stomach, revealing the effects of the dying host. The muscular lining no longer convulsed. The undigested contents of the intestines were backing up into the stomach and seeping into a pile, actually raising the nose cone of the submersible. Jonas looked up. Twenty feet above the stomach entrance, seawater poured into the esophagus, the only possible way out.

Jonas dropped to his knees, bracing his shoulders beneath the nose cone of the AG I. With all his strength, he stood up, sliding the torpedo-shaped sub sideways until it was leaning at an angle against the now-vertical lining of the stomach.

Blindly, Jonas relocated the tail section, now sinking beneath three feet of deformed, half-digested whale blubber. He dug with his arms, scooping a hole in the fat. His hands found the outer hatch and yanked it open. Squeezing through the blubber, he forced his head, then his arms, through the hatch and into the dry chamber. Finally, he managed to wriggle his entire body inside the torpedo-shaped submersible, the slick coating on his wet suit lubricating the tight fit. Jonas secured the hatch beneath his feet, then stood upright within the eight-foot-long capsule. Directing the exterior light upward, he relocated the entrance of the stomach. With one burst of fuel left, he knew the AG I had to make it into the esophagus.

Jonas heaved his body to his left, shifting the position of the submersible, lining up the nose cone beneath his intended target as best he could. He strapped himself into the pilot's harness, then reached toward the latch that would ignite the fuel. Turning it counterclockwise, he pulled.

What little remained of the hydrogen fuel ignited, propelling the submersible upward along the stomach lining like a rocket scaling a wall. Jonas gripped the joystick, aiming for the esophageal opening. The nose of the AG I slipped and plunged through the lubricated entrance of the stomach and into the water-filled canal that was the creature's esophagus.

WHUMMMMP! The AG I slammed to a halt. The exterior light revealed a chamber immersed in seawater and blood. The dead predator's mouth was open, the sea slowly infiltrating the

Meg's lifeless body. Jonas could make out the cavernous opening of the gullet looming ahead.

The AG I could not enter the esophagus. Jonas realized the sub's wider tail-fin section must have caught fast on the upper stomach's muscular lining. Jonas panicked as he felt the submersible begin to slip back into the digestive chamber whence it had come. He pulled the fuel latch again . . . nothing. Jonas was out of fuel. Nothing remained to prevent the AG I from sliding back down into the stomach.

In frustration, Jonas slammed his right fist downward, hitting a metal box. The escape pod! He tore open the lid, grabbed the lever, and pulled.

The AG I shuddered from the detonation that separated the internal Lexan glass torpedo-shaped escape pod from the heavier tail section of the submersible. The clear cylinder was propelled through the flooded chamber of the esophagus, its positive buoyancy assisting it upward.

The canal widened. The exterior light attached to the base of the escape pod illuminated the internal arches of the Megalodon's gullet that supported the cavernous chamber like the walls of an underwater cathedral. The escape pod shot upward, spinning out of control in a twisting funnel of water and blood. The buoyant cylinder continued to rise, approaching the open maw of the dead Meg.

Only one thing could halt Jonas Taylor's exit from his twenty-ton prison. Looming ahead, the Megalodon's lifeless jaws still bristled with row upon row of lethal nine-inch fangs.

Jonas lay in total darkness, save for the twisting exterior light of the pod. The jaws were locked open, but not hyperextended, leaving the gates of hell at less than half their potential diameter. Jonas held tight as countless primeval teeth leapt at him.

WHACK!

Jonas grimaced as the Lexan pod wedged sideways in between

the half-closed jaws. The vessel was horizontal, immobilized between the razor-sharp points of the creature's upper and lower
teeth. Failing to clear the open maw, the pod and its reluctant
pilot were held captive within the locked jaws of their dead host,
as its 42,000-pound frame plummeted hopelessly into the abyss.

OUT OF THE FRYING PAN

The lifeless form of the female Megalodon descended tail-first, her glow disappearing into the black waters of the Monterey Bay Canyon. Trapped between its jaws, the AG I's seven-foot-long escape pod remained wedged in triangular prison bars, its condemned man losing sight of the surface. Jonas glanced quickly at his depth gauge. Eleven hundred feet and sinking fast.

He had to free up the pod. Assuming a push-up position, Jonas launched his frame upward, slamming his back against the interior of the sub. The pod shuddered against the fangs of the monster, the vessel sliding a good six inches farther out of the jaws of death. Encouraged, Jonas smashed upward again, and again, each time slipping the pod a little bit closer to freedom.

At last, with a terrible scrape of bone on bulletproof plastic, the escape pod popped free from the death grip of the Megalodon and rose like a helium balloon toward the surface.

Jonas breathed an enormous sigh of relief. The pod would rise at a rate of sixty feet per minute, allowing for proper decompression.

Then he saw the cracks begin to spread, water seeping through the damaged shell of the escape pod.

Mac could swim no farther. Unable to catch his breath, his legs numb, he sensed the creature circling, felt the current generated by its mass before actually spotting the three-foot triangular dorsal fin.

"Get the hell out of here, you midget," he yelled at the thirteen-foot predator. The caudal fin slashed back and forth along the surface even as the harness dropped upon Mac's head from above.

Startled, Mac looked up to see the Navy helicopter. He slipped one arm into the harness and frantically signaled to the crew to pull him out of the water. The conical head of the shark rose out of the sea just as the pilot was yanked upward.

Mac looked up at his rescuers, a smile on his face, tears welling in his eyes. "Well, what do you know—the good ol' U.S. Navy. I can't believe it! Saving my sorry ass after all these years." He shook his head. "Lord, you do have a sense of humor after all."

The Lexan torpedo continued rising, the integrity of the escape pod in serious jeopardy. At five hundred and thirty-eight feet, what had been a tiny crack suddenly lengthened above Jonas's head. Physically and mentally drained, he could only watch as the six-inch-long crack began circling the circumference of the cylinder.

The satanical face of the Megalodon continued sinking into the canyon below. Jonas watched as the glow diminished, then disappeared entirely into darkness. He had escaped certain death twice. But to survive this day, he needed one more miracle.

Pressure. Oxygen. Pressure and oxygen. The all-consuming mantra entered his mind. For some reason the pod was rising at too fast a pace. Within his bloodstream, Jonas knew, nitrogen bubbles were beginning to form.

Four hundred feet. The seven-foot-long Lexan tube continued to hurtle upward like a glass missile. The cracks within the plastic had branched out into several different sections. A fine spray of water soaked the interior of the pod. Jonas knew that when the crack completely encircled the escape pod, the integrity of the structure would collapse under the tremendous pressures.

CRAAAACK. Only three feet separated the ends of the fissure. Anxious, Jonas began calculating. How deep was my best dive? What was the maximum depth he could tolerate? One hundred and twenty feet? One-thirty? He checked the oxygen tank still strapped around his chest. Not good news: less than three minutes of air remained.

At three hundred feet, the torpedo-shaped pod began vibrating.

"Terry, get out of the damn water now!" screamed DeMarco.

Terry ignored him, her face down in the water, breathing through the snorkel. The Megalodon was dead, that she knew. But her heart told her that Jonas had survived. She watched as the white glow disappeared.

André Dupont sat on the transom as Leon Barre and the trawler's captain disassembled one of the engines. André felt dazed and depressed. All his efforts to save the creature—the lobbying, the expense—all for naught. The greatest predator of all time . . . lost.

"I could have died today," he whispered to himself. "For

what? To save my killer? What would the Society tell my wife and children? 'Ah, Marie, you should be a proud widow. André died in the most noble of fashions, giving his life to feed an endangered species.' "

Dupont stood, stretching his sore back. The setting sun still shone strong enough to warm his skin. He watched the golden-yellow beam blaze a path from the horizon across the dark Pacific to the trawler. That was when he sighted the fin.

"Hey! Hey . . . Shark! SHARK!"

The bone-chilling water of the Pacific continued to fill the escape pod, the additional weight slowing the ascent significantly. Jonas shivered in his wet suit. He was afraid to move. He glanced at the depth gauge: two hundred feet. The fissure had completed its journey around the circumference of the vessel. The vibrations were reaching a fever pitch, exterior pressures encouraging cracks in the damaged chamber. He looked up, still unable to see the surface. At this depth, if the escape pod split open he would not survive.

Carefully, he donned his mask and prepared the regulator. He strapped the oxygen tank across his chest with the Velcro fasteners. Slow movements, he reminded himself. Don't panic. Force yourself to relax. Slow-kick to the surface. The empty tank will tow you topside. Use as little energy as possible. Don't close your eyes. Don't fall asleep, or you'll never wake up.

CRAAAACK.

I'm too deep . . .

The three-foot fin circled the fishing trawler. Eleven men as one screamed for Terry to get out of the water.

"That's a great white, no doubt," said Steve Tabor. "Looks

like a female, maybe thirteen feet. She's attracted by all that blood. We gotta get Terry out of the water fast."

The trawler's captain went below and returned with a shotgun. The dorsal fin circled the girl. The captain took aim.

Terry disappeared below the waves.

At one hundred and forty-two feet, the escape pod cracked open, showering Jonas with freezing seawater and crushing him with the pressure of more than four atmospheres. His nose began bleeding as he pushed his way out of the hatch. His faceplate cracked.

His legs began scissors-kicking. The air tank was pulling him up rapidly . . . too fast! He wasn't decompressing properly. Jonas stopped kicking.

Eighty feet. His body was like lead, no longer moving. The oxygen tank, barely strapped to his chest, had expelled nearly all of its air. Now its extreme buoyancy accelerated him upward at a dangerous pace. Jonas gazed through heavy eyes at the Velcro strap straining to hold the tank to his chest. Watched as it began tearing away. He tried to reattach it, but his arms were no longer his to control.

At fifty-eight feet, Jonas ran out of air. The two ends of the Velcro separated. The empty tank rocketed away from his chest, sailing high above his head. Jonas closed his eyes and bit hard into the regulator. Since he could not reach the tank with his hands, he struggled to maintain the connection to the buoyant canister with his teeth. He felt drunk.

At thirty-three feet, Jonas blacked out. The regulator slipped from his mouth. The tank escaped to the surface.

Jonas felt nothing, no pain, no fear. *I'm dreaming.* He looked up and saw a bright light. He was flying, moving toward the light without his body, no more pain, no more fear.

I'm in heaven.

Terry Tanaka grabbed Jonas's wrist just as his body began slipping back into the abyss. She kicked hard, pulling water with her left hand. To her right, the shark circled above her. She swam harder.

As her face broke the surface, Terry pulled Jonas's head out of the ocean. He was blue, no sign of breathing. She saw the dorsal fin eight feet away, accelerating toward her as the triangular snout broke water.

The fishing net arced through the air, its lead weights dropping it around and beneath the predator. The creature twisted, attempting to escape, but the big fisherman had pulled the net taut. The shark was trapped.

Terry pulled Jonas to the boat. A dozen hands dragged them on board. David Adashek began resuscitating him. DeMarco wrapped him in blankets, feeling for a pulse. Yes, but very weak.

Jonas coughed up water. Adashek rolled him onto his side, allowing him to expel the seawater and vomit. Terry bent over him, massaging his neck. Exhausted, Jonas squinted against the golden sunlight of dusk.

"Try not to move," she said, stroking his hair. "The Coast Guard's on its way. They're going to tow us into the lagoon. We have a recompression chamber on site at the Institute." She smiled at him, tears in her eyes.

Jonas looked at her beautiful face, smiling through the pain. *I am in heaven,* he thought.

The shark thrashed back and forth within the fishing net, five feet below the surface, unable to free itself. André Dupont followed the captain throughout the boat, attempting to reason with him.

"Captain, you can't kill it," yelled Dupont. "It's a protected species!"

"Look at my boat. She's busted up. I'll kill this fish, stuff it, and sell it to some tourist from New York for twenty thousand. You gonna give me that much, Frenchy?"

Dupont rolled his eyes. "Harm that shark, and you're going to prison!"

The captain's response was interrupted by the Coast Guard.

The 110-foot Coast Guard patrol boat *Manitou* arrived and tossed a towline to the disabled fishing trawler. Leon Barre attached it to the ship's bow. Within seconds, the line went taut, and the trawler was in tow behind the ship, heading into the Tanaka Lagoon. The two-thousand-pound predator continued thrashing within the net.

The massive doors separating the Monterey Bay Sanctuary from the lagoon had been left open for the *Kiku*. The *Manitou* entered the entrance to the canal.

Jonas was leaning against the transom when the sharp pains began in his elbows. Within seconds, every joint was on fire, stabbing pains running throughout his body.

Terry grabbed him. "Jonas, what is it?"

"Bends. How far?"

They had entered the lagoon, the Coast Guard towing the fishing trawler toward the dock, situated at the north side of the artificial lake.

"A few minutes. Lean against the transom. I'm going to make sure they have an ambulance at the dock."

Jonas nodded.

The pain began increasing; he felt dizzy, nauseous. His joints felt as if the Megalodon's teeth were biting down. Opening his eyes, he focused on the great white being towed along the left side of the stern.

Masao Tanaka was waiting at the dock in a wheelchair, his head heavily bandaged, an orderly by his side. Mac was there, along with a team of paramedics standing ready to rush Jonas into the recompression chamber.

Terry saw her father and ran to the bow. She waved. Tears of joy flowed down Masao cheeks.

Jonas leaned back against the transom, doubling again in pain. He could feel himself beginning to lose consciousness. He tried to focus on the predator in the water. She was struggling fiercely, twisting within the confines of the fishing net. Her white hide cast a soft glow in the growing dusk.

For a brief moment, man and beast made eye contact. The creature's eyes were blue-gray. Jonas stared incredulously at the baby Megalodon. He closed his eyes and smiled. And then the pain became overwhelming and the paleontologist lost consciousness as the two paramedics loaded him into the ambulance.

Author's Note

A tremendous amount of research went into the making of this novel in order to maintain a high degree of realism. The author wishes to acknowledge and recommend *Great White Shark* by Richard Ellis and John E. McCosker (Stanford University Press, 1991) for further reading and as an excellent source of information on both Megalodons and great whites.